Six Houses Down

six
houses
DOWN

a novel

Kari Rimbey

NEW YORK

LONDON • NASHVILLE • MELBOURNE • VANCOUVER

Six Houses Down

A Novel

Published in New York, New York, by Morgan James Publishing. Morgan James is a trademark of Morgan James, LLC. www.MorganJamesPublishing.com

Publisher's Note: This novel is a work of fiction. Names, characters, places, and incidents are either products of the author's imagination or used fictitiously. All characters are fictional, and any similarity to people living or dead is purely coincidental.

ISBN 9781642792324 paperback
ISBN 9781642792331 eBook
Library of Congress Control Number: 2018910323

Cover Design by:
Rachel Lopez
www.r2cdesign.com

Interior Design by:
Chris Treccani
www.3dogcreative.net

Morgan James is a proud partner of Habitat for Humanity Peninsula and Greater Williamsburg. Partners in building since 2006.

Get involved today! Visit
MorganJamesPublishing.com/giving-back

CHAPTER 1

"I don't understand why you can't stay just a little longer. You said you'd be home for three weeks this time." Sharon Webster pulled on the end of her sleeve as she watched her husband prepare to leave again. "Can't you start work on this next project from DC?"

"I wish I could, but there are pre-bid meetings with contractors and design questions, among other things I have to be in Sorrento for." Bill placed a freshly cleaned shirt in his suitcase. "The Italian government moved the project up, not me. I don't *want* to be away from you and Stewart. I'm sorry, Sharon; I have to leave in the morning." He reached for her. "Come here."

Sharon sunk into his chest and tried to find comfort in the strong arms wrapped around her, but her gut twisted as if she hadn't eaten in days. Every time Bill came home, he had to leave early. The first time it was one or two days, then a week, and now two weeks. A question that seeded itself several months earlier needled her: did he really have to leave?

"Why don't we go out for dinner tonight?" Bill suggested. "We could go to the station and get a burger. Stewart will do okay there, don't you think? There's a lot to see; the space is wide open; and we can sit away from the crowd. He could check out the charter buses." Bill looked at her as if one night away from the house was all she needed to pull her out of the he's-leaving-again blues.

Sharon nodded, afraid that resistance on her part would only make things worse.

"We could walk down Independence Avenue and follow the path around the water. It would be good for Stewart to get out. He'd like that, right?" Bill's exaggerated optimism wasn't helping.

"He probably would," she replied, forcing a smile.

* * *

Stewart hopped in place as Bill unlocked the car in the alley.

1

"Somebody's happy to get out of the house." Bill helped him hook his seatbelt and then slid into the driver's seat. "Are you ready to go to Union Station and see the buses?"

Her son chuckled and tapped his fingers on his legs. To make room for the joy coming from the back seat, Sharon forced the disappointment over Bill's early departure aside and winked at Stewart. He smiled and pressed his face against the window. Tall for a five-year-old, he was a mini version of his father. While they waited at the stop sign, Bill reached back and poked Stewart in the side, causing an eruption of pleasure-induced squeals. If she could only freeze this moment in time. For the next several miles, her son continued to clap his hands and bounce his legs on the edge of the seat.

After parking at Union Station, the three of them rode the escalator to the bus deck. Bill held their son's hand while they walked the length of the terminal. Stewart thrust a hand at every empty bus in the long row, as if completing an inventory.

"Which one is your favorite? Which bus do you like better than all the other ones?" Bill asked, looking back and forth along the row. "How about Mom? Maybe she has a favorite?"

Sharon pointed down the sidewalk. "I like the red, white, and blue one."

Stewart seemed to study his options and then yanked on his father's arm, pulling him down the row to a black bus emblazoned with a lightning bolt.

"That is a nice one. Good choice, son. Come on." Bill pulled on his hand. "Let's go get something to eat."

Stewart jerked his hand free and darted across the lot.

"Stewart, wait!" Sharon yelled.

Both her and Bill leapt forward in pursuit of their runaway son.

"Stewart, stop!" Bill demanded.

A station attendant blew hard on his whistle. "Get back to the sidewalk! You have to cross at the crosswalk!" he barked.

When Stewart didn't comply, the attendant blew his whistle again and ran toward him. "Get back on the sidewalk!"

Stewart screamed and ran between two empty busses. The closer the attendant got to him, the louder he screeched, like a trapped animal in fear of imminent demise. Bill reached his son before the attendant did, scooped him up with one arm, and motioned for the attendant to back off. Sharon regretted leaving the house as she watched Stewart kick and slap his father.

"That's enough!" Bill scolded, setting him down on his feet.

Stewart covered his ears and hunched down on the sidewalk. The parking attendant speared Bill with an expression of accusation and kept a steely glare on him, cocking his head back and waiting a few seconds before turning to walk away.

"Come on, honey. It's okay." Sharon patted Stewart's shoulder and tried to ignore the offense boiling off her husband.

Bill threw his hands in the air. "That idiot thought I was going to hit Stewart!"

"Don't worry about him; he doesn't know what's going on here. Let's get something to eat." Sharon helped Stewart to his feet.

"What *is* going on?" Bill raked a hand through his hair. "When did he start freaking out like that?"

"It's all right. Can we go eat now?" She steered Stewart toward the crosswalk.

"It's *not* all right." Bill looked at her as if she should have the answers to their son's temperament.

Heat crept up her neck. "Is this supposed to be my fault—since your gone all the time? He's getting older and more independent; that's *what's going on*. Not to mention the obvious—he's scared to death!" She spun around and marched Stewart back to the car.

Sharon felt a distance growing between her and Bill as they ate drive-through burgers on the way home, exchanging impersonal small talk like a telephone survey. She studied their son for signs of distress. He hummed, held a plain burger in one hand, and pulled on the door handle with the other.

"The door is locked, right?"

Bill rolled his eyes. "Of course it is."

Sharon put her burger back in the paper bag. She wasn't hungry. By the time they were home, Stewart seemed as if nothing out of the ordinary had happened and sorted a box of cars in the living room. Sharon busied herself washing a counter that was already clean, and Bill sat with his head in his hands at the kitchen table.

"I'm sorry," her husband said without looking at her.

Sharon wished they'd stayed home. "It's okay. Me, too."

"I know," he mumbled.

It wasn't okay, but she'd say anything to smooth things over before he left for Italy. Sharon couldn't tell what bothered Bill more, what he'd said that hurt her or her own caustic response about him being gone all the time, but she wouldn't ask.

CHAPTER 2

Nearly a month had passed since Bill left for Sorrento, Italy. They'd had several hour-long phone conversations laced with remorse over the situation at Union Station, and Sharon felt like things were on the mend between them. He would be coming home soon. The thought of it infused her with energy.

Everything's going to work out, she told herself as she made Stewart's lunch, keeping an eye on her son through one of two kitchen windows affording a clear view of the tiny backyard. Stewart sat in a sandbox big enough for two children, but it never held more than one. She watched as he played in silence, raking his fingers back and forth through the tan grit. The morning was warmer than usual for a late-September day in Washington, DC. A few blocks down from the tidy line of brick row houses, the sounds of the city buzzed by, but Sharon and her son would stay close to home. The screen door squeaked as she stepped outside.

"Honey," she said as she knelt down beside the sandbox and placed a gentle hand on Stewart's shoulder. "Are you hungry? Why don't you come inside now and have a sandwich?" She brushed a silky, blond curl behind his ear.

Stewart stood and followed her, his bare feet depositing grains of sand across a twelve-foot patch of soft grass. He stepped through the screen door with the nagging spring, sat on his step stool at the kitchen table, and tapped a crystal bird hanging within easy reach from the latch on the window sash. The high-noon sun would soon send a brief finger of golden light through the single pane and then fade away behind the houses across the alley.

"Can you wash your hands?" Sharon reminded him.

He tromped over to the stool in front of the kitchen sink and pumped out a stream of green soap. Thick liquid puddled in his cupped palm, and he drew a thin layer of soap down each finger. Sharon noticed the distraction and let him linger for a minute.

"Your sandwich is ready."

Stewart looked over at the table but continued to press the dispenser and watch the soap drip off his fingers.

She patted him on the shoulder. "Can you rub your hands together and rinse them? The sun will shine on your bird soon."

He quickly rubbed his hands and rushed to the table.

"Wait, Stewart. We need to *rinse* your hands." Sharon placed a firm hand on his chest, leaned over, and nudged him toward the sink.

A piercing scream filled the kitchen as Stewart flung his arms in frantic panic, his eyes wild as he clawed at her hair.

"You're all right. Let me help you." She tried to calm him with a steady voice, firmly holding his shoulders and guiding him back to the sink.

Stewart moaned as she rubbed his hands under the water.

"See? All rinsed off." She held out a dishtowel. "Can you dry your hands?"

He batted at the towel, hurried to his seat by the window, and proceeded to shove bite-sized cubes of cheese sandwich into his mouth in rapid succession. Sharon dabbed splotches of liquid soap off her shirt and pants, pulled the band out of her auburn hair, and combed the loose strands back into place with her fingers before noticing Stewart's packed cheeks.

"Careful. Don't put so much in your mouth."

Swallowing hard, he forced barely chewed globs of bread and cheese down his throat. "Uhn, uuuuuuuhn," he whined.

The problem frequent, Sharon calmly handed him his cup of milk. "Here, honey, take a drink."

A large belch followed several big gulps.

"Excuse you," she teased, as Stewart laughed at the funny sound. "I see you have your father's sense of humor."

A sliver of sunlight hit the top of the window, reflected off the white kitchen wall, and inched its way toward the crystal bird. Sharon purchased the figurine several weeks ago at a moving sale a few houses down from their own. After hanging the bird in the kitchen window, she encouraged her son to notice the rainbow display. What she thought would be a temporary pleasure had become a lunchtime ritual, if the day offered the necessary sunshine.

"Can you eat that last bite of sandwich?"

Six Houses Down

Stewart swallowed the last cube of cheese and bread without chewing and watched wide-eyed as the sun hit the facets cut into the crystal bird, casting a dozen tiny rainbows on the wall. He tapped the bird, sending flickers of light dancing and twirling on the temporary screen. Clapping and jumping, he joined the swaying colors, complete with a song of guttural chants.

"Boog, boog, boog, boog," he spun around and swatted at the rainbows on the wall. Soon the colored lights were gone. He rocked slowly, tilting his head to the side and rubbing his eyes.

"Are you ready for a book?"

Following her to the coffee table by the brown velour couch in the living room, her son watched as she held up several books for him to consider. He tapped his choice, one of his favorites, and climbed up on the couch beside her for their familiar pre-nap routine. Sharon read *One Fish, Two Fish, Red Fish, Blue Fish* six times before he fell asleep.

She cradled her son, who would have objected to the restriction of movement if he were awake, and admired his innocent face. What would it be like if this precious little boy of hers could open his sleepy eyes and tell her he loved her. "Lord, could you let him tell me he loves me, just one time?" She brushed a patch of bushy, blond curls away from his forehead, gently pressing her cheek against his warm skin and breathing in the scent of him. "I love you, little man," she whispered before laying him back on the couch and spreading his favorite blanket over him. He looked even younger when he slept, covered in quilted, yellow corduroy squares, his long lashes fanning the top of his sun-kissed cheeks.

A familiar buzz sounded as Sharon's cell phone vibrated on the kitchen counter. Desperate to talk to Bill, she raced for the phone before it could switch to voice mail. Checking the caller ID, her chest tightened in anticipation. It's him.

"Hello, Bill," she whispered as she slipped out the back door so she wouldn't wake Stewart. "Are you on your way home?"

"Hi, sweetheart. I just needed to hear your voice. I wish you and Stewart could be here. It's beautiful in Sorrento. You would love it. How's everything there?"

Sharon noticed he didn't answer her question. A heaviness threatened any hope that he was calling to tell her he was headed home. "I wish we could be with you, too. Will you be here for Stewart's birthday?"

"That's right; his birthday is coming up. I can't believe he's going to be six years old already. What's he up to? Is he doing better with the kids at group?"

"No . . . we stopped going to group a week ago. The other mothers didn't want their kids playing with him anymore."

"Why not?" Bill sounded offended.

"He's having frequent meltdowns. There's really no way to know when he's going to have an outburst, and he's attacked several kids."

"You need to go," Bill said with a tone of urgency. "Group is as much for you as it is for him. They're supposed to know how to deal with those kinds of things."

Sharon rubbed her arm, sensing the control she tried to place on her emotions slipping. "It's just easier to stay home. He was so much better when you were here. Can you please come home . . . soon?"

"What if you try a different group?"

"Bill, are you coming home?" She continued to rub her arm, afraid she already knew the answer.

"I'm sorry, sweetheart. I want to, but I can't. I have to be in Palermo in a couple weeks, and I'm going to be pressed for time. I'm a week behind schedule as it is. Sorry this is so tough on you. I honestly thought I'd have more time between these projects. What about trying church again, maybe a different one? Can you search online for one with a program for special needs kids?"

"I'd rather do that when you're here to go with me. Stewart isn't doing well with new places and people right now. When will you be able to come home?" She ran a hand across the back of her neck.

"I can't really say. It could be a long stretch this time."

"Bill . . . I can't do this anymore." Sharon started to cry. "Stewart needs you—I need you."

"Please don't cry, honey. I'd be there if I could. I love you."

"I love you, too. I have to go." The second Sharon hung up, she dropped to the step and leaned on the screen door, releasing a torrent of tears she'd been holding back. Did he really love her? Why was he so quick to accept a promotion taking him away from her and Stewart? Maybe that's all he wanted—to get away, regretting that he ever married her. Something she kept buried in the far recesses of her mind tried to surface: was there someone else?

"No, he wouldn't do that. Get a hold of yourself," she whispered as she stood and pulled the screen door open.

Stewart continued to sleep as she slipped past him into the bathroom and washed her face. After several deep breaths and a good look at her reflection, she returned to the kitchen, pulled out her computer, and typed in a search: work at home in Washington, DC.

"Let's see . . . audio transcription . . . no . . . dog sitter . . . sales, definitely not . . . online instructor . . . laundry service subcontractor." Sharon clicked the description on the laundry service and read all the fine print. The steamer and cleaning bags were supplied along with an in-home tutorial on the commercial garment steamer. It wasn't what Bill suggested, but she could press uniforms by the kitchen window and watch Stewart play in the yard at the same time. Something about it appealed to her. One call later, she had a job with On the Spot Cleaners. They would be delivering hangers, uniforms, a roll of plastic bags, and a steamer the next day.

Stewart marched through the kitchen, headed for the door.

"Wait. Do you want to get something new to play with?"

She pulled a drawer open, full of miscellaneous utensils, cups, and bowls. He made a quick selection, followed her outside, and lined up measuring cups on a mound of sand. His best days were those spent playing outside in the fresh air.

With a reel mower from the storage shed against the house, Sharon made several passes over their small patch of grass.

"I'm going inside now. Are you done playing?"

Stewart thrust a hand toward her, a gesture she interpreted as *definitely not.*

After going back in the house, she was careful to check on him every few minutes. A locked gate, leading to the alley, secured the chain-link fence bordering their small backyard, but her son would soon be big enough to climb over it. Two months earlier, she had left the gate unlocked after bringing groceries into the house from the car and went back out seconds later to find Stewart gone.

Racing through the open gate, Sharon found him meandering down the fence-lined alley. She yelled for him to stop, which proved to be the wrong thing to do. Stewart turned and looked at her for a split second before spinning around and running in a full-on sprint toward a busy intersection. She bolted after him, covered the twenty yards between them in record-breaking time, grabbed his arm, and bent forward to catch her breath. With a tight grip on Stewart's wrist, she pulled him back to the open gate. A combined mess of fear and anger, she'd scolded him and then instantly regretted it, knowing he didn't understand the danger. One of her worst fears was not being able to find him. Unfortunately, one of his favorite games was hiding from her.

Sharon changed over a load of laundry, her internal timer reminding her that several minutes had passed and it was time to check on Stewart again. The back door was open, and the sound of his contented hum drifted through the screen door, affording her assurance of his well-being. She poured a drink for both of them. With cups in hand, she headed outside to relax for a few minutes, wanting to take advantage of one of the last summer days of the season. The screen door squeaked as she pushed it open with her elbow.

"I have a drink for you, Stew—" She stood in shocked surprise. A little girl, with the fairest skin and the brightest red hair she'd ever seen, sat busily playing in the sandbox with her son. Sharon's eyes darted to the gate. It was still locked.

The mystery guest looked up and smiled at her as if she belonged there. "Hi . . . I'm Stacey. We moved into our new house over there." The little girl pointed down the alley. "Well, it's not really *our* house, but we live there now." Stacey proceeded to fill a bowl with sand while she continued with her introduction: "I'm five, but I'm gonna to be six this year, 'cause my birthday's comin' up soon. Well, not really soon. And I have to go to school now 'cause I'm in kindergarten, but I don't go today 'cause there's no school today, and I don't have any school till after lunch, so I can play here on those other days, too."

Sharon tried to sort through both the impressive monologue for a five-year-old and the confusion over Stacey's sudden appearance. "Hello, Stacey. My name is Mrs. Webster." She set the drinks on the kitchen step and looked over the locked gate and down the alley for someone missing a child, but she didn't see anyone. "Does your mother know where you are?"

"Nope," Stacey answered, continuing to dig in the sand with Stewart, who seemed pleased to have a surprise guest to play with.

"Do you think we should go tell her where you are? She might be worried." Sharon checked the alley again.

"She's not 'cause she's at work. My mommy works at the ginormous station." Stacey leveled a freshly molded hill of sand. "She sells tickets so people can go on those outside buses that people like to ride to see stuff." She reached for one of Stewart's plastic cups. "I like to ride on top 'cause it's super fun, and sometimes we go with Uncle Shane. He's my uncle 'cause he's my mommy's brother, but I don't have a brother."

Sharon thought it unlikely the little girl was left to fend for herself. "Who is taking care of you today while your mother is at work?" She covered the short distance from the fence to the sandbox in a few steps.

The little girl pursed her lips together. "Nanna May watches me mostly, 'specially when Earl's gone, but she can't move very good. I told her I have to meet a new friend and then come back." Stacey continued to dig in the sand. "Oh, yeah, Nanna May says I can't stay too long 'cause I talk too much 'bout stuff and people get tired of hearing me."

Sharon stifled a laugh and pulled a lawn chair closer to the sandbox so she could intervene if her son became temperamental. The last thing she wanted was to send the little girl home with a bruise from an unexpected slap.

"Your boy doesn't talk, does he?"

"This is Stewart, and no, he doesn't talk right now. You know, I should have a little visit with Nanna May if you're going to play with Stewart."

"So, that's your name, little boy? You're a picture bowl." She nodded her head as if the observation was obvious.

Intrigued by the five-year-old's logic, Sharon asked her why she thought that.

"You know, if you put *stew* and *art* together, it's sort of like a bowl of something and a picture." She tilted her head to inspect the progress in the sand.

"You're a smart little girl, aren't you, Stacey?"

"I already know that. My mommy says I'm not s'pposed to say it to other kids, though, 'cause it makes 'em feel bad. I can read books, but the other kids in my class can't read 'cause they haven't learned yet, and it's okay if your boy can't talk. My Uncle Shane doesn't talk either, least not with his mouth."

Sharon would have liked the precocious little girl to stay but was suspicious that her grandmother might not be aware her little charge was gone. "Can you tell me where you live so I can visit with your grandmother?"

"Nanna May isn't my grandma. Her name is just Nanna May 'cause that's what people call her. You can write a note, and I can give it to her. My teacher sends notes with me lots of times. Mostly they say I did a good job listening, but sometimes they don't say that."

"That's a good idea." Sharon stood to retrieve a pen and paper and then hesitated. Stewart seemed to be in good spirits. Maybe she could chance leaving them alone together for a few seconds. She grabbed the pen by the phone and searched a drawer for a pad of paper, all the while listening through the screen door, her ear tuned in on the mood in the sandbox. Hurrying back outside, she sat next to the kids as they played and wrote a quick note:

We enjoyed Stacey's company today and would like you to know she is more than welcome to visit us again. However, I would like to discuss with you the special needs of my five-year-old son, Stewart, and a few concerns you might want to be aware of before Stacey becomes used to playing with him.
Sincerely,
Sharon Webster

Sharon included her name and phone number at the bottom of the page, hoping the note would make it into an adult's hand before the little girl returned to play.

"Here you go, Stacey. Can you take this home and give it to Nanna May right away?" Sharon held out the folded paper. "We would really like it if you could come back and play again soon."

Stacey stood up, brushed the sand off her teal green pants, took the note, and stuffed it in her boot. Turning to Stewart, she offered her hand for a handshake. "It was super nice to meet you, Stewart. Thanks for playing with me."

He looked at her briefly before Stacey grabbed his hand and put it in hers to show him how to shake hands. Sharon jumped forward, sure her son would jerk his hand away and follow through with a swift slap to her face, but he seemed at ease with the intrusion and continued pumping his hand up and down after Stacey released it.

"That's how we say hello and goodbye to new people, just like at church, and Stewart, you're one of my new friends now." She turned and offered her hand to Sharon.

Regretting that she had to send the bright little girl away, Sharon shook her hand before unlocking the gate so Stacey could go home.

"How did you come into the yard, Stacey?"

"I just came in the usual way," she replied with her hands raised at her sides, as if the answer was obvious.

"Of course." Sharon grinned, not having a clue what *the usual way* referred to. She stood at the fence watching the little red-haired girl skip down the alley, expecting her to turn into one of the backyards several doors away, but she continued on, turning out of sight five or six row houses down.

Returning to her chair, Sharon picked up her glass of tea. The ice had melted, but the tea was still cool enough to quench her thirst. She handed Stewart his cup. "Would you like a drink?"

He emptied half of the cup's contents, handed it back to her, and continued to play, his attention on a small bucket he was filling and dumping.

"That was a nice little girl. Wouldn't you like it if she came back to play with you again?"

He smiled and looked at her briefly before shifting his attention back to the sand.

"It's really important you're nice to Stacey, and be careful not to hit her when you're angry, okay? If you hit her, she won't be able to play with you." Sharon studied his face, hoping to detect a spark of understanding.

Stewart looked past her and chuckled.

CHAPTER 3

On Sunday, the crisp morning gave way to that perfect temperature that begs everyone to go outside and enjoy it. The parks and bike paths would be crowded, and swarms of tourists would filter through the historic sights of downtown DC.

Stewart finished his cereal, and when it came time to choose her son's clothes for the day, Sharon noticed he'd skipped the rejection process they usually went through. The crystal bird performed its much-appreciated rainbow display, and Stewart ate his lunch without flares of temper or complaint. Finished with a short nap, he appeared to be in high spirits as he headed out the door to play. Sharon pulled a small trampoline from the storage shed and placed it in the grass. He played on it for half an hour before settling into the sandbox.

"I'll be right back, honey." Sharon went in the house to search for a book to read, feeling the heaviness of disappointment stalking her. Stacey hadn't returned to play with her son. It was possible that the note caused enough concern to keep the potential playmate from ever coming back, the friendship already discouraged.

It was nothing new. A few well-meaning mothers, from the church they used to attend, were willing to come to play dates Sharon had planned at a nearby park, but even they soon drifted off in favor of other, more accommodating friendships. They offered excuses at first but eventually moved on completely. She didn't blame them. As soon as a potential friend was on the receiving end of one of Stewart's short-tempered slaps, the offended child's desire to play with him soon soured, and they would move on. She had heard so many versions of sympathetic apologies that Stacey's absence shouldn't affect her; the rejection from the support group and church friends had seeded itself so deeply that staying away from people altogether had started to appeal to her.

Sharon glanced through the window again, surprised to see that Stewart was no longer in the sandbox. Instead, he stood with his face tightly pressed against the chain-link fence, trying to see down the alley through slivers of space between the thin, white-plastic strips woven in and out of the metal links.

Releasing a deep sigh, Sharon set her book on the counter and stepped outside. Stewart turned to face her. The look of anticipation on his face broke her heart.

"Are you looking for Stacey?" She walked over and bent down beside him.

He shifted his attention back to the alley. His lack of frustration with her question was evidence that she guessed correctly.

"It would be nice if she could play with you again, but she might not be able to come back." Not wanting to give her son any false hope, she tried to distract him by offering to search the kitchen utensil drawer for something new to play with in the sandbox.

He turned and shuffled with sagging shoulders and heavy steps through the noisy screen door. Sharon tried to interest him in an old, wire-handled strainer, which he accepted. The sifting sand held his attention for fifteen minutes while Sharon stood by the window, pressing her first batch of shirts. Stewart came inside on his own, stood by her, and shared a few soft, mournful moans she recognized as boredom. She turned off the steamer and unplugged it. The uniforms could wait until later that night, after Stewart went to bed.

"Why don't we go find a puzzle?"

They went into the small living room, and Sharon held up a few of his favorites. He tapped one with brightly colored and textured letters, touching each piece as she named them. Halfway through the puzzle, she noticed the carpet held his interest more than the puzzle. He raked lines in the pile with his fingers and moaned.

"I know—you can watch one of your shows." She tried to sound excited about the option. Stewart stood up and awkwardly danced, bobbing his head up and down in agreement. The videos were saved for especially trying days. One of the most helpful things she had learned over the last two years, since Stewart had been diagnosed with autism spectrum disorder, was how music affected him. Whenever he was particularly moody or melancholy, the happy tunes would soothe him. He would listen to "I'm in the Lord's Army" twenty times in a row, rocking back and forth as the children marched across the screen. However, she regretted showing him the repeat button on the remote, not appreciating the cadence nearly as much as he did, but if it made him happy, it was worth it.

Sharon sifted through a pile of mail, throwing the majority away without opening it. One of the envelopes caught her eye.

Parent's Night Out the heading read in bold letters. Skilled caregivers were offering a night of respite and a chance for special needs children to socialize. It was an opportunity she wouldn't take advantage of. With a heavy heart, she read over the activities available while parents enjoyed a couple hours of alone time. The socialization would be good for Stewart, but not wanting to go anywhere alone, she slipped the letter into the wastebasket with the rest of the junk mail. The letter conjured difficult memories: therapists offering little hope that her son would ever develop communication skills other than gestures, moans, or grunts and Bill's endless search for the perfect specialist to unlock the confused passages in his son's mind. If Bill were home, he would have encouraged her to let Stewart spend a few hours without her hovering over him, but he wasn't home.

Stewart had finally let the DVD advance to the next song, and the welcome change reminded her that the mental path she was on could use a change as well. The reality of her son's diagnosis had been easier for her to accept than for Bill, but it didn't mean she'd given up hope. She continued to work with him daily, always watching for signs of progress but not defeated if they weren't achieved.

When evening came, Sharon was content to see the day end. This particular Sunday seemed longer than most days, stretched out by the disappointment that the little red-haired girl had not returned to play. Sharon tucked Stewart into bed and retired early herself.

* * *

On Monday morning, gray clouds blocked the rising sun, and a light rain sent trails of water down the kitchen window. Sharon stirred several eggs together before pouring them into a hot skillet, interrupting the quietness with sizzles and pops. She filled a small bowl with dry cereal and set it on the table in front of Stewart's chair, waiting until he woke up to add the milk. The day's pile of shirts, covered in plastic and draped over a heavy wooden chair, seemed larger than usual. The number of items pressed determined her wages, so she challenged herself to view the extra workload as beneficial. She scooped half the eggs onto a small plate and sat across from the milkless cereal and the red metal stepstool that Stewart preferred to sit on.

A large wooden chair, which now held uniforms, used to hold Bill. Five months ago, he'd accepted a promotion at Davis Engineering, an electronics manufacturing firm he'd been with for three years before they were married. The promotion came with a potentially significant increase in income; however, it also had its downside: year-round travel. Over the last five months, Bill had been home a total of twenty-two days. The time spent at home seemed to dwindle as his project bids became more and more successful. His absence left her wondering if he still cared for her. As far as their financial needs were concerned, he was faithful, and she tried to be grateful that his job enabled her to stay home with Stewart. The wages from her new job weren't a necessity, but she couldn't help feeling she might need the extra income someday.

As she ate her eggs, a garbage truck rumbled down the alley. Sharon watched the dimly lit figures empty the cans of all the unwanted things, items broken, worn out, or no longer useful.

"I'm sorry, Lord," she prayed, disappointed with herself. "Instead of feeling thankful, I'm feeling as useless as the contents poured from the cans, emptied of their worth and destined to be discarded." Sharon's conscience needled her, so she amended her prayer with an apology. "I'll try to be more thankful tomorrow."

Stewart shuffled into the kitchen, wearing his superhero pajamas and sporting skewed hair and tired eyes. He climbed up on the red step stool by his bowl and ate a few dry pieces of cereal before she covered the rest with milk. Sharon warmed the cooked eggs and placed them on the table in front of him. He grabbed the eggs with his hands and pushed them into his mouth.

"Stewart, here, use your fork." She poked a few pieces on his fork and handed it to him. He pulled each piece off with his fingers and popped them into his mouth.

"I see someone is going to have an attitude today." She ran her hand through his messy hair and kissed him briefly on the forehead.

He copied her gesture, running his own hand through his hair, before returning his attention to the cereal in front of him. Ignoring the large spoon next to his bowl, he used his hand to shovel milk-soaked squares into his mouth. Sharon considered pressing him to use his spoon but decided to let it pass this time, not willing to start the day off with conflict.

Sitting across from her son, Sharon watched the changing sky. The rain stopped and patches of sunlight began to filter through fading, gray clouds.

"Look, it might be a nice day after all. Let's hurry and get you dressed so we can go for a walk." Eager to bury her doldrums, she thought the change in scenery would be good for both of them.

Early morning, before the sidewalks and streets were busy, proved to be the best time to take a walk around the block. Stewart would be free to stroll down the sidewalk without bikes and skateboards making him nervous, the empty streets offering relief from screeching brakes, honking horns, and revving engines. She helped Stewart with his rain boots and snapped his yellow jacket before heading out to survey the perimeter around the block. Every puddle would be analyzed, the depth measured by how far the murky water rose on Stewart's green boots.

As they made their way down the long line of row houses, Sharon pointed out landmarks like a tour guide, hoping Stewart would be familiar with the area should he ever leave the house without her noticing and need to find his way home. After walking most of the way around the block, they turned down the alley. Sharon wondered which house Stacey might be living in and then pushed the thought aside. They may never see the little girl again.

"Look, Stewart, this big, prickly tree is only three houses away from our house."

They took a few seconds to feel the pointed needles on the evergreen tree before continuing down the alley, stopping when they reached the gate at their own backyard. Parked past the gate, Sharon's beige Subaru sat surrounded by brown, overgrown grass.

She reached over the gate to unlock it and noticed something lodged in the grass between the car and the fence. "What's this, Stewart?" she asked, including him in her investigation. It appeared that a folding step stool had been left for the next time a short yet ingenious little redhead might need it.

"We'd better leave this here, just in case someone wants to come into our yard again the *usual way*." Sharon smiled, hoping the stool would be used again. After locking the gate, she removed the cover from Stewart's sandbox and headed back inside with their jackets.

"I'll be right back."

The late morning air felt warmer than when they left, and the change of scenery had provided a needed boost to her mood. As she walked back through the kitchen, she jerked her head up, surprised to hear familiar chatter through the screen door.

"And then I found this shovel and thought we could play with it in your sandbox."

The singsong, pixy-like voice was music to her ears. Sharon hurried to the door. "Hello, Stacey. We missed you yesterday. I'm glad you came back to visit us."

"Hi, Mrs. Webster. I brought a shovel for your boy and me to play with. It's plastic, so it's okay for Stewart to play with, least that's what Nanna May said when she gave it to me." She got up and brushed the sand off her animal-print leggings before stepping out of the sandbox. "I got something." Stacey pulled a folded piece of paper out of her pink cowboy boot and gave it to Sharon. "I couldn't play here yesterday 'cause we go to Sunday school with Nanna May and Earl. The Bible stories are fun, and I like Mrs. Diller lots—she's my teacher—but the crafts are lame 'cause all they have is crayons. They should have markers for older kids or play dough or something, but they don't." She swung her long, red hair back over her shoulder, returned to the sandbox, and shoveled sand into a plastic bowl.

Sharon situated a lawn chair next to the two children, ready to intervene if she had to. She unfolded the note and read Nanna May's reply:

Dear Sharon,

You are a breath of fresh air to a weary old soul. Thank you so much for your kind note. You are probably wondering how I can let Stacey roam the neighborhood looking for new lands to conquer. I heard from a reliable source that our neighborhood did not have a single soul living in it that I needed to fret over. You see, a policeman and his wife moved in a few doors down from yours, and they seem to have the scoop on all their neighbors already.

Anyway, my only concern is that Stacey might overstay her welcome. She won't hesitate to speak her mind, so if she has a problem playing with your Stewart, she can just get herself back home. That won't be likely, though, since she's bored out of her mind with nothing but an old woman to entertain her, and she talks my ear off by breakfast. That girl has a bigger vocabulary than Noah Webster. I would have come over today with Stacey to talk to you in person, but I don't get out much anymore. You and Stewart can come and visit anytime. In fact, I'd love to see the both of you.

Nanna May

A phone number and address were listed at the bottom of the page. Sharon would call and tell the elderly woman how much she enjoyed having a playmate for her son. She tucked the note in her pocket and thanked Stacey for bringing it with her.

Stewart seemed pleased that his new friend had returned to play. Stacey chatted on and on, commentating in great detail about the imagined events unfolding in the sandbox.

"And then the princess walked to the castle, and the prince dug a huge moat to catch all the bad guys, " she continued the never-ending monologue.

The two children were playing so well together that Sharon felt all would be well if she slipped into the kitchen for a few minutes. As she put dry dishes in the cupboard, she realized that Nanna May's challenge with Stacey's abundant verbal skills would become her blessing. The screen door provided an ample avenue for sound to travel from the sandbox to the kitchen, a second-by-second reminder that the kids were still where she expected them to be and content.

"No, Stewart! You can't grab things! You wait your turn!" Stacey yelled.

Sharon was already running for the screen door when she heard Stewart's angry, shrill scream followed by the familiar sound of a hand slapping hard on skin. When she reached the door, she expected to see a crying little girl huddled in a corner of the sandbox. Stewart had done what she had feared, and now Stacey's fair skin would sport a red welt, inflicted by her temperamental son. Just as she reached for the handle on the door, she saw Stacey rear back and land a solid slap on Stewart's arm. Sharon stood in conflicted surprise, watching to see what would happen next.

Stewart grabbed his arm. He'd never been on the receiving end of a hard slap, and he moaned his clear dissatisfaction with the exchange, "Muuuuuh."

"What do you 'spect, Stewart? It's not nice to hit, but I had to hit you back to make things fair. If you hit me, I will hit you back every time. Did you hear me, Stewart? Ev-er-y time! Now . . . you need to tell me you're sorry." Stacey folded her arms.

Sharon stepped back away from the door and continued to watch and listen, hoping Nanna May would accept the red mark on Stacey's arm as easily as Stacey did. Having never been slapped before, Stewart appeared as if the return in kind both surprised him and informed him of the natural consequences of slapping his new friend, a lesson he seemed to understand instantly since he returned to playing without the coveted shovel. Sharon watched them from the door as Stacey explained the meaning of *sorry* to Stewart and promised if he did what she said, he could have the shovel. A minute later, Stewart was playing with the shovel and accompanying Stacey's singsong commentary with happy, guttural chants.

"Stacey, would you like to stay for lunch? I could make you a sandwich," Sharon offered as she stepped through the squeaky screen door.

"No, thank you, I have to go home for lunch. Nanna May said I'm not s'posed to ask for stuff to eat here 'cause we have lots of food at our own house." She stood up and brushed the sand off her pants. "Then I have to get on the bus 'cause, remember, I go to school when I'm all done with lunch."

Smiling at her frank reply, Sharon walked over and unlocked the gate. When Stacey stepped into the alley, Sharon noticed the stool was pulled closer to the fence. "You know, Stacey, if you want, you can come to the front door so you don't have to climb over the fence."

"The usual way works fine for me," she replied. "Thank you for letting me play with your boy again."

"I have another note for Nanna May. Can you give this to her?" Sharon handed the folded paper to Stacey.

"Yep." Stacey took the note, tucked it in one of her pink boots, then skipped down the alley, singing an impromptu song about cats and rats and hats and anything else that seemed to rhyme.

Sharon and Stewart would have to walk down the block and have a visit with Nanna May. She hoped the slap on Stacey's arm wouldn't put an end to the little girl's visits. After lunch, she called the number at the bottom of Nanna May's note.

"Clarks' residence . . . this is Anna."

"Hello, this is Sharon Webster. I live down the block from you and—"

Anna interrupted her, "Oh, yes, are you Stewart's mom, where Stacey has been playing? I'm Stacey's mom, Anna Hayes."

"Yes, hello," Sharon answered timidly. Anna didn't sound upset about the slap, but her voice had a commanding, no-nonsense tone to it. Sharon asked if tomorrow morning would be a good time for Stewart and her to come over for a short visit, maybe around ten o'clock. She could hear Anna relaying the message.

"Nanna May says come on over; that's a good time for her. She's looking forward to meeting you guys. I'm sorry I won't be here. I have to work, but thanks for letting my daughter play over there with your son." After a short visit, Anna hung up, leaving Sharon with the impression that Stacey hadn't mentioned being hit. Tomorrow morning, she'd have to tell Nanna May what happened.

CHAPTER 4

At ten o'clock the next morning, Sharon and Stewart headed down the block to find the address on Nanna May's note. Anna had given her a quick description of the house, along with a future plan to meet her and Stewart. As they walked past familiar houses with unfamiliar people, Sharon wondered how long they had lived on the same block as Nanna May without ever meeting. So many people were coming and going that knowing one's neighbors had become a thing of the past.

Six houses down, they came to the number listed on the note and knocked on the front door. An elderly black man with friendly eyes and graying hair opened the door, but before he had a chance to say anything, Sharon was apologizing.

"I'm sorry, I thought this was where Nanna May and Stacey lived." She fumbled with the note and checked the address, "I must have the wrong number." She backed away from the door.

The older man chuckled, "You got the right house, missy. Come on in. My name's Earl, Earl Clark. You must be Sharon. And this little guy here must be Stewart. Hello there, young man. It's real nice to meet you both."

Sharon noticed the elderly gentleman was aware of her son's limitations but not uncomfortable with him. She considered her own reaction, assuming she must have had the wrong house because a black man answered the door. His friendly nature pushed her embarrassment aside as he announced their arrival.

"May . . . Maybeline, you have yourself some good lookin' company for a change." He waved for them to follow him through the short entry into the living room, similar in size to their own, and offered them a seat.

Pictures of family and friends covered a floral-papered wall, many of them decades old. Judging by the haphazard way the frames on the periphery had been added to the once symmetrical display, the collection must have grown over the years. Sharon and Stewart sat on a worn leather sofa with a brightly colored afghan draped over the back. Two recliners were situated across from the sofa, and a picture of an old man praying over his simple meal of broth and bread hung on the far wall. Sharon thought the room seemed comfortable but aged.

"I'll be there before the sun goes down. Don't be thinkin' I forgot about you two," Nanna May's rich, deep voice greeted them from around the corner.

"I'll be right back," Earl said, stepping out to assist his wife.

A large, elderly black woman wearing a long, orange-and-brown floral dress and comfortable slippers slowly made her way into the living room from the kitchen, holding on to her husband's arm for support. It was apparent arthritis had taken its toll on her aging body.

"Well now, just look at the two of you. Earl and I are so glad you could come by. I knew when the step stool disappeared that Stacey found herself a fence to scale. She must a been casin' your place for a couple days before she decided to enter the premises. I hope she hasn't been no trouble."

"No, not at all; we're happy to have her. I had a concern, though, with something that happened yesterday," Sharon started to explain.

Earl came back in the room with two tall glasses of sweet tea and a juice box for Stewart.

Sharon thanked him and handed the juice box to her son. "Here, Stewart, can you hold this?"

He smiled and grabbed the small box with both hands. Sharon was relieved that he seemed comfortable enough in the new surroundings and content to stay seated next to her.

The kitchen door slammed, and small boots thumped toward the living room.

"You're here already! Fantastic!" Stacey leaned on the elderly woman she called Nanna May.

"Well, there goes my chance to visit." Nanna May teased her little charge with a tickle.

That must have been Earl's cue to collect Stacey and Stewart since he shuttled them off to the backyard without an explanation. As Stacey skipped toward the back door, Sharon noticed a trio of faint red lines on her upper arm. She wouldn't be able to think about anything else until she had a chance to explain the slapping incident.

"Mrs. Clark, I'm sorry about—"

"Sugar, you just call me Nanna May like everybody else does. Now, I bet you're wantin' to discuss the redness on Stacey's arm. I did read your note, and thank you for sendin' it."

Sharon dove in with an explanation, "Yes, I'm so sorry. You see, Stewart hits whenever he gets angry and—"

Nanna may nodded her head and interrupted Sharon again, "Now, the story I was told by little Miss Stacey included a slap right back at your son. I'm not a big fan of hittin', but as long as there's no real harm bein' done, it don't hurt kids none to get bumped around a bit by their friends. That's how they learn to live with each other. There's too many kids bein' raised like a bunch of sissies these days. They go a bawlin' to their mommas whenever they get what's comin' to 'em."

Sharon didn't know how to respond. If Stacey were her daughter, she might have been more offended, like the previous mothers who were not keen on their children playing with Stewart any longer. "If Stacey still wants to come over to play, I can watch the kids more closely to make sure she doesn't get hit again," Sharon offered.

"You know what? Judgin' by the size of Stewart and the amount of vim and vinegar in our Stacey, I'm fairly certain she can hold her own. Now, if you don't want two kids scufflin' at your place, I sure do understand, but as far as I'm concerned, a few well-placed slaps between the two of them will probably toughen 'em up some so the good Lord can prepare them for the next bit of discomfort life swings their way. Of course, I don't have no patience for bullies, but a bump here and there 'cause a couple of kids are expressin' their selfish human natures isn't somethin' to get one's panties all twisted up over." Nanna May swiped her hand through the air like it was nothing.

Sharon, not sure what to say, didn't disagree with the older woman's logic, but never had she heard someone say it was beneficial for kids to hit each other as long as they were friends.

"If you agree we've got that business settled, tell me 'bout yourself. What brought you to DC?" The elderly woman settled back in her recliner and folded her hands on her ample lap.

It didn't take long before a comfortable flow of conversation drifted back and forth as if they'd known each other for years. Sharon told her that she and her husband met in DC, skipping the most recent details so she wouldn't insinuate anything about her disappointment with his absence.

Nanna May explained that Stacey and her mother, Anna Hayes, moved in a few weeks ago and Stacey's mother had taken a job at Union Station with a tour bus company. Anna's brother, Shane Hayes, was going to Gallaudet University and working on his doctorate.

She continued to share the story behind the Hayes trio and their arrival at the Clark house. "Anna and Shane's folks died in a car accident when a drunk driver came up on the freeway goin' the wrong direction and hit them head-on. Their parents had life insurance and all, but lawyers managed to weasel most of it out them kids before they ever saw any of it. Anna was only a freshman in college, and her brother was a junior in high school when the accident happened. Then Anna dropped out of college and got a job to support herself and Shane. She was determined to see her brother go to college." Nanna May sat quietly for a moment, slowly shaking her head.

Sharon patiently waited, allowing her new acquaintance to collect her thoughts and hoping the story wasn't over.

"That's a lot on a young momma's plate. The Lord blessed that brother of hers with brains, though, and his smarts earned him a scholarship for most of his four years of college."

Sharon felt sorry for them. Apparently, life had dealt them an unfair hand. "So, Anna never married? I don't mean to pry, but I noticed she and her brother have the same last name."

"It ain't no secret," Nanna May replied. "Anna got pregnant shortly after the accident, and the young man she was seein' promised to marry her before Stacey was born, but then done changed his tune and run off." Nanna May's empathy for their misfortune was apparent.

Sharon wanted to know more but felt it would be impolite to ask.

"You see," Nanna May continued, "Shane is deaf and has been since birth, but he's one smart young man. That fiancé gave some excuse about not wantin' to be responsible for him, so he made Anna choose between him and her brother. You can see how that went down. If you ask me, Stacey's daddy never was gonna marry Anna. There was a problem with Stacey before she was born, but I'll let her tell you about that. No . . . baby daddy was only using Anna's brother as an excuse. He wasn't interested in havin' no babies—just makin' em."

Nanna May shook her head in disgust. "That boy, he knew Shane was gonna to be on his own soon, bein' all full of brilliance and brains. Shane bein' deaf wasn't gonna slow him down none. No way. Baby-daddy went to church and all, but he tried to make Anna take the blame for him not marryin' her, all while lookin' for an excuse to run off with somebody else. I heard he had a silk tongue, sellin' himself as some kind of gentleman with a good-boy haircut and all. As smooth as the devil himself, that's what he was." Nanna May clucked her tongue and took a drink of her tea.

"Poor girl. Anna was an easy target when her parents died. Accordin' to our friends in Michigan, he had his parents thinkin' she hustled him. They had some money, and he claimed Anna got pregnant so she could tap into their bank account. It sounds like they should have spent some of it gettin' their boy some lessons in manners. My daddy always told me, *just 'cause a boy is in church don't mean church is in the boy.* Seemed to me what that boy needed was a good ol' fashioned whoopin'. I'd of givin' it to him myself, but I hear they don't parcel those out to kids these days. Anyways, Anna is a good momma. She'll do fine once she gets her feet under her."

"If you don't mind my asking, how did they end up living here, with you and Earl?" Sharon hoped the question wasn't too invasive.

"They went to a church in Grand Rapids, Michigan, with some friends of ours who had Anna give us a call. They were lookin' to get somethin' worked out for the three of them to come to DC when Gallaudet accepted Shane into their graduate program. Our spare room was bein' vacated, so we told them to come on over. Anna and Stacey live here, and Shane stays at the university. He comes over every once in a while, when he's not busy with his research. Anna and Stacey couldn't afford to be here if they had to be on their own, at least not for another half a year or so."

"So, you didn't know them until they came to live with you?" Sharon wondered how the elderly couple could be so trusting.

"Not one bit, but we could trust our friends who told us they were good kids, and their parents were good folks, too. That was enough for us. Little Stacey should have come with a disclaimer, though. Them young preachers like to say the Lord won't give us any more than we can handle, but they got it all backward. What they should be preachin' is that the good Lord gives us all kinds a things we can't handle. If we could take care of things on our own, we wouldn't need to call on Jesus for no help. So, when I prayed, *Lord Jesus, help me with this chatter box*, he done sent her down to your place."

Nanna May laughed at herself, a deep, happy rumble that filled the room with an irresistible wave, capturing Sharon with its contagious melody. It had been too long since she had laughed like that, far too long. Sharon couldn't remember the last time she had been so at ease with someone.

"You see, sugar, you and Stewart are both answers to my prayers, and the good Lord knows I'm gonna thank him every day so you don't change your mind about lettin' Stacey come over to play."

Sharon felt a sense of relief, assured that Nanna May and Earl, and likely Anna as well, were comfortable with the new friend arrangement. She checked the time on her watch. An hour and a half had passed by in what seemed like minutes.

"Oh—we need to get going." Sure they had overstayed their welcome, Sharon apologized, "I'll show myself through the kitchen, if you don't mind, and get Stewart. I had no idea we had been here so long."

"Why not stay for lunch? Earl makes a mean grilled cheese sandwich," Nanna May offered.

"Thank you, but I need to get Stewart home for a nap before he turns into a bear. It was so nice to meet you, Nanna May. I enjoyed our visit."

"You don't stay away too long now; I like the company. Earl's good lookin' and all, but he's heard all my stories, so you two come on back here any time."

"I'd love to," Sharon replied honestly, encouraging Nanna May to stay seated while she showed herself to the backyard. As she passed through the kitchen, she glanced at the cluttered refrigerator door. Stacey's artwork was on display, held in place by a variety of magnets. A phrase on one of them seemed familiar: *All things work together for good.* If that were only true, Sharon thought as she pulled the back door open.

Earl trimmed a shrub, and Stacey and Stewart collected the trimmings and threw them in a cardboard box. Somehow, the chore was a game.

"I see you're gonna take my helper away," the older man said with an easy grin.

"Thank you for watching him. I hope he wasn't any trouble."

"Trouble? No, ma'am, he's no trouble at all. It's kind a nice havin' a man 'round the house. All these girls give me the itches." He scratched at his sides, encouraging high-pitched giggles from Stacey.

Sharon and Stewart left through the Clarks' back gate and walked up the alley toward home.

"That was a nice visit, wasn't it, Stewart?" She brushed her hand through his thick hair.

He patted her arm and chuckled. She could tell he agreed.

* * *

November ushered in cooler days and sunless early mornings. Sharon found it more difficult to get up with it still dark outside but was glad to have the last shirt pressed. She covered the uniforms with plastic and hung them by the front door, ready for pickup. It was still early, and Stewart would likely sleep for another hour or so.

She made herself a cup of coffee, lifted the wrap covering a plate of pecan rolls on the kitchen counter, and coaxed the plastic to release the thick caramel sauce sticking to it. Cutting one of the rolls in half, she placed it on a small plate and secured the sugarcoated wrap back in place. A few seconds in the microwave produced a sweet aroma of home-baked bread and roasted, caramel-covered pecans. Sharon wondered if she should even indulge in the butter-soaked sweet roll.

Nanna May had sent the rolls home with her yesterday, insisting she and Stewart could use a little more meat on their bones. She savored the first gooey bite. How could there be so much pleasure in the calorie-laden sugar overload? The answer was obvious. It was because of the hands that made it. Nanna May poured her own recipe of sweetness over everything she touched. Sharon placed another bite in her mouth and grinned. Her elderly friend's sweetness included a bit of spice as well. Nanna May had an authoritative edge to her, but it was evident her selfless compassion ruled her heart and dictated her life's course. Sharon felt fortunate to have stumbled onto that course. Her own burdens now seemed a bit lighter, lifted by the new friendships six houses down.

There was much to be thankful for. Stacey was aware of Stewart's limitations and quick temper and had determined him worth befriending. Her son had made a friend—not just any friend but his first *real* friend. The little fireball had been a literal forced entry into their lives, and the encroachment opened the door for a friendship of her own, something she had not had since attending church nearly a year ago and maybe not even then.

* * *

Sharon and Bill started going to church several years after they were married. Bill attributed his interest in attending church to his grandmother, who took him with her to Sunday school many times. When he was younger, he'd noticed a marked difference between his parents' and his grandmother's priorities. He had asked Sharon if she was interested in visiting a church when she became pregnant, and although she had not gone before, it seemed like a good idea at the time.

They considered a handful of people friends of theirs, mostly professionals and a few stay-at-home new mothers, similar in age and just starting families. However, when challenged with less-than-perfect circumstances, the bonds of friendship would prove to be loosely tied. Once Stewart was born, two of Sharon's closest friends opted to foster relationships with other women since they liked to travel and had fewer restrictions on their time. Several others, with children similar in age to Stewart, made an effort to stay in touch but became uncomfortable with her son's disorder and moved on as well, eventually untying any small thread that had once connected them. After Stewart turned four, they made it to church only on the occasional Sunday. By then, the only things shared between Sharon and her waning friendships were smiles and pleasantries. She tried not to blame them, since she had given up trying to foster any meaningful friendships herself. Stewart's fits of temper had steadily grown more unpredictable, making it easier for her and Bill to choose seclusion over discomfort. Bill stayed in touch with a few of the men, most of them business connections. After her husband accepted his promotion, which unfortunately became synonymous with being absent, she stopped going to church altogether.

"Thank you, Lord, for Stacey, Nanna May, and Earl," Sharon prayed as she rinsed the sticky caramel off her plate.

* * *

Nearly every weekday, like clockwork, Stacey would show up at the Webster' house around ten in the morning. If it was a rainy day, the front doorbell would ring, and the two kids would play inside until eleven o'clock, the customary time for Stacey to head home for lunch. Sharon and Stewart had a new Friday routine of walking to the Clarks' house around ten thirty in the morning. His anticipation of the visit had overridden his previous anxiety caused by the late-morning traffic sounds. Stewart would benefit from the change in scenery, and Sharon would enjoy a visit with Nanna May.

Earl, who was generally home in the mornings, unless working on something at their church, would take the kids outside and somehow convince them that helping him in the yard was great fun. This freed up his wife to enjoy Sharon's company. One day, he had them make letters with blades of grass they pulled from the walkway. Stewart, the keeper of the pulled grass, provided Stacey with a continuous supply of letter-forming material.

The two playmates didn't always stay out of trouble. On one of their earlier visits, Earl needed to do a few things without children in tow and gave them some crackers to snack on while he looked for something in the basement. In less than ten minutes, Stacey and Stewart used their crackers to make a trail of crumbs leading up to the back door and into the house for the *soldiers* in the yard to follow inside. Several hundred ants made their way into the house before their marching orders were swiftly altered with a call for an about face, enforced by Earl and the kitchen broom.

CHAPTER 5

The phone on the kitchen counter rang. Sharon dried her hands and reached across the counter by the fourth ring. Over the last two months, the twenty or so calls she'd answered were telemarketers or strangers in search of opinions but rarely her husband. Bill's last few calls had ended badly, one to apologize for missing Stewart's birthday and the other to tell her he wouldn't make it home in October.

"Hello," she answered, bothered by the likely intrusion.

"Sharon, it's Bill. How are you, sweetheart?"

Caught off guard, it took her a few seconds to respond.

"Are you there, Sharon?"

"Yes, Bill—I'm here. I haven't seen you for so long. Are you coming home?" Maybe her worries had been unfounded over these past few months.

"I'd like to, but I'm headed to Brazil in a few days. What do you think about you and Stewart flying down to Sao Paulo for a week and joining me?"

Sharon was hesitant to answer. Bill had to know how difficult it would be for Stewart to travel. A flight that long in an enclosed, unfamiliar space would surely overwhelm their son worse now than it had on their trip home from Mexico, just over two years ago.

"Do you have a break in your schedule? It would be nice if we could spend some time with you, but can you fly home? Please, Bill, even if it's for a couple weeks. Can you make it home for Thanksgiving?" She wanted so badly to see him. "You know I would meet you down in Brazil tomorrow if I could, but Stewart wouldn't be able to handle being on an airplane for that long."

"That's all right; I understand. I wouldn't have much time away from meetings anyway, but I miss you and Stewart. I was hoping it might work out this time." He sounded disappointed.

"Just fly home then, even for a few days—please—we miss you, too." Sharon was sorry she had fallen back into the same pleading conversation that dominated the last few calls, but she was desperate to see him.

"I'm sorry, Sharon. I can't. I have a redesign to finish before a meeting next week, then another meeting in Sao Paulo with a selection committee to finalize a contract. I don't even have three free days in a row, or I would come home."

Sharon burst into tears and covered the phone with her hand.

"Sweetheart, are you crying? I'm so sorry . . . I love you, Sharon."

"No, I'm all right, Bill," she sniffed, not wanting him to hang up yet. "Do you think you might be able to come home after you're done in Brazil? That would give me something to look forward to."

"Sharon, I'm sorry. I can't promise anything right now. We're swamped with the company expansion, but this is the only year I have to be away from home for so long. Please hang in there with me through this one tough year, okay, honey?"

"All right," she replied, trying not to sound defeated.

"How is Stewart?

"He has a new friend, a feisty, little redheaded girl. She's good for him, though, and can handle his limitations." Sharon tried hard to disguise her disappointment and talk about other things, but her throat began to tighten.

"He has a friend . . . That's great. Where does she live?"

Sharon could detect relief in his voice, obviously preferring to talk about anything other than his absence.

"Just down the block. She and her mother are staying with the Clarks. Do you know them?" Sharon rubbed the back of her neck in an attempt to relieve building tension.

"Yeah, I do. I had a few visits with Earl when I put in the chain-link fence a couple years back. I saw him a few times when he went for a walk down the alley, and I remember him being a friendly man. I think he started working at one of the museums. Never met his wife, though."

Sharon didn't want to talk about the goings-on in the neighborhood and couldn't maintain her composure any longer. "Bill, I'm sorry, but I really need you to come home. Get a different job if you have to, but I can't be here without you any longer." She hated each desperate word as it left her mouth.

"Sharon, you know I love you and Stewart, and I would come home if I could, but if I don't finish these contracts, I won't get paid. Can you give me until December? I can be home for at least a few days at Christmas time," he offered.

"A few days? . . . Bill . . . if you loved us, you could give us more than a few days at Christmas time!" Sharon's true feelings had forced their way to the surface and quickly shifted from disappointment to anger.

"Do you want me to come home for a few days or not at all?" he asked her, sounding exasperated.

"I'm sorry, Bill. I don't want to talk to you again unless you're calling to tell me you're coming home to stay." Sharon hung up the phone, instantly regretting her hasty, angry words.

She cried on and off for the next two days, trying to reserve any energy she had for the care of her son. The reality that her marriage could be irreparable began to weigh heavily on her, but her concerns didn't stop there. Trying to resist a question that could no longer be kept in the back of her mind, Sharon allowed the nagging thoughts to resurface. Was her husband having an affair? Would another woman be with him, taking her place?

An acrid taste worked its way up her throat and into her mouth. Her conscience warned her that she was overreacting, so to put her mind at ease, she decided to call Bill. When Stewart was ready for his nap, she would slip into the backyard with her cell phone, call her husband, and tell him she regretted what she had said to him two days earlier.

* * *

Bill boarded his flight for Sao Paulo and took his seat in first class. He had a ticket for coach, but the flight had been overbooked, so he was upgraded to a first class seat. A smartly dressed woman sat by the window next to his seat, slowly twizzling a stir stick in her mixed drink. As soon as he took his seat and reached for the seatbelt, a friendly attendant offered to get him a drink as well.

"Yes, please. I'll take a ginger ale," Bill replied.

The woman sitting next to him put her hand on his leg. "What's the matter, sweetie, you're not the designated driver."

Bill was instantly uncomfortable with the woman's overfamiliarity. "I tend to get really nauseous when I fly, so I'll stick to soda for now." He patted his stomach, even though it was a lie.

She lifted her permanent eyebrows and removed her manicured hand from his leg. "Are you going to Brazil for business, pleasure, or both?" she asked with a glint in her eye.

"Business," he replied, thinking this was going to be a torturously long flight.

She continued to stare at him, clearly waiting for him to engage her with the same question, so he reluctantly asked her where she was going, which turned out to be a huge mistake. After she introduced herself as an executive assistant at a pharmaceutical company, Jacinta spent the next hour filling him in on the benefits headed his way in the field of bioengineering.

"You know, Bill, you appear to have been blessed with quality genetics yourself. At first glance, I'd suppose you to be about . . . twenty-six or -seven, but if I really looked at you with my trained eye, I'd say you are . . . thirty-three years old?"

Jacinta was right, and Bill was curious to know how she could tell. She ordered her third drink and was clearly pleased to have finally captured his attention.

"Well, for instance," she said as she brushed her hand over his ear and held his hair loosely away from his temple, "the difference in skin tone and texture around the ear, and also just under the hairline, reveals a wealth of information. If you hadn't been a sun lover, you'd appear to be even younger."

He was uncomfortable with the apparent invitation to touch him and decided a trip to the bathroom was in order. When he returned, he made it obvious he wanted to change the subject. When she moved in for round two, he interrupted her.

"So, Jacinta, do you have any children?" he asked, assuming the platonic question might remind her he was not combining business with pleasure on this trip.

"None and no husband either, since you're asking, at least not anymore."

She tried to get him to order a drink, but he declined. Somehow, his platonic question had morphed into an indecent proposal.

"I have a wife—yes I do—a wife and a son," he blurted out awkwardly when Jacinta drew several fingertips across the back of his hand. A narrow seat soaked in an unidentifiable liquid between two crying toddlers suddenly seemed preferable to his luxury leather recliner. Jacinta was a predator in a skirt and was unfortunately ordering another drink. Deciding another distraction was in order, Bill stood up and slid his jacket off before pulling his computer out of the overhead compartment.

"It's been a pleasure visiting with you, but I won't bother you anymore. I need to get a few things buttoned up before we land. He felt somewhat guilty, acting as if the remaining seven hours of the flight would barely give him enough time to complete his important work, but the diversionary tactic was worth it. Unfortunately, he underestimated Jacinta's ability to keep her eye on the prize.

After her fourth drink, she went in for the kill. "You know, before you can button things up, they need to be unbuttoned . . . Am I right?" She started to move toward him with an apparent willingness to conquer. "I have a luxury condo with plenty of room for a visitor . . . only minutes from the airport."

The alcohol on Jacinta's breath scented the air as Bill realized he would not be able to keep her at bay without being unpleasantly blunt.

"I'm sorry, miss; I am happily married. And, as attractive as you are, I would really appreciate it if you would save your . . . attentions for someone more . . . receptive." He pushed her hand off his leg and leaned toward the isle, intent to study his computer until the inebriated passenger next to him accepted the rebuff. Several minutes and one ginger ale later, he left his seat to use the restroom, careful to lock the screen on his computer.

The cell phone in Bill's blazer pocket vibrated. Jacinta glanced at the blazer lying across the back of the empty seat next to her and then at the restroom door. His phone continued to buzz. On the fourth ring, she slipped her hand into the pocket, retrieved the phone, and looked at the caller ID. "Sharon. Huh?" she scoffed and answered the call with the silkiest voice she could manage. "Hello, can I help you?"

"Oh . . . I'm calling Bill Webster. Sorry, maybe I dialed the wrong number."

"You don't have the wrong number, honey bun, but Bill is busy right now. We're on our way to Sao Paulo, and he has a few things he needs to *button up*," Jacinta said with a tipsy giggle, "but I can give him a message, if you'd like?" She kept an eye on the restroom door.

"No . . . thank you . . . I'll try again later."

The restroom door opened just as Jacinta ended the call. She slipped Bill's cell phone back in his blazer pocket and faced the window. When he returned to his seat, Bill noticed she wore a smug grin on her face and figured the alcohol she'd consumed was working its magic. Jacinta ordered another drink and kept her hands to herself. Relieved he was no longer the object of her affection, he reclined the back of his chair, finally able to relax.

* * *

The cell phone still in her hand, Sharon struggled to breathe, her stomach twisting into painful knots, her worst fears now validated. Bill was on his way to Brazil with another woman. With one hand on the screen door, Sharon felt as if the ground had turned to waves beneath her. She stared at the silent phone in her hand before letting it slip through her fingers and shatter on the concrete step.

CHAPTER 6

When Sharon and Stewart showed up at the Clark house for a Friday morning visit, Anna Hayes greeted them, explaining that she had a rare day off. Stacey looked just like her mother, with the same fiery red hair and freckled nose, but Sharon was surprised to see how petite Anna was. They visited comfortably, and then Anna suggested the four of them go on a bus tour. The following week was predicted to be unseasonably warm for November, and the crush of tourists wouldn't begin until the week after that. Since Anna worked for the tour company at Union Station, the tickets were complimentary. Sharon accepted the offer. It had been a long time since she and Stewart had spent a day out of the house just for fun. She could stay up late and get up early the next morning to have the uniforms pressed in time for pickup. Anna made arrangements to cover her shift and planned the trip for the following Monday morning.

The weekend flew by, the anticipation of a new friend shortening the hours. The welcome distraction gave Sharon enough energy to tackle everything on her to-do list before their day of fun. Monday morning, Sharon helped Stewart move at a steady pace through their morning routine without any emotional flare-ups.

They met Anna and Stacey at the curb as their new friend pulled up in a faded gray sedan that could have been Anna's car since high school. A mascot sticker of an angry Saint Bernard, as faded as the car, clung to the middle of the rear window. After making the necessary adjustments to booster seats and seatbelts, the four tourists-for-a-day headed off to Union Station. Anna was an interesting person with an abundance of energy and a sarcastic wit. After a short time in the car, Sharon could tell where Stacey's extroverted personality came from.

To free up an avenue for conversation, Anna handed her phone to Stacey, who was happy to scroll through pictures with Stewart. She commanded his full attention as she slid her finger across the screen.

"That's my uncle. His name is Uncle Shane. Can you see him, Stewart? He has my same hair, just like my mommy."

Sharon was curious and asked to see the little picture on Anna's phone.

"You can make it bigger if you want to," Stacey said. "If it's too small for your eyes, hand it to me. I can fix it for you." Stacey spread two fingers across the screen to fill the space with the picture and handed the phone back to Sharon.

"Thank you. Oh, yes. Very nice."

The three of them did have the same bright-red hair and fair skin, but Shane had the lion's share of the freckles, along with a big, bright smile and friendly sky-blue eyes. Sharon wondered if Anna at one time wore the same easy smile as her brother, but life's circumstances had forced her to trade it in for the responsibility she seemed to be made of.

Anna filled Sharon in on her brother, every so often reminding Stacey not to interrupt. Nanna May had shared some of the information with her already, but she didn't mind hearing it again from Anna. Shane was busy in the doctoral program at Gallaudet University and lived there as well. Clearly proud of her brother, Anna spent the next five minutes sharing several of his impressive accomplishments. Sharon found the information on Anna's brother interesting but couldn't help being curious about Stacey's father. She would keep her curiosity to herself, though, knowing that it was not her place to ask.

Stacey piped up from the back seat, "Can I talk yet, Mommy?"

"Go ahead; you have two minutes," she replied, partially annoyed.

Sharon smiled at the time limit. It took only minutes after first meeting Stacey to realize the five-year-old's verbal skills were highly developed, but the gift of gab was not always encouraged by her mother.

"Uncle Shane makes an 'O' with his hand and tells me my hair is orange. He's silly and likes to tease me. He calls me Ginger with his hands, but he knows my name is Stacey." She rattled on for several minutes, talking faster when she sensed her two minutes were almost up.

"Why don't you show Stewart how to sign your name, Stacey?" Anna said, clearly trying to shift her daughter's attention to the confines of the back seat.

"I already showed him before."

"Well, show him again," Anna encouraged, with a hint of warning.

* * *

With car parked and kids unloaded, they headed toward the entrance to Union Station. Following Anna through the crowded building to the waiting row of tour buses was easier than Sharon expected. They took the least-traveled path, skirting around the crowds rather than pushing through them. Anna thought of every detail, including blankets for the children so they would be comfortable riding on the top deck of the bus.

Sharon welcomed the crisp, early November air on her face as the bus moved along the National Mall in historic DC. She reached over to make sure Stewart's hat was covering his ears and then allowed herself to relax and enjoy the scenery. The world's tallest obelisk towered above them, climbing toward the clouds at a height exceeding 550 feet and casting a sundial's long, shadowed hand to the northwest.

"Look at that big thing, Stewart." Stacey pointed to the sky. "That's Washington's Monument."

"Stacey—the *Washington* Monument," Anna corrected.

"It's *Washington's* because it's his," her daughter challenged.

Anna shook her head, and Sharon chuckled. Stacey took it upon herself to be their personal tour guide, bolstered by Stewart's enthusiastic reaction whenever she pointed something out to him. Sharon didn't mind the somewhat factual commentary since it was perfect entertainment for Stewart, but Anna was clearly bothered with the constant chatter. Sharon didn't fault her for it. Anna wasn't much younger than her, maybe twenty-seven or twenty-eight years old, and had experienced more than her share of disappointments, but Sharon would give anything for Stewart to be a chatterbox like Stacey.

"Look, Stewart; we're going to stop by the animals. It's so cool, and Earl works there, too. It's a national story museum."

Stewart laughed and tapped his hand on the seat in front of him. "*Natural history*, Stacey," Anna corrected.

"Mommy, that's what I already said!" her daughter shot back.

"Stacey Hayes!" Anna gave her feisty daughter a stern look of disapproval. "That's not okay."

With shoulders slumped, Stacey offered her mother a monotone apology. Stacey's shame instantly forgotten, they stepped off the bus and headed to the museum's entrance.

"Next," a woman called, waving for Stewart to step forward through the metal detector.

Walking over to the attendant, Sharon sent Stewart through and opened his backpack for the woman to inspect. He waved a hand back and forth, agitated by the unfamiliar activity around him. Sharon pointed out Anna and Stacey waiting for them, and the distraction was enough to settle him down.

The foursome continued to move through the first exhibit at a comfortable pace, unhindered by the sparse number of visitors. When they paused to admire an amazing display of cats, Stewart stood motionless, apparently enthralled by a snarling tiger.

"Stewart, come on. There's more better stuff where the bugs are. Hurry up," Stacey prodded.

"Has he ever been to the museum?" Anna asked.

"Not when he was old enough to remember. I think he was asleep in his stroller for most of it," Sharon replied, not mentioning that Bill had been the designated stroller pusher that day.

Stewart was only two years old, and they had spent most of the day walking around the tidal basin, admiring the memorials and each other. She tried to resist taking a trip down memory lane, but if there were days worth remembering, that would be one of them.

"No way! Look at that spider!" Stacey waited for a turn to hold a giant tarantula.

Stewart watched with intense interest as the hairy spider was carefully placed on Stacey's hand. He seemed to be mesmerized by the eight-legged creature crawling up her arm and stood unusually frozen in place.

"Take it . . . Go ahead and take it . . . Take it!" Stacey ordered the young man from the museum. She tried to remain brave but wasn't interested in letting the spider continue to move up her arm.

"Would you like a turn?" the young man asked Stewart.

He seemed eager to hold the spider, but Sharon was uncertain how her son would react once the creature was placed on his hand. She wasn't sure she could grab it if he suddenly changed his mind. The museum attendant set the compliant spider on Stewart's open palm. It took a few tiny steps up his wrist. Stewart gently stroked its fuzzy back and switched it carefully onto his other hand.

"Look at him," Anna said with a smile.

She was surprised herself and relieved she would not have to save a suddenly ejected spider. She continued to watch her son handle the harmless, hairy beast with uncommon ease. His turn over, Stewart reluctantly handed the spider to the next child in line.

"What is it with boys and bugs?" Anna mused. "They just go together . . . like moths to a flame."

Stacy had a few thoughts on the matter. "Boys always like bugs, but I'm not afraid of them. And boys like other gross stuff, too," she informed everyone, until seeing the unmistakable *that's enough* look on her mother's face.

"Bu, bu, bu," Stewart chanted.

He instantly had Sharon's full attention. Not wanting to distract him with her own excitement but hoping for a repeated response, she asked him, "Did you like the bugs, honey?"

"Bu, bu, bu," he repeated, accompanied by an exuberant expression of hopping and clapping.

"Bug-g-g-g," Stacey corrected.

Her mother tapped her on her shoulder and shook her head, appearing embarrassed that her daughter didn't know better. "Sorry," Anna whispered.

"It's all right," Sharon assured her, wondering if the past two months spent playing with his talkative friend might have produced unnoticed progress.

Six Houses Down

Sharon and Stewart stayed at the live insect zoo while Anna took Stacey to view the other exhibits. An hour later, they returned, but Stewart was noncompliant when it was time to go. Sharon coaxed him into leaving by bribing him with a stop at the gift shop. She purchased a book on insects and a large plastic beetle. A sliver of hope tried to seed itself, but she remained careful, not wanting to set herself up for disappointment. They would look at the book together when they got home, and she would try to encourage a repeat performance. The question would not leave her mind the rest of the day: was her son finally trying to talk?

* * *

After thanking Anna for the fun day on the tour bus and the visit to the museum, Sharon helped her sleepy son out of the car and said goodbye to Stacey. Over the next few days, Stewart would pore over the pictures in his new book on insects and play on the couch with his plastic beetle. Unfortunately, he was not interested in repeating the sounds he made at the museum, leaving Sharon to speculate that he was merely imitating a sound rather than comprehending its meaning.

* * *

One week before Thanksgiving, the phone rang. Sharon's nerves jumped, reacting to every ring of the phone as if it were Bill.

"Hey, Sharon, it's Anna."

Sharon's heart sank momentarily as it did with every call that wasn't from her husband, but she quickly shifted from disappointment to surprise, this being the first time Anna had called her.

"Hi, Anna." She hoped everything was all right with their friends down the block.

Anna called to see if Sharon and Stewart would like to join them for Thanksgiving. Afraid to add to an already crowded house, Sharon gratefully declined.

45

"Are you sure?" Anna pressed, "We all go to the church and get together in the fellowship hall, so there's plenty of room for everyone. The Clarks will be there, of course, along with a few of their friends—or more like twenty. My brother won't be able to make it, though, so I would really like it if you and Stewart could come. Besides, Stacey needs someone to play with, or if we can be honest here, someone to talk to . . . continuously."

It wasn't difficult for Sharon to be convinced to join them. Anna offered to pick her and Stewart up a few minutes before noon and refused her offer to bring anything. Grateful for the invitation, Sharon looked at the calendar by the phone, wondering if she should call Bill to make sure he wouldn't be coming home. She pushed the thought aside, fearing the possibility that a woman might answer his phone again.

* * *

Returning home from a day of feasting at the church, Stewart and Sharon were overfed and tired. Nanna May insisted on Sharon bring a tray of leftovers home, complete with enough food for several days and dessert as well. She set the tray on the kitchen counter and allowed her son to keep the two cookies he had absconded with when she wasn't looking.

"You sneaky boy," she teased as she pulled the plastic back over the tray and arranged a spot for it in the refrigerator. "Why don't you sit at the table to eat those?"

He flashed a guilty grin and climbed up onto his step stool, apparently pleased the discovery of his heist would not end in the forfeiture of his loot.

Sharon tried to maintain her resolve not to check the phone for messages, but the temptation had proved too great. She glanced at the phone on the counter and saw the number one flashing on the screen. Instantly regretting not being home when he called, she pressed the button.

You have one new message, the machine reminded her before playing a computer-generated voice pleading with her to consider sending a generous donation for the holidays. She deleted the message before it could finish its appeal. How long would she continue to allow disappointment to control her? Several seconds of unfulfilled expectation had trumped the pleasure of an entire day with friends. She considered disconnecting the landline but decided to wait since she hadn't yet replaced her broken cell phone. There were months of prepaid time remaining, but the cost of the new phone caused her to question if she really needed it. If Bill didn't bother to call her soon, she would disconnect the landline and save herself from the anxiety it caused her. One week later, she called the phone company and cancelled her service.

* * *

"Five down," Sharon mumbled as she hung a uniform on a wire hanger, pulled another shirt from the pile on the chair, and checked the time. Stewart would wake up soon. As she finished steaming the sixth shirt, the disconnected phone on the counter caught her eye. She wrapped the cord around the useless phone and stashed it in a rarely used, high kitchen cupboard, out of sight and mind. Since Stewart was still asleep, she removed the pictures of Bill from the living room wall and put them in a box in her bedroom closet.

A constant worry demanded her attention and threatened her with the likelihood that the automatic deposits to her checking account would soon be as nonexistent as Bill's phone calls. It was time for her to consider how she might take care of her son alone; she knew the pressing she took in was not going to bring in enough money to stay in their house for long.

Every month, Bill had deposited ample funds to cover the mortgage and all of the bills. Until they stopped coming, she would keep steaming uniforms. Over the last few months, she had saved a few thousand dollars, including the money saved by disconnecting the phone and parking her unused car in the alley. The funds would be there should she and Stewart need them. Sharon was fully aware of her obsessive tendency to be self-sufficient, and she didn't need her college textbooks to explain the reason why. It had been obvious to her since she was twelve years old and unsure of many things.

47

* * *

When her parents, Robert and Shirley Henderson, divorced, Sharon was an only child. Even though both her mother and father profusely promised to offer the same love they shared with her before irreconcilable differences changed everything, her world fell apart, shattering her sense of self-worth and leaving her questioning everything she trusted. Her father moved out and remarried, leaving Sharon to bounce back and forth from home to home every six months until she turned fifteen. Four months after her father's second set of forever promises, he and his new wife had a baby boy.

The visits with her father began to feel like an intrusion, the new family seemingly frustrated with her interruption in their schedule. When her father called to ask her if she would be interested in attending a camp for half of the summer, she stopped visiting him, making excuses until she was eighteen. He continued to send her money throughout her teen years and paid for most of her college, as if taking care of her financial needs covered his fatherly obligations.

Six years had gone by since she last heard her father's voice, calling to congratulate her when she graduated from college and apologizing that he wouldn't be able to come to the ceremony. She had not seen or heard from him after that. A Christmas card would show up in the mail slot every year, complete with manufactured sentiments and his name listed at the bottom, signed in someone else's hand.

Her mother, Shirley Henderson, also remarried and had two more children, a boy and a girl. Her new stepfather was friendly enough, but after she turned fifteen, he was a little too friendly. Certain her mother would think her accusation exaggerated, she kept the incident to herself, considering the advance her stepfather had made toward her as no real damage done. Not interested in giving him another chance, she moved in with one of her girlfriends to avoid being near her stepfather.

When her mother questioned her, Sharon concocted a lengthy explanation about needing her freedom. Her mother seemed too eager to comply and quickly agreed to give her the space she wanted. They spoke on the phone several times a month for the next three years, and then her mother suddenly stopped calling. A month after her high school graduation, Sharon received a hundred dollar bill wrapped in a handwritten note. It was from her mother, and the note simply stated that she loved her. Sharon noticed the missing return address on the envelope. When she tried to call and thank her, the phone number was no longer in service. She was suspicious her mother's second marriage had ended badly.

A marked improvement to her sense of well-being, Sharon's college years were a step in the right direction. She made a few close friends and poured herself into her studies, earning her top marks in her class. There was no mystery in her desire to pursue a degree in counseling and psychology. She had determined the things missing in her own life, and the disappointments she had experienced would serve to produce a level of understanding that other counselors would not be able to tap into. What she did not plan on, however, was that her previous, difficult circumstances were destined to repeat themselves, leaving her abandoned again.

The empty phone jack above the kitchen counter reminded her it was time to move on. If Bill needed to tell her anything of great importance, he could mail it in a letter.

CHAPTER 7

The beach in Mumbai, India, was crowded with locals and tourists. Several camels adorned with bright red and yellow tassel-edged fabric provided rides for tourists along the shore. Bill had always wanted to visit Mumbai, and now his job would keep him here for several months. Traveling had been part of his childhood, and his parent's passion for exotic and faraway places naturally became his own. Before he was sixteen, he had visited several South American and four European countries. By the time he graduated from college, he had a list of twenty *must see* destinations, and Mumbai was one of them.

He stood on the hot sand and looked westward toward the Arabian Sea. Gone was the excitement he remembered as a traveling young man, carefree and full of wonder. Disappointment needled him, but the reason for his unmet expectations had nothing to do with the scenery. He was trying to be free, independent and free, but this *freedom* felt more like bondage.

A young boy's shrill scream interrupted Bill's thoughts. He looked down the beach in time to witness a young Indian boy's father snatch him up and march toward the water's edge for a quick dunk in the surf. The boy clearly felt the price was worth it as he returned to taunting and running from his father, the scenario playing out several times until the boy ran to his mother for rest and safety. Bill continued to observe the family, entertained by the small boy who was energized moments later for another game of catch and release. That was freedom, Bill thought to himself, guiltless freedom.

His own family could not be farther away. Bill had left his wife and son off his *must see* list for nearly half a year, the guilt of it robbing any pleasure he might have experienced in India. Within a few months, he would head to Beijing, China, another destination on his list, but his passion for travel was long gone. Bill wanted to be with Sharon and Stewart, asleep at home in DC, on the other side of the world from where he was at that moment. It was the very place he had thought he needed to escape from.

Six Houses Down

Back at his hotel room, he kicked his sandals off and drained a tall glass of ice water, the ninety-degree day leaving him parched. As he brushed the sand off his loose, white cotton pants, he couldn't shake the image of the young boy with his father on the beach. He would have given anything for that man to be him, the mother Sharon, and the spirited boy Stewart.

* * *

Bill recalled the day he and Sharon sat across from Stewart's doctor and tried to process the reality that their son had autism spectrum disorder. They had some concerns earlier, shortly after a family trip to Mexico, when they noticed their son was not progressing like other children. At first, they were advised not to be overly concerned, the doctor assuring them that some boys develop language skills later than others. When Stewart became excessively agitated and aggressive, they began to search for answers. It was devastating when they found one.

Over the next year and a half after Stewart's diagnosis, Bill poured himself into research on the disorder, trying to *fix* the problem by switching Stewart from one therapist to another. Sharon appeared to handle their son's limitations with far more patience than he had, and before long, he retreated into his job, secretly mourning the life he thought he would be robbed of. Bill winced at the thought that his lifelong passion for world travel was the catalyst for leaving his family behind. When it became clear that his son had an aversion to things unfamiliar, travel was no longer an option, unless he could go without him, and so he did. The reality of what he was doing uncomfortably reminded him of his own childhood disappointments, waving goodbye to his parents as they left for months at a time.

Bill's dreams of travel were not the only things that felt as if they were slipping away. Most of their closest friends distanced themselves, slowly at first, uncomfortable with his son's aggressive tendencies. After being *advised* several times on a particular Sunday morning that they needed to learn how to discipline their son, Bill's discouragement began to foster anger. That was the last Sunday Bill bothered going to church. The invitations to join his parents in their travels had suspiciously stopped as well. Bill's father had gone so far as to suggest they put Stewart in a home since he would be happy as long as he was fed and comfortable. Sharon had lost all respect for the senior Mr. Webster, and Bill had to do a bit of damage control to assure her that he and his father were not like-minded. Sharon's concerns might have been well founded after all. He would never consider putting his son in a home, but he had abandoned Stewart just the same. Over the last year, he had fallen into the addiction of selfishness, and now his job depended on it.

His first trip away from home was a temporary position to see if he was cut out for the promotion Davis Engineering was offering him. It was like an alcoholic's first drink, a justifiably small amount of guilt and pure pleasure to the senses. That first trip took him to the beautiful Seychelles Islands in the Indian Ocean. Tourism was booming, and they were in need of significant infrastructure upgrades to accommodate the influx of people, along with the electronic protection systems his company was known for. Compared to the disappointment at home, the Islands were intoxicating. He had secured his first contract and wanted the promotion more than anything. He used his best sales tactics to sell the idea to Sharon. The promotion would be a win-win situation for the whole family, he assured her. When she reluctantly agreed, he sold his truck to pad their savings account for emergencies or the chance that his ability to secure project bids wasn't always successful.

Each new destination away from home tipped the scales more heavily on the guilt side and less on the pleasure side until he was locked in a vicious cycle. The more he was gone, the harder it became to return home for only a handful of days, spending the majority of the precious time offering Sharon lamentations and excuses for leaving again, weeks or months at a time.

He asked her to join him when he was in Brazil, but they would have been on their own most of the time, and he knew it was too difficult for Stewart to travel that far. Several of his last calls home turned into heartfelt apologies that fell flat when there was no offer to mend the situation. It became more and more difficult to call, each conversation turning into a reminder that he had chosen his job over his family. He told himself when the guilt was first setting in that he needed this position to provide for them, but he knew better. Sharon never wanted expensive things, and he could find a job that paid less and kept him home where he belonged. An ache growing inside of him felt as if a band was being pulled tight around his chest. He failed them both.

* * *

Standing at the window of his hotel room, Bill stood watching black and yellow taxis swarm like bees on the Mumbai streets below; so many people had places to go. He looked over his schedule for the next few weeks and wrote down the names of several people he needed to call. Sharon should have been on that list. Replaying the last conversation he had with her over and over in his mind, he came to the realization of what he needed to do. He hoped it wouldn't be too hard on her or that he would regret his hasty decision. When all the dust settled, it would prove to be the right thing for all of them. Bill searched the internet for a company in Washington, DC, and made the necessary arrangements. He would have liked to call Sharon and talk over the details with her so she would know what to expect but didn't want to take the chance that she would try to talk him out of it.

* * *

The market in Mumbai smelled of lamb and chicken as Bill wove through the mix of locals and tourists. When he stopped at a booth to purchase fruit, two women dominated the vendor, haggling over the price of beaded necklaces. The vendor's wife, not interested in losing a sale, took on the women and gestured for her husband to help him instead.

As the Indian merchant wrapped the mangos and bananas he'd purchased, Bill asked him about the oil-burning clay lamp on the roof of his booth. The friendly man smiled, his teeth gleaming a brilliant white against his dark-brown skin.

In broken English the man replied, "American, yes?"

"Yes," Bill replied.

"Is Christmas time coming soon, you know. The lamp is for peoples to know Yeshua. He is really good. I tell you, my friend, Yeshua is the light of the world . . . yes?"

"Yes, yes he is," Bill said, nodding in friendly agreement. He thanked the merchant and wished him a Merry Christmas, not missing the instant commonality he had with a total stranger, based solely on their faith in Jesus. After making one final purchase from another vendor, Bill returned to his hotel and collected the things he would need for his meeting. One last look at his schedule reminded him it was two weeks before Christmas.

* * *

Five days before Christmas, Anna stopped by the Webster's house to talk to Sharon.

"You know, it would be a lot more convenient to get a hold of you if you answered your phone," she scolded as she hurried to close the door in an effort to keep the swirling snow from blowing into the house.

"I'm sorry. Didn't I tell you my phone isn't working? But if it was, I wouldn't get to see you as often. You'd just text me, and then I'd miss out on all the interesting things that come to mind when you're forced to communicate with a real person."

"Good point . . . inconvenient, but justified." Anna rubbed her hands together. "Why is it so cold in here? Is something wrong with your furnace?"

"Sorry. Come in here." Sharon waved her shivering friend into the living room. "I have a space heater that travels around the house with us." Sharon didn't want to bother Anna with the fact that the furnace was in fine working order but the heating bill had been so high she had turned the thermostat down to fifty-five degrees and opted to move the little heater around to make sure her son was warm enough.

Anna sat on the couch and warmed her hands by the radiant heater, which provided a decent degree of warmth for Stewart to play in.

"How are things going, Sharon?" Anna asked with a serious expression.

"They're good. What's on your mind?" she replied, able to sense that Anna was worried about something.

"I came to ask if you and Stewart would like to come with us to church on Christmas Eve, and then maybe you could join us for dinner on Christmas Day, too. We really want you two to come, so let's say you're coming. Now that we have that settled, is everything all right with . . . things?" Anna asked again.

"Was I a part of that conversation you just had there?" Sharon asked, trying to avoid answering Anna's question.

"Sharon, is your house so cold because you can't pay your electric bill?" Anna asked her, getting right to the point.

With a sigh of relief, Sharon explained the misunderstanding. "No, no, Anna, we have plenty of money. That is sweet of you to worry about us, but honestly, I'm a little over the top when it comes to saving for . . . emergencies or, you know, unplanned expenditures."

"Is that why you didn't replace your phone, to save money? Wouldn't you need to *call* someone if you had an emergency?" Anna pressed her and then instantly backed off the interrogation. "Sorry. Never mind. Now you know where Stacey gets her propensity toward annoyance."

"That's all right. I should replace my phone, but I keep putting it off." She still had six months of service remaining. It was unlikely, however, that she would spend any money on a new phone. "Thank you for being worried about me, but everything is fine."

Before Anna returned home, Sharon agreed to join them for the Christmas Eve service and dinner on Christmas Day as well, knowing Stewart would enjoy himself. She didn't recall being given the opportunity to decline but appreciated Anna's insistence that she and Stewart be included in their holiday celebrations. Even though Sharon felt a little railroaded, she also felt cared for, which meant more to her than Anna would ever know.

CHAPTER 8

Only four days until Christmas, Sharon reminded herself as she pulled down the attic stairs folded into the ceiling. Pushing aside a tote full of Bill's clothes, she retrieved a plastic Christmas tree and a box of ornaments. Once she showed Stewart how to hang the figurines on the branches, he remained content to arrange and rearrange the colorful decorations. Sharon tried to resist a nagging menace, her own dark thoughts haunting her with questions she could not answer. Who was Bill going to be with this Christmas?

A loud thumping at the entry startled her. Not expecting anyone, she pulled the front door open and came face to face with a frazzled mailman wearing a Santa hat.

"Hello, I have a certified letter for Sharon Webster," he informed her.

"That's me." She took the pen he offered and signed the soggy paper on the clipboard. The weight and size of the envelope in her hand suggested official contents. Was this what she had been dreading? She closed the door and inspected the oversized envelope. The sight of gold embossed letters on the upper left corner punched her in the stomach: *DC Attorney at Law.*

The letter felt as if it weighed a hundred pounds as she carried it to the kitchen and set it on the table. She was tempted to leave it there unopened. The nagging menace returned with a vengeance.

What's going to happen to Stewart? If you sign those, how will you know what you're agreeing to? She tried to counter the mental jab. The waiting is finally over. You knew this was coming.

Sharon left the letter on the table and joined Stewart in the living room. She wished she could hold him, but his nearness was still a comfort to her. Finished with his redecorating of the tabletop Christmas tree, she tried to interest him in a book, but he chose to arrange his collection of metal cars instead. Knowing the wait would do more harm than good, she returned to the kitchen, slumped down in her chair at the table, and picked up the linen letter in front of her. She tore the top open, pulled the folded document out, and read the first line. Her trembling hands blurred the words on the page.

In boldface, the first line read, *Your child may have certain legal rights.* She dropped the letter and buried her face in her hands, sobbing as the tension of mind and body escaped like water from a breached dam. A personal injury lawyer was interested in cashing in on the malpractice insurance of any obstetrician unfortunate enough to have delivered a child with an impairment of any kind. These were not divorce papers. They were a lawyer's desperate attempt to use special needs children as a potential paycheck. Wondering how the lawyer had gotten her name, she threw the letter in the trash, mentally and physically stressed over a piece of junk mail.

* * *

On Christmas Eve, Anna and Stacey waited in the entry of the Webster' home for Sharon and Stewart to bundle up and make the short trip to the church. When they opened the door to leave, a flurry of icy air threatened to deposit a fine layer of white powder in the house. With the door hastily shut behind them, fresh snow swirled on the sidewalk at their feet as they hurried to the car.

"My glove!" Stacey yelled in panic. "It's in the house."

Sharon tossed her key to Anna and buckled Stewart in the back seat while the missing glove was retrieved. Not wanting to leave a puddle of melted snow in Anna's car, Sharon tried to shake off her boots before she closed the car door, but the powdery snow continued to blow through the open door, frustrating her efforts.

"Don't worry about the snow," Anna said as she jumped in the car and handed Sharon her house key. "There's no keeping it out in this weather."

"You get to go to our church tonight, Stewart," Stacey announced as Anna pulled into traffic at the end of the block. It's fun 'cause everyone dances; then, we get to turn the lights out and hold candles. They have real fire on them, so you have to hold super still."

Anna giggled. "You look like you're in shock, Mrs. Webster," she teased.

Sharon and Stewart had been invited to join them for church several times before, but she declined the invitations, sure Stewart would be a distraction and unable to sit quietly through a sermon. Anna assured her the variety of music and other things they would have going on would hold his attention, and she trusted Anna not to put her in an uncomfortable situation. Sharon wondered if her idea of comfort might be drastically different from Anna's.

"You know what else, Mrs. Webster?" Stacey asked, without waiting for a response. "There aren't hardly any people with our same skin at our church. Our friends at church have other skin, like Nanna May and Earl, 'cause they're Samaritans."

Anna shook her head. "Stacey, our friends aren't black because they're Samaritans. That's just the name of our church."

"Then what color are Samaritans?" Stacey challenged, as if her own logic could out-reason her mother's.

Anna and Sharon couldn't resist laughing, and soon the contagious nature of giggles had infected all of them, including Stewart, who was always fond of joining in on a good laugh.

* * *

The cabin lights came on as the pilot announced the plane would be landing in Washington, DC, in twenty minutes. Bill rubbed his sleepless eyes and checked the time. He'd been in the air for nearly eighteen hours. Once landed, he hurried toward the parking garage, weaving through travel-weary passengers as they trudged down the long corridor. With keys in hand, he tossed his carry-on in the back seat of the rented sedan and drove away from the airport. Tapping a hand on the steering wheel while waiting for the stoplight, he glanced at the clock again, then glared at the offensive red signal.

"Come on. Change already." He barely had enough time to pick up the gift he'd ordered for Stewart several weeks ago. Zigzagging through traffic, his impatience earned him several stern looks along with honks of disapproval. With growing anxiety, he parked the rental car in the mall parking lot and hurried into the gift shop, with only minutes to spare before closing time. With gift in hand, he jumped back in the car and set the brightly wrapped box next to the gift he purchased for Sharon in Mumbai and headed for home.

His heart thumped hard in his chest, wondering how Sharon would react to his unannounced appearance. He hoped she wouldn't be too upset that he had to return the day after Christmas, but he needed to see her and Stewart, even if leaving again proved to be painful. He pulled up to the house, surprised to see the lights off. A quick look at his phone informed him it was only seven thirty. The front door was always locked for Stewart's safety, so he rang the bell. No one answered. Relieved to find he still had a house key on his keychain, he turned the rarely used key and stepped through the front door.

"Sharon . . . Stewart . . . is anyone home?" Of course they weren't there, but it felt good to say their names out loud. He pulled his cell phone out of his pocket and tapped in Sharon's cell number. Disappointed to find she was out of service, he reluctantly left a voice message. "Sharon, honey, I'm at the house. I can't wait to see you and Stewart. I'll be here when you get home." He tried to sound as joyful as possible and waited to tell her he would have to leave again.

Maybe it was better this way. She would be prepared to see him, and since he was already there, she couldn't tell him not to come. He slid his phone back in his pocket, wondering if they might have gone somewhere for Christmas Eve, maybe a concert or a play, but thought it unlikely. They were probably at the store.

Bill slid his coat and boots off and flipped the light on in the living room. Something was missing. He rubbed his hands together, wondering why it was so cold in the house, and then noticed what was different—the pictures of him on the wall. His throat tightened as he looked around the house. Several men's work shirts, fresh from the cleaners and covered in plastic, hung by the front door. He tried to reconcile what he was seeing, but there was no way around it. Sharon was seeing another man. His absence had created an emotional vacuum she was desperate to fill, and he was the one to blame.

Exhaustion and disappointment assaulted his senses, forcing him to consider what his next move would be. After deciding the house was cold because his wife and son were gone for the holidays, he pushed his tired feet into his boots at the front door and pulled his coat back on. He had waited too long, and now they were enjoying the company of someone that had time for them. Salty tears stung his tired eyes as he retrieved the presents he had brought for his wife and son and placed them in the entryway before closing the door behind him. He drove to a nearby hotel and called the airlines. In less than ten hours, he would be on the next flight back to Mumbai.

* * *

Stewart enjoyed the music at the church, but the intensity threatened to overwhelm him until Earl handed Sharon a pair of earplugs. As soon as Stewart cooperated and left the plugs in his ears, he settled down, clapping and swaying to the music. After the service, Sharon said goodbye to Nanna May and Earl, at the same time trying to keep Stewart on the sidewalk and away from the cars in the parking lot.

"Here you go," Earl said, handing Sharon two small gift bags with curled red and green ribbons. "Merry Christmas. If I was you, I wouldn't wait to open up them bags," he said with a wink.

Nanna May thanked Sharon again for the hand-painted ornaments she'd delivered a week earlier. "You are some artist. Now give me a hug and promise me we'll see you two tomorrow."

Sharon assured the Clarks that she and Stewart were looking forward to joining them again for Christmas dinner back at the church. As she was saying goodbye, she noticed Anna was annoyed by something. The mounds of shoveled snow along the sidewalk had proved to be too much of a temptation, and both children had packed their boots in a matter of seconds.

"I'm sorry we didn't get to see Shane tonight," Nanna May said to Anna. "I thought he was gonna join us."

While Anna dumped snow out of one of Stacey's boots, she told the Clarks that Shane was sick and wished he could have come but would unfortunately spend Christmas Day trying to recuperate.

"Stewart, stop!" Sharon yelled as her son ran down the sidewalk and boarded a shuttle bus.

"Hello, young man," the driver said to him. "And where might you be goin' tonight?"

Close behind him, Anna stepped onto the shuttle and gently pulled Stewart toward the exit, "Sorry, Ben," she said to the driver, "looks like he would rather go with you tonight."

"No problem, Anna. You have a Merry Christmas now," he said before closing the door on the small bus.

With snow dumped out of boots and children securely buckled in, Anna drove Sharon and Stewart back home. Sharon thanked Anna as she collected Stewart, a booster seat, and gift bags and hurried toward the house.

As they made their way to the front door, she noticed something on the walkway—fresh footprints in the snow. Someone had been at her door only minutes earlier, and it appeared as if the mystery visitor had stayed awhile before leaving. As she turned the key in the lock, she became afraid of what she might find. Her pulse quickened as she pulled Stewart behind her, opened the door, and quickly turned the light on in the entry.

With a huge sigh of grateful relief, she closed the door behind her. "That Anna." She moved the presents out of the entry. "She's just as sneaky as her daughter." Sharon was sure Stacey's missing glove was merely a cover and Anna had left their front door unlocked on purpose.

Stewart inspected the brightly colored packages with intense interest and chanted happy guttural sounds. Sharon handed him a small present with his name on it.

"Here, honey, you take this one over to the couch. It looks like Earl was Santa tonight after we left with Anna and Stacey." She moved the other packages into the living room, placed them next to their plastic Christmas tree, and turned the space heater on. It was eight o'clock and time for Stewart to get ready for bed, but she wouldn't make him wait to open the gift in his hands.

"You can open this one tonight, and then we'll save the others for tomorrow." She encouraged him to pull the wrapping off the small box.

Stewart tore the shiny red paper and looked at her for confirmation that he was indeed allowed to tear it.

"Go ahead. It's a present, not a book. You can tear it open."

When the small box was opened, Sharon expected to find a small toy but was shocked at the gift inside. For a second, she thought the box held a live animal, and then she laughed at her own reaction. Stewart didn't hesitate to pull the gray fur-covered toy out of its wrapping and roll it over in his hands for a thorough inspection. He pet the soft fur with rapt attention and then startled when the furry critter uncoiled in his hand.

Sharon was as surprised as her son by the lifelike mystery creature. She searched the box for instructions but didn't find any. They would soon figure out the toy was touch and motion activated. After a half hour of discovering an abundance of responses, Sharon moved the heater into Stewart's bedroom and made a reluctant son go to bed.

"You can keep the toy by your pillow, but you need to go to sleep, all right?"

Stewart set the furry ball next to his head and pulled his blanket tight to his shoulder. Sharon tried to hide her knowing smile. His eagerness to lie down wouldn't last, but she didn't blame him, nor did she expect him to keep his hands off his new toy. For another hour, she could hear random beeps and giggles coming from his room. She let him be. This was Christmas Eve, and her son was happy.

* * *

"Merry Christmas," Bill grumped as he unpacked the few things he'd brought with him in his carry-on and checked his phone again. Sharon had not returned his call. He spent the first few hours back at the hotel waiting for his phone to ring before calling her again. When her voice message recording came on, he hung up, not wanting to leave another message. Bill's stomach reminded him he had not eaten in almost ten hours, but it was too late to get anything. Maybe sleep would give him a reprieve from all that ailed him. The hotel bed did not offer Bill any comfort, his mind wandering in and out of a variety of unsettling scenarios Sharon and Stewart could be in. He finally fell asleep several hours later.

"*It's over,*" he heard a voice say, startling him awake.

He lay in the dimly lit hotel room, sensing a darkness that desired to rule him, but he tried to resist it. A thought came to him: *Cast all of your cares on him, for he cares for you.*

Who was he to cast his cares on God? He did not deserve any divine help. Again, the phrase came to mind as if his thoughts were not his own: *he cares for you.*

"Lord, help me, please," Bill prayed, not considering himself worthy. "If you can forgive me, please help me fix what I have broken."

It was still dark when Bill awoke early the next morning. The lights of Washington, DC, reflected off a fresh covering of snow, tempting him to admire nature's Christmas display as he made his way to the parking lot. He turned his attention to the phone in his pocket, checking one last time for a returned call or text before going back to the airport, but he found what he had expected— nothing.

Two hours later, he was flying over the Atlantic Ocean, back to Mumbai, India. He noticed the time, reminding himself he would lose a day as the plane headed east to the other side of the world. If there ever was a day he was willing to lose, it was this one.

CHAPTER 9

Early Christmas morning, Sharon hurried to throw on a thick robe and a pair of warm wool socks. She peeked in on her son, assuming Stewart would sleep in since he had stayed up so late playing with his new toy. Part of her wished her friends had not been so generous, knowing the gift he'd opened the night before was a considerable expense for someone on a limited budget. She had made ornaments for the Clarks and the Hayes and delivered them over a week ago, but she was now embarrassed by their simplicity. Pushing unfavorable thoughts aside, she challenged herself to focus on the things she was thankful for. It would be her gift to herself, except for one other thing. Rubbing her hands together, she moved the thermostat up to sixty-eight degrees.

Sharon checked on her son, still asleep at nine o'clock. After pouring her second cup of coffee, she wandered back into the living room, which was slowly warming up to a comfortable temperature. Feeling somewhat childish, she admired the gifts that her friends had given her and Stewart. It wasn't the thrill over the potential contents in the packages that gave her so much pleasure but rather the reminder that she had friends who cared enough to give them. She bent down by the plastic tree and picked up the gift bag Earl gave her the night before. She carefully unwrapped the tissue paper, discovering a stack of almond shortbread cookies drizzled with chocolate. Taking one and wrapping the rest up for later, she set the bag on the kitchen counter and savored each bite of the crispy cookie, likely one of Nanna May's many specialties.

At 9:15, Sharon was determined it was time for Stewart to wake up. She walked down the short hallway and pushed his bedroom door open. He continued to sleep soundly, unlike most children his age on Christmas morning, who were up before the sun and would have ripped their presents open by now. She hoped her son would like the gift she chose for him, but it would be difficult to compete with the furry critter perched next to his pillow.

She reached for the interesting toy sitting inches away from his face. Picking it up carefully, she set it on her palm, unsure of how they managed to turn it on the night before. She poked at it a few times and then shook it gently. Maybe Stewart had played with it long enough to run the batteries down. She reached over to set the toy back on his bed, but without warning, it opened up in her hand and made a high-pitched chirping sound, followed by her own startled chirp and an accidental furry landing on her son's forehead. He was awake now.

Stewart blinked a few times, rubbed his eyes, and then searched for the toy that had pulled him from his slumber. Luckily, he was more interested in the toy's whereabouts than the abrupt wake-up call.

"Merry Christmas, honey," Sharon said as she coaxed him out of bed and into the kitchen for some breakfast.

As soon as he finished, Sharon felt like an eager child herself, anxious to see her son's reaction to the gift she had for him.

"You have two more presents to open. Do you want to go find them by the tree?"

Stewart clapped his hands and hurried to the living room. Sharon pointed out the gift she'd placed there earlier that morning. He pulled the paper off, inspected all moving parts and pieces, and then set it on the coffee table, unimpressed.

"Look here. It's a record player," she said as she placed one of the colorful plastic disks in place and wound up the toy player.

Metal tines plucked the grooved disk, chiming the tune "(How Much Is) That Doggie in the Window?" Stewart was instantly thrilled and was content to play every song on the double-sided disks several times before his interest waned.

"You have another gift. That one is from Nanna May and Earl and Anna and Stacey." She pointed at the gift bag that looked similar to the one she opened earlier. If his present turned out to be cookies as well, she would let him eat one.

Stewart pulled the ribbons free and looked into the bag. He had a look of confusion on his face as he pulled a handful of shredded paper out of the bag and set it on the coffee table.

"Keep looking, honey. I think there's something else in there."

He checked the bag again before turning it over and dumping its contents on the floor. Several brightly colored plastic frogs fell to the carpet, catching his attention. Sharon, relieved to see he had not dumped cookies on the floor, watched her son as he arranged his frogs and records and then retrieved his furry critter from the couch, adding it to the procession on the coffee table.

As she watched her son play, Sharon picked up the last gift, temporarily distracted by the lettering of her name on the silver label. Earl's handwriting was very similar to Bill's. Pushing the thought aside, she set the gift on her lap, pulled the taped seam apart, and slid the contents out of the tissue cover.

"Oh, my," she gasped as she brushed her hand over a beautiful silken ivory shawl with an intricately woven magenta border on either end. It was too much. The shawl had to of cost a fortune. She couldn't understand why her friends would have purchased such an extravagant gift. They seemed to be frugal people, not unlike herself. The mystery would have to be figured out later that day at Christmas dinner, but until then, she would be thankful rather than working up things to fret over.

Wrapping the soft shawl around her shoulders, she brushed the magenta border across her cheek. Never before had she felt anything so soft. As she sat watching her son arrange his new toys, she couldn't help wondering how Bill would be spending Christmas Day, wishing he could be there with her and Stewart and again regretting her hastily spoken words the last time he called. She had told him not to come home if he couldn't stay, and she now wondered if her angry words had predetermined his absence this Christmas Day and every one hereafter. Stop! No drifting back to your list of regrets. Folding the soft shawl and draping it across her bed, she pushed the thoughts of her husband away, not willing to let life's disappointments ruin the holiday.

Sharon pulled a pan of fresh-baked rolls out of the oven and set them in a basket to take to the church. Anna and Stacey would be there soon, so she helped Stewart dress and brush his hair, and then she opened her closet. Sifting through her sparse collection of functional, comfortable clothes, she realized she hadn't bothered adding anything holiday worthy for several years. A black dress, covered in plastic for ages, seemed appropriate, but it was now a size too big. She ran her hand across the shawl lying on her bed and pulled on a pair of black dress pants and a simple ivory sweater. Wrapping the silken shawl around her shoulders, she scrutinized her reflection in the mirror. Her face looked pale next to the bright magenta border. A light dusting of blush on her cheek and a touch of color on her lips seemed to brighten her up enough to be presentable. She heard a car pull up in front of the house and hurried to find Stewart and connect him with his boots before the doorbell rang.

Still missing one boot, Sharon answered the door. "Come on in. We're almost—oh—Steve—hi." She gave him a big hug, surprised and pleased to find a friend she hadn't seen in months standing there.

"Merry Christmas. You look as beautiful as ever, luv. Are you headed out?"

"Some friends have invited me to join them for Christmas dinner. You should wait and meet them. Besides, it's so good to see you." She hugged him again, not wanting him to go.

When he finally looked her in the eye, she thought she detected an unspoken concern. He likely knew about Bill's unfaithfulness and wondered if she did as well.

"Come in, Steve, I want to know what you've been up to. Stewart will be happy to see you, too." Sharon stepped back and pulled the door open, but Steve hesitated and didn't step through it.

"Uh . . . I won't keep you. Sharon . . . I wanted to give this to you and make sure everything . . . um . . . that you were having a jolly Christmas." Steve handed her an envelope. He hugged her one last time and kissed her cheek. "I've gotta go. Bye, luv."

Sharon noticed his accent was more pronounced than usual, something he was known to do when he was nervous. He did seem distracted but put on a good show of holiday cheer, even if he did know what Bill was up to. Unfaithful thoughts of her own invited her to ponder the possibility of spending more time with Steve. The guilt of it had her offering her own conscience a justification— What if he's lonely, too? She pushed the thoughts from her mind, uncomfortable that she had welcomed them so easily.

Anna arrived moments after Steve drove away. Once they were all in the car and ready to head to the church, Anna stared at Sharon as if something was wrong.

Kari Rimbey

"What? Did I forget something?" Sharon asked.

"Um, I'm sorry, but do I know you?" Anna teased.

"Oh, stop it," Sharon replied. "I had to add a tiny bit of color so I wouldn't look like a ghost next to this beautiful shawl somebody extremely generous gave me for Christmas." She pulled her coat open and held an end of the silken fabric for Anna to see. She looked at her friend with suspicion.

"Wow, that's amazing. Who gave it to you?"

"Like you don't know." Sharon tucked the end of the shawl back into her coat.

"I don't."

"So, you didn't leave my door unlocked so some mystery Santa could leave presents for me and Stewart in the house last night?"

"No . . . honest, I didn't. So you don't know who left them for you?" Anna seemed curious herself.

"You know, I might. A friend came by before you got here, and you know what, it would be like him to leave us Christmas gifts." It made sense that Steve could be the mystery Santa. In fact, he was her emergency contact while Bill was gone, and Bill would have left a house key with him. If she had known, she could have thanked him.

"He handed this to me as he was leaving," Sharon said as she pulled the envelope out of her purse.

"Open it." Anna looked at her with shameless curiosity. "I want to know what it is."

"Open it! Open it!" Stacey chanted from the back seat of the car.

"I'm afraid you might be disappointed. It might be my new insurance card," she said as she tore the top open.

"What is it?" Stacey asked.

"I'm not sure. It looks like tickets to a play. There are three tickets in here." Sharon read the note that came with it:

68

Merry Christmas, Sharon,

I thought you and Stewart might like to see this production of The Lion, the Witch, and the Wardrobe. *The performances are autism sensory friendly, so I think Stewart would enjoy it.*

Love, Steve

"I love that story," Stacey cheered. "Can I go?"

"Stacey," Anna interrupted, "It's not good manners to ask." Anna apologized.

Sharon insisted Stacey could use the other ticket, or better yet, they could buy one more and all four of them could go. It was odd there were three in the first place. Maybe Steve had intended to go.

* * *

Sharon added the rolls she brought with her to the large buffet line at the church and visited with a few familiar faces from the night before. Everyone took a seat at a long table, and Earl prayed over the feast, thanking God for his ever-expanding family. He then cast a joyful mood over the dinner when he claimed they were also responsible for his ever-expanding waistline.

Sharon and Stewart enjoyed the traditional Clark Christmas dinner. Over thirty people came to the church to share the meal together, all with stories to tell about Nanna May and Earl. The common thread in this unusual family was that the Clarks had drawn them all together with their love and generosity.

As the children played games at the end of the room, Sharon tried to listen to the different stories shared around her, but her thoughts kept drifting back to the mystery gift giver. Why would Steve leave gifts anonymously, just to show up the next day and give her and Stewart another one? Had he intended to use the third ticket to the play? Why didn't he say anything about going with them? She pushed the thoughts away and focused her attention on the people sharing around the table.

"I was a newborn when the Clarks took me in," a man shared, seated next to Sharon. "They're the only parents I ever knew."

He had people laughing with his stories, including Nanna May and Earl.

"When I was about sixteen, I told Nanna May that I knew I wasn't special and wouldn't amount to a hill a beans because I was adopted. Well, she came at me waving her I-don't-think-so finger and said, 'We got us two presidents and two first ladies that were adopted, and they made it to the White House in this very city, young man, so if you don't amount to a hill a beans, it'll be your own fault.'"

Everyone laughed, most confessing they were familiar with the wave of the I-don't-think-so finger.

Anna informed Sharon that the man was a successful surgeon and had offered to build the Clarks a custom home, but they refused his offer, preferring to stay where they are now. Sharon was warmed by the thought that she and Stewart were invited to be part of the Clark family get-together and wondered if she would one day have something interesting to share, besides the benefit of having stumbled onto the path of her loving friends.

* * *

Bill's plane landed back in Mumbai in the early morning hours. He found a taxi and returned to his hotel room for much-needed rest. After several hours of mental torment and the inability to fall asleep, he pulled his clothes back on and walked to a nearby convenience store. The clerk didn't speak English, so Bill wandered around the store looking for a familiar liquid sleep-aid. He purchased what he needed and smelled the contents. When he returned to the hotel, he decided to ask the night receptionist to translate the label on the bottle before he trusted his intuition. The woman informed him that the bottle held brake fluid.

Unbelievable, I could have killed myself. He threw the bottle of green liquid in the trashcan and returned to his room. The next morning, Bill made his way through the market to the vendor he purchased mangos and bananas from earlier in the week. The Indian man remembered him and greeted him with a smile.

"*Mere dost ritarn* . . . my friend returns . . . yes? You have Merry Christmas?"
Bill offered him a half-hearted smile and avoided the question.

"Here is your fruit. And here, I give you this. You are my brother in Yeshua, so I give you gift. Is very good. You make tea. It help you with heavy eye. Remember Yeshua . . . he care for you."

Bill accepted the small package and thanked the merchant, trusting that this mystery tea was a better option than the last substance he tried to medicate himself with. He returned to his hotel room, boiled some water, and poured it over the mixture of crushed leaves and stems from the small paper bag. The tea didn't smell bad but neither did the brake fluid. He let it sit and steep for a minute as he looked over his schedule for his last week in Mumbai. A few final meetings remained to secure another contract for Davis Engineering.

With eyes so tired his lids nearly stuck to his eyeballs, Bill looked at the cup of tea before bringing it to his mouth. The merchant's words replayed in his mind—*he cares for you*—prompting him to wonder if the repeated phrase was merely a coincidence or if he was to believe, after everything he had done, that God really did care for him. He took a few sips of the hot liquid and waited several minutes to see if his stomach would warn him against sending any more of the foreign substance in its direction. He finished the cup of tea and noticed a mild, spicy aftertaste. For the time being, it seemed to agree with him. Feeling much better an hour later, Bill decided to spend his one free day taking in the city rather than wallowing in his failings.

He took a cab to several historical sites and, by the day's end, felt much better. Before the sun went down, he went for a jog along the sea, his thoughts fixed on Sharon and Stewart. He wondered where they were, but another question weighed more heavily on him: who were they with?

That night, Bill wrote Sharon a letter. It was helpful to unpack his thoughts with the pen in his hand, pouring his heart out on the paper in front of him. *I was there. Why didn't you answer when I called you?* he wrote. When he finished the three-page letter, he sealed it in an envelope, ready to mail the next day. He struggled to determine what he should do, fearing Sharon had already given up on him.

Kari Rimbey

Sharon pulled a picture album down from a high shelf in the living room and brushed a thin layer of dust off its leather cover. She felt a twinge of guilt when her son recognized the picture album in her hands and reached for it with eager anticipation. She had sequestered it to the top shelf out of Stewart's reach and, more importantly, out of her sight, not wanting to be reminded of the way things used to be or could have been.

Stewart sat on the couch beside her and opened the cover. He inspected one of the larger pictures on the first page—she and Bill on their wedding day. The happy couple smiled at them from seven years in the past. Pointing at the picture of Bill, Stewart laughed and then returned to the image with rapt attention. Sharon's heart sank as she watched her son inspecting the pictures of his father, working his way slowly through the plastic-covered pages.

The longer Bill stayed away, the more she tried to cleanse the reminder of him from their home. The clothes he left behind had been boxed up and placed in the attic, along with his books and travel memorabilia that once filled several shelves in the living room. The pictures of him on the living room wall followed the first exodus of Bill's possessions a few weeks before Christmas. The purge had given her a sense of control and justice until she noticed her son searching for the missing pictures, rubbing his hands on the wall where the face of his father used to be.

As much as she wanted to forget Bill, she couldn't deprive her son the memories of his father. They would likely fade over time, but for now, she would indulge him and pretend to enjoy the pictures as much as he did. One particular group of photographs held Stewart's attention the longest. Stewart briefly looked at her with questioning eyes, as if to ask where the man in the picture went, and then returned to the images of the three of them vacationing in Mexico over two years ago.

Bill had hired a photographer to follow them around for a few hours while they played at the beach. The pictures portrayed the perfect family, young and vibrant with their first child, enjoying a measure of wealth and full of hope for the future. The display was not a charade, like many professionally manipulated scenes; it was a moment of blissful ignorance frozen in time.

"Look, Stewart," she said, pointing to the three-year-old boy on the glossy paper, "this little guy playing in the sand is you." Her lilting voice veiled a wound that had just been salted. The woman in the picture thought she had been gifted a perfect life. Sharon wasn't sure if her son understood that the little boy was him, but he laughed and pointed at the three of them, wanting a running commentary on every detail in the scene.

"There's Daddy with a bucket of water, and Mommy is laughing because you and daddy are funny."

Stewart insisted they look through the album several times before his need for a nap overcame his interest in the pictures. She set the album on the table in front of the couch and retrieved her son's favorite blanket. It wasn't long before Stewart was sound asleep.

Picking up the album, Sharon went to place it back on the high shelf. She hesitated, trying to fight off an urge to look through the pictures once again, but the urge won. She carried the album into the kitchen and sat at the small table by the window, flipping the cover to reveal the first page.

A vibrant woman, seven years younger than she, with long, auburn hair and greenish-blue eyes, smiled back at her, full of life and hope for the future. A handsome young man with a mop of blond curly hair, generous-sized ears, and an easy smile held his bride close, both with expressions full of love and pride. In the background, a sunset with hues of orange and yellow reflected off a beautiful, white-sanded Jamaican beach. The picture of their elopement looked like a travel advertisement or one of those pictures already in the album when you buy it, as if it had yet to be replaced with one of her own.

Flipping a few more pages into the book, a loose picture, tucked underneath the others, slid partially into view. Sharon teased it out, careful not to damage the plastic cover. Upon closer inspection, she recognized the image. It wasn't a wedding picture but a basket of tomatoes with a note that read, "Sharon, will you fall for me again?"

CHAPTER 10

Sharon flipped through the next few pages. She and Bill had an unusual first-encounter story, which he was quick to share with anyone that asked. She'd always let him tell his version since it was mostly true. He didn't embellish or exaggerate it, but there were a few facts he had never been privy to. In fact, he enjoyed his version so much that she didn't have the heart to change it.

* * *

Six months before their elopement to Jamaica, late in the afternoon, Sharon was backing out of a grocery store parking lot. The sun was low and over her right shoulder. A large, white box truck, advertising mattresses, pulled in next to her, blocking the view and blinding her with reflected sunlight. She crept back a few feet and someone honked. Frustrated, she hit the brakes and let him pass by. Still not able to see if anyone was coming, she attempted to back up again. After creeping back a few more feet without any repercussions, she gave the car a little gas.

Thump. "No!" Sharon had hit someone, not a car—a person. She threw her door open before realizing she hadn't put the car in park. Shaking, she grabbed the shifter, shoved it forward, and flipped the key to turn off the engine. With heart racing, she yelled repeatedly, "I'm sorry! I'm sorry!" as she jumped out of the car.

The loud groaning of an injured man could be heard coming from the ground behind her bumper. Sharon ran around the back corner of the car and slipped in a pile of spilled tomatoes. *Thunk.* She landed with a hard hit to the back of her head on the black pavement, knocking her out cold.

Bill couldn't believe it. The young woman that just hit him lay motionless on the ground a few feet away.

"Miss . . . miss can you hear me?" Nothing.

Six Houses Down

"Heavens to Betsy!" A man in his seventies, pushing a cart with only a gallon of milk in it, was the first person to find the unlucky couple. "Son, can you tell me what happened?"

"Check on her!" Bill again tried to get her to respond. "She slipped and hit her head." He scooted himself closer toward the unconscious young woman, pain shooting through his left leg, which was obviously broken. "Miss, can you hear me?" Still nothing.

"This doesn't look good, young man. If it's all right with you, I'm going to call 911."

"Yes . . . call." Bill looked around as best he could for his own phone but couldn't find it anywhere.

"Walter," a woman's authoritative voice called from a short distance away, "if you leave the milk in the sun like that, it's going to sour. Why isn't it in the car yet?"

Bill could hear the sound of chunky heels approaching and then coming to a startled, sudden stop.

"Land's sake, what happened here?" the woman asked, getting a closer look at the unconscious young woman.

"There's been an accident," her husband replied. "I'm calling an ambulance . . . wait . . . Is this thing on, Marge?" He handed the phone to his wife, who was wearing a plaid dress that matched her husband's shorts.

She grunted in disgust and grabbed the phone from him.

"Can you give me the phone . . . please? I can call . . . Maybe I should call for you," Bill said as he watched them fiddle with their phone, the waiting driving him crazy. "Please give me the phone!" Bill reached a hand toward the couple. "It'll be easier if I talk to them."

The woman looked surprised but quickly handed him the phone. He punched in 911 and gave the operator the information she needed. After verifying that Sharon was breathing, Bill gave the phone back to the couple, thanking them politely.

A few more people gathered to inspect the injured, and within minutes, several sirens could be heard making their way toward them. A police officer pushed through the growing crowd, making room for the emergency vehicles and trying to get a response from the injured young woman.

As two ambulances pulled up, the woman was regaining consciousness.

"Oh, no!" she moaned, reaching behind her throbbing head and feeling a patch of sticky, matted hair. "What happened?"

"Don't move, miss," one of the paramedics instructed as he placed a cervical collar around her neck and asked her a few questions she struggled to answer.

"Can you tell me your name?"

"Sharon . . . Hen . . . um . . . Henderson."

"And how old are you, Sharon?" the paramedic asked as he placed her on the gurney.

"Um . . . twenty-three . . . no, twenty-four . . . I think." She didn't sound very convinced.

Before the door closed on the back of the ambulance, Sharon looked down at Bill as a paramedic fitted a support under his leg. Bill heard her groan, likely just realizing what she'd done.

* * *

Bill looked at the clock on the wall in the emergency room. He had been at the hospital for an hour and a half and was again waiting in an exam room for results of tests and X-rays. A doctor walked past the curtain separating him from another patient and approached Bill.

"Hello, Mr. Webster, my name is Dr. Gupta. It looks like you have a tibial-fibular fracture. In other words, both of the bones in your lower left leg are broken."

Bill figured as much but didn't look forward to having them set back in place. On the other side of the curtain, someone retched and vomit splattered on the floor. The Indian doctor quickly stepped to the other side of the bed and informed him he would be going into surgery soon. Bill thanked him, and Dr. Gupta watched the floor as he stepped away from the curtain.

A pair of legs in light-blue scrubs and a mop soon appeared on the other side of the curtain.

"Is there anything I can get for you, Sharon?" the person with the blue legs asked.

When the scrubs disappeared, Bill reached over and pulled the curtain back. "Hello, there, my name is Bill . . . How are you doing?" His intentions were to calm the young woman who had hit him.

Sharon squinted, apparently struggling to focus on his face. "Are you the guy I hit in the tomatoes?"

Bill tried to suppress a laugh. "You don't need to worry about my tomatoes. What's your name again?" he asked, taking mental notes of her long, auburn hair and greenish-blue eyes that likely reflected a timid nature when given the ability to focus.

A middle-aged nurse sporting short, dyed, black hair with a thick stripe of gray on either side of her part walked by, her rubber shoes chirping as she turned and retraced her steps.

"Don't mess with this curtain, sir," she demanded, pulling the blue speckled wall back into place.

Her brightly colored jellybean top didn't seem to fit her demeanor. Bill thought a scrub covered with angry emoticons would have been more appropriate. He waited until the windshield-wiper squeak of her rubber shoes on the waxed floor faded down the hallway before reaching over and pulling the curtain back again.

Sharon looked surprised but also amused at his defiance. "You're going to get in trouble," she smiled at him and then squinted again.

"It'll be worth it," he replied, spreading a charming, mischievous grin across his face. "I wanted to tell you the accident wasn't entirely your fault."

"It wasn't?"

"No, it wasn't. I was parked next to you in the red pickup."

"I don't remember a red pickup. Did I hit that, too?" She looked confused again as she tried to focus on his face.

"No . . . you see, I was walking behind the car that honked at you and was on my—"

"Sir!" The nurse returned and bore into him with a hard stare. "This emergency room is not a dating service. You'll leave this curtain in place, or I'll have you moved!" For added measure, she scowled at him while she jerked the curtain shut, making him feel like he was twelve years old instead of twenty-five.

Bill could hear a muffled giggle coming from the other side of the curtain.

"Don't encourage him, miss," the nurse said in a huff. "We have a strict privacy policy here."

Waiting less than a minute, Bill slid the curtain back again. "How did she know I was the one who pulled it back?"

Sharon looked at him with a tight-lipped grin and glanced behind her. "I don't think my arms are long enough to reach it, so that makes me the innocent bystander."

"Good point, miss," he said, imitating the grumpy nurse. "As I was saying before Nurse Ratched showed up, I was walking behind the car that honked at you. As soon as they pulled forward, I started to text on my phone and cut across to my truck. Since my eyes were glued to my phone, I didn't see you back up. Next thing I knew, I was under your car. If I would have been watching where I was going, I could have easily avoided you. I'm pretty sure I stepped right under your bumper."

"It's still my fault. I don't know why I didn't see you. I'm usually very careful." She closed her eyes as if needing to stifle a fresh wave of pain.

Bill saw a flash of multi-colored jellybeans, and the curtain was yanked past his face.

"That's it! It doesn't appear you're accustomed to following the rules, young man," the disgruntled nurse scolded as she readied his gurney for transport, bumping the frame with her stout derrière. His leg shifted slightly, causing him to wince at the instant, sharp pain shooting through his broken leg. Her happy, jellybean-printed scrub was an evil disguise. Before marching off down the hall to look for someone to help her move the reprobate, she offered him a smirk rather than an apology, making him wonder if she bumped him on purpose.

A pair of legs in darker blue scrubs appeared on Sharon's side of the curtain. "Hello, Sharon, I'm Dr. Hardie. How are you feeling, given the circumstances?"

"All right, I guess."

Bill listened closely, eager to hear where Sharon would be shuttled off to and hoping the bump on her head hadn't turned out to be a more serious injury.

"Well, we'd like to have you stay overnight, just to keep an eye on you," the doctor said in a friendly, encouraging tone. "You have what we call a grade-three concussion. It's a pretty solid bump on the noggin, but you'll probably be out of here tomorrow, if all goes well. All right, sweetie?"

"Yes, thank you." Sharon sounded nervous but trusting.

The doctor went over a few more details before asking Sharon if there was anything else she could do for her.

"If it's all right, I'd like to see the guy I ran over."

"Oh, uh . . . where is this guy?" Dr. Hardie asked.

"He's right over there on the other side of the curtain. We were talking, but the nurse, I believe her name is Miss Ratched—"

The doctor burst out laughing. "Wait, did you say the nurse's name was Miss Ratched?" She continued to laugh at the character reference from *One Flew over the Cuckoo's Nest*. "I know exactly which nurse you're referring to."

Bill chuckled on the other side of the fabric divider. The doctor pulled the curtain back and peeked at Mr. Funny with friendly suspicion. He offered a guilty grin to the doctor, who had short, tightly curled salt-and-pepper hair and smile-lined eyes.

"Is this the guy you wanted to see?"

"Yes," Sharon replied, looking confused at their reactions.

"I'm sorry," Bill said, trying not to laugh. "I thought she had seen the movie. See, I got in a little bit of trouble from the nurse for pulling the curtain back . . . a few times."

Dr. Hardie appeared amused. "No problem. You made my day—Miss Ratched—that's awesome."

A young medical student rounded the corner, "Hello, sir. Are you Bill Webster?"

"That's me."

"It looks like they're ready for you in surgery. You're probably tired of waiting and ready to get this leg taken care of, aren't you?" The friendly young woman had a bedside manner opposite that of Nurse Ratched.

"I suppose so, but the company in here wasn't all bad." He glanced over at Sharon with a flirtatious grin. "I hope we can finish this conversation later."

She responded with a shy smile and an instant flush of warm red across her face as she watched the nurse whisk him away to surgery.

"So, Sharon Henderson," Dr. Hardie said with a knowing grin, "you may have hit him, but he was hitting on you. Who knows why these accidents happen sometimes?" The doctor gave her a teasing wink as she turned to leave. "See you tomorrow, hon."

* * *

The day after the accident, Sharon assured Dr. Hardie she was comfortable taking a taxi home and didn't want to call anyone to come pick her up. She left with a concussion and a list of dos and don'ts for the next few weeks. Thanking the nurse for wheeling her to the entrance, she carefully made her way down the sidewalk toward a row of waiting taxis. Out of the corner of her eye, she caught sight of Bill adjusting his balance on his good leg and holding the open door of a red pickup. Trying not to make herself obvious, she subtly glanced his way and could see a man close to Bill's age standing ready to assist him. She wasn't sure if he saw her and figured she looked awful if he did.

"Hey, Sharon . . . it is Sharon, right?" Bill hobbled toward her on a new pair of crutches and casted left leg.

"Yes, Sharon Henderson. I'm sorry, did you get my insurance information?" She reached into her purse for something to write on.

"I'm not worried about that; I'm more worried about you." He hesitated and then offered to share a taxi. "I have a few questions I need to ask you, and I don't want to hold you up, so if you don't mind, we can share a cab."

Sharon could see Bill's friend waiting for him four or five cars down the sidewalk, looking their direction and probably wondering what Bill was up to.

"Sure, we can share a cab, but did you have someone coming to pick you up?" She pretended not to notice the red pickup.

"I did, but I can give him a call. Here, how about this one?" He opened the door on a small SUV taxi, a little higher off the ground and easier to get into.

They slid into the cab, and she gave the driver her address. Sharon thought she saw him wave to his friend before setting his crutches at their feet and closing the door.

"Wait," Bill said, "is your car still at the grocery store? I can help you get it if it's still there."

"That's all right. I'm not sure you're in any condition to drive." She pointed at the bulky cast on his leg. "And I have strict orders not to."

"This won't keep me from driving as long as your car doesn't have a manual transmission and I can move the seat back far enough."

"I think my car does have a transmission," she said, a little uncertain.

Bill smiled, "I bet it does. Why don't we check it out?" He redirected the cab driver, and they headed toward the grocery store.

Sharon glanced over to see Bill's friend with his hands held palms-up by his sides. Bill appeared not to notice the confused man standing by the red truck.

As the taxi drove away from the hospital, Bill asked her if she had her car keys. She searched her purse several times, not finding them anywhere. When they reached the grocery store, the taxi wove through a few rows of parked cars before coming to a stop behind a tan Subaru.

"Could your keys still be in the car?"

She slid out of the taxi, peered through the driver-side window, and, with exasperation, put her hands on her head. "They are."

Bill grabbed his crutches and carefully maneuvered himself out of the taxi and onto his good leg.

With slumped shoulders, Sharon asked him how they were going to get in.

He reached in front of her and tried the door handle. It opened. Covering her forehead with her hand, she hoped the concussion was excuse enough for her stupidity.

"I can drive this," Bill said as he hobbled over to pay the driver.

Sharon tried to pay the fare herself, but Bill had it paid before she could get her wallet out. Making his way around her car, Bill said he heard a beep coming from the trunk. Taking a closer look, he saw his cell phone lodged between her car's bumper and trunk and was able to pull it free. It had a low battery but was still in one piece. It beeped again, and Sharron offered to plug it into the charger.

"That would be great. I have a good friend I really need to call." He slid his crutches into the back seat.

"Are you sure you want to try this?" she asked again as he struggled to make room for his casted leg. "I wish we had someone with my legs and your brains."

"That would be a deadly combination indeed." He slid the seat all the way back. "If you find someone like that, will you give me her number?" he teased.

Her quiet laugh validated his wit, but she couldn't think of anything to say in response, wishing she had his quick sense of humor.

"Okay, ready to go. Where to?" he asked.

Sharon suddenly felt self-conscious with Bill so close to her in the small space. Stumbling over her answer, she tried to recall the number of her address. She had given it to the taxi driver only minutes earlier, but for some reason, being alone with Bill in her car affected her memory. A little frustrated and embarrassed, she pointed the direction they needed to go. "It's that way, just a few blocks."

"I'm not sure I can trust you to ride in your car, with me, to your place," he said, obviously trying to ease her nerves.

Turning away from him, she looked out the window to hide her flushed face and tried to work up a humorous response with her fuzzy cognitive skills, "Well, Bob."

"It's Bill—definitely not Bob," he said with exaggerated offense.

"Yes, that's what I said. Now . . . if I did anything untoward, I'd probably forget it, so I think you're safe," she teased.

"How does that make *me* safe, and what exactly does *untoward* mean?" he asked, clearly not a novice when it came to the art of flirtation and distraction.

Thoroughly enjoying the banter, she replied, "You know, inappropriate."

"Wait . . . you're already thinking of doing inappropriate things to me? We just met!"

Sharon laughed hard, her face flushed with a fresh wave of heat. A pain in the back of her head reminded her not to get carried away. "Turn left at the next intersection," she instructed, trying to stifle a giggle.

A few blocks farther, Bill parked her tan Subaru outside her apartment.

"How are you getting home?"

He grabbed his phone and tapped a contact. "I'll call a friend of mine. He was expecting to give me a ride anyways." He turned and looked directly at her. "What? Why are you smiling at me like that?"

"No reason." He didn't need to know she was on to his scheme. At least he was telling the truth, except for the fact that his friend had been at the hospital ready to give him a ride home fifteen minutes earlier.

"Do I have something on my face?" he asked, feigning embarrassment and checking his appearance in the rear-view mirror, "Is it the whiskers? No—it's the ears, isn't it? You just noticed how big my ears are, didn't you?"

"No!" She laughed again, holding the back of her head.

"That's enough, young lady. You need a break from me." He tapped his phone and set it down. "A friend of mine will be here in a few minutes. I wish I could help you up the stairs to your apartment, but if I tried, we'd both be back in the hospital. You rest for a few days, and then I'll expect a call from you."

"You will?" She took the keys he held out. "What will I say?"

"You'll offer to take me out for dinner to replace all of my obliterated groceries that were spilled when you tried to mow me over, including the tomatoes that are responsible for your concussion. Deal?"

"Deal," she said with a shy smile, fishing her phone from her purse.

He entered his contact information and collected hers as well. "You better call me . . . I know where you live." His smile was sincere and friendly. "You let me know when you feel up to it, okay?"

"I will," she answered, not disappointed that the good-looking guy she'd backed into was pressuring her for a date.

A red pickup pulled in next to them and the same friend from the hospital parking lot walked over to help him. Bill grabbed the open door of the Subaru and pulled himself up on his good leg.

"Thanks for coming." Bill retrieved the crutches from the back seat. "Sharon, this is Steve Davis, longtime cohort in crime since college. We both work for his cousin. Steve . . . Sharon, who is none of your business," Bill said jokingly.

"Hello, pleasure to meet you," Steve said with a friendly smile.

Sharon greeted Bill's friend, fairly certain she detected a subtle English accent. Steve was taller than he appeared when she first saw him at the hospital and shockingly good looking with lady-killer eyes.

"Are we sporting scruffs now?" Steve teased, rubbing Bill's chin. "It looks good on you, mate. It might even get you noticed by the ladies for a change."

"We need to get going, Steve," Bill said pushing his friend toward the truck, suddenly in a hurry. Then he hesitated. "Sharon has a considerable bump on her head, and she lives up those—"

Steve cut him off. "Would you fancy letting me help you to your door, Sharon?"

She shyly placed her hand around the arm he offered and walked with Bill's friend up the short flight of stairs.

"She doesn't need you to help her inside," Bill instructed, as he leaned against the truck.

"Cheers then, Sharon. Watch out for this one," Steve warned, pointing at Bill as he turned to go back down.

"It was nice to meet you, Steve." She couldn't help thinking he was probably used to getting more than his share of attention.

"Call me," Bill reminded her as he opened the passenger door.

She smiled and replied with a wave as he closed the door and rolled down the window. She thought she heard Steve asking him if he was seriously picking up girls from the hospital now, but Bill didn't respond to his question and waved goodbye as they drove away.

CHAPTER 11

Sharon looked at his number on her list of contacts for the tenth time. Did Bill really want her to call him, or was he simply humoring her? He did enter her number in his phone as well and hadn't called. Two weeks after the accident, she finally got up the nerve to call the man she ran into.

"Hello, Bill, this is Sharon. Do you remember me?"

"Sharon . . . hi. I was afraid you forgot all about me, but with your concussion and all, you have a good excuse. I'm so glad you called. How are you doing?" He sounded genuinely pleased to hear from her.

"Pretty good. I was wondering if you were hungry." Sharon rolled her eyes, feeling like everything she said sounded foolish. How did he trap her into asking him out, anyways? He should be calling her.

"Famished," he replied. "In fact, if I don't have authentic French food soon, I might die. What are you hungry for?"

"French food?" Why not take the bait and follow his lead since he was purposefully making it easy for her?

"Oh . . . I don't know . . . okay, French food sounds good. Are you thinking tonight, tomorrow, or both?" he prodded.

"Either is fine with me," she offered, eager to please, but she had intended to go out the following day.

"Perfect. I'll swing by and pick you up. How about seven o'clock tonight?" Bill asked.

"Do you need me to drive?"

"I've got it covered. I'll see you at seven then, okay?"

"Yes, seven," she agreed.

"I'm looking forward to it. See ya soon, and, Sharon, thanks again for calling."

* * *

Bill hung up the phone and checked the time. It was just past two. He tapped in a number on his phone.

"Hi, Steve. Hey, I'm not going to make it tonight . . . Yeah, something came up that I can't miss . . . Yes, the girl from the hospital . . . No, you can't come with us. Nice try."

* * *

A yellow Hummer taxicab pulled up next to Sharon's car a few minutes before seven. She walked down the stairs outside of her apartment, not certain if the cab was for her. Bill opened the back door and stepped out, pulling one crutch from the back seat.

"Hi there. Ready to go?" He flashed a friendly smile.

"Hello," she replied shyly, suddenly self-conscious and thinking he was a little out of her league.

He had one black boat shoe on, a pair of loose khaki cargo shorts that gave him room to navigate his casted leg, and a black button-up shirt with rolled sleeves. His curly blond hair, still slightly damp, was coerced to curl over the top of his ears.

"I would have come up to your apartment to get you, but we would have missed dinner." He lifted the crutch as evidence for his lack of chivalry.

"I'm sure you're a perfect gentleman." She took a seat next to him in the over-the-top cab, trying not to make it obvious that she enjoyed the clean scent of his damp hair and faint, woodsy aftershave.

"Perfect might be a slight exaggeration. Before you think too highly of me, you should know this cab is a free ride. It didn't cost me a cent."

"How did you swing that?" Sharon was a bit relieved to know he wasn't accustomed to impressing his dates with extravagant displays of wealth—or debt. She'd often been accused of being unnecessarily frugal, a trait she wasn't ashamed of.

"A buddy of mine started a business with three of these Hummers. I introduced him to a potential investor that eventually gave him the start-up capital he needed to get the business *rolling*. Did you catch that?"

"Yes, I did. Pun intended?" she asked him with a good-for-you look in her eyes.

"Yes, pun always intended." Bill offered her a sly grin. "And, as a thank you for the introduction, he gifted me one year of VIP cab rides. I wasn't sure I'd ever collect on the gift, but circumstances being what they are, I graciously accepted the door-to-door pampering."

"A timely gift. It's nice of you to share it with the assailant that left you in this miserable state."

"Tell me, Sharon, do I look miserable?" He held her gaze rather intently.

"No, not at all." Shifting her eyes to her lap, she could feel heat creeping up her neck. He most definitely appeared to be the opposite of miserable.

"Don't worry about the leg, okay? If I had known you before the accident, I would have jumped behind your car on purpose, just to coerce you to go out with me. You know, use the victim card to my advantage. You look beautiful, by the way."

Not expecting his compliment to be thrown into the conversation, she struggled to respond. The heat on her neck moved across her face as she offered him a shy smile in reply.

* * *

They enjoyed the small French restaurant, a favorite of his, and visited comfortably for several hours before he suggested they go.

"I'm enjoying that lucid look in your eyes and don't want you to lose it on account of me keeping you out too late."

She smiled at his reference to her previously diminished mental capacity. "Thank you, Bill, or was it Bob?"

He laughed a little too loudly for the table next to them. "Sorry. Good one." He leaned in close to her and whispered something about ruining the ambiance.

"We'd better go before you get us kicked out of here." He wouldn't let her pay for dinner, taking the blame for coercing her into going out with him.

The yellow Hummer was waiting for them a few yards down the sidewalk from the restaurant. Bill opened the door for her, balancing on his right foot. She carefully stepped around him, close enough to catch his warm, woodsy scent again. He placed his hand gently on her elbow, as if he could steady her if she were to slip. The entire evening was worth that one touch of his hand. She straightened her skirt as he maneuvered himself onto the seat beside her.

"You know, I only have a few months left of VIP treatment, and it would be a shame to waste this Hummer on myself. Would you like to ride around with me in this thing next weekend? Maybe I'll have graduated to a boot so we can get around a little easier. What do you think?"

"I would like that." She couldn't help but smile, flattered that he had taken the initiative to secure another date.

Bill kept his silliness to a minimum the rest of the drive home. Their injuries had finally taken a back seat in their conversation, and they were comfortably getting to know one another. All too soon, they arrived at her apartment.

"Thanks again, I had a really good time." Sharon tried to persuade him to stay seated while she stepped out of the Hummer.

"I'll call you," he reminded her as he stood by the open cab door. He watched her make her way up the stairs and waved before scooting back into the cab.

* * *

"I'll call you Mrs. Webster for the rest of your life," he whispered as the taxi drove him home. She had unexpectedly effected a few chemical changes in his brain. Instinctively, he felt like he needed to start building some kind of spectacular nest to gain her approval and encourage her to entertain a long-term relationship. You're getting ahead of yourself, his internal voice warned him. You're a long ways away from nest building. His broken leg would keep him from dancing around her like a prairie rooster, so he would be limited to dining out for now.

Bill knew Sharon would be on his mind for hours or, more likely, days: her light floral scent, the way she laughed at his jokes—never minding if they were funny or not—her understated modesty in her purple cotton dress, and the way she blushed every time he complimented her. "Oh, man, Bill, you are such a goner."

"Sorry, sir?" the taxi driver replied. "I didn't catch that."

"Nothing . . . talking to myself."

* * *

Sharon pulled out her new black dress, purchased two days earlier in anticipation of a special milestone date. There were several things worth celebrating: Bill would finally have a boot-free leg; they had enjoyed four months of getting to know one another, their mutual attraction unmistakable; and this particular date would be an anniversary of sorts as they revisited the quaint French restaurant that marked the beginning of their growing relationship. When they made plans for this special dinner, Sharon and Bill laughed over the fact that the parking lot at the grocery store was their real beginning, but they decided the restaurant would be a better marker for a romantic trip down memory lane.

Nervously checking her reflection in the mirror one last time, Sharon tried to coax her long, wavy hair away from her face. Before she could tame her loose mane into a ponytail, she heard a familiar tap on her apartment door and pulled it open

"Hello—oh, wow—you look beautiful." Bill shook his head. "Are you sure you want to be seen with me?"

Sharon blushed at the compliment. "You know I do."

He didn't reply but stood silent, staring and grinning, like a boy waiting for a caramel apple at the fair.

"What?" she asked. "You're making me nervous."

"If you knew what I was thinking, you should be nervous," Bill teased. "So, we'd better get out of here."

The free service of the Hummer taxi no longer available, Bill drove Sharon to dinner in his red pickup. She preferred it to the taxi, just the two of them, his eyes on the road and her eyes on him.

They enjoyed their meal and shared a dessert, taking an hour and a half to eat the small dish of crème brulee, and then, to her surprise, Bill ordered the "chef's special."

"Are you still hungry?"

The chef returned with a small basket of tomatoes and set it in front of her. "What's this?"

"Open the card," he said softly, his hands sweaty and shaking.

She reached into the basket of tomatoes and pulled out a small card that read, "*Sharon, will you fall for me again? I love you—Bill.*" She looked at him with wide-open eyes, not sure what the note meant.

Bill pulled a small box from his pocket and got down on one knee beside her. "Sharon, I want you all to myself forever . . . I love you . . . Will you marry me?"

Sharon stood to her feet and started to cry. She pulled on his arms so he would stand up and relieve his recently boot-free leg. "Yes . . . of course . . . yes, I love you, too." She wrapped her arms around his neck.

He pulled her close and gently kissed her. Pulling back to see her face, he reached up to wipe a tear off her cheek and kissed her again. "I love you, Sharon," he whispered into her ear before releasing one arm and handing her a handkerchief he had in his shirt pocket.

Overwhelmed by his proposal, she smiled at him and dabbed at her eyes before noticing the letters S.Y.W. embroidered on the soft cotton fabric. "Sharon Yvonne Webster. I don't remember telling you my middle name."

"I stalked you a little bit online. Is that going to be a deal breaker?" He looked at her with a crooked grin.

"Not a chance," she replied, basking in the reality of the moment.

"Sharon?"

"Yes?"

"Were you interested in this ring?" He picked up the black satin box from their table.

"Oh . . . the ring! Yes . . . oh, my, it's so beautiful, thank you." She smiled at him, her eyes drinking in every detail.

He took her left hand and slid the solitaire diamond onto her slender finger. "It looks good on you." He continued to hold her hand in his. "I'm so glad you fell for me—again."

"Are you going to be cheesy our entire married life?" she teased, dabbing her eyes again with the handkerchief.

"Likely. Is that going to work for you?"

"Yes, yes it is." She felt like the luckiest girl in the world.

* * *

Sharon closed the picture album, her thoughts a mixture of fond memories and fresh rejection. She returned the book to the high shelf in the living room and walked back into the kitchen to press another shirt.

CHAPTER 12

Bill checked his bags and boarded the plane that would have him in Beijing, China, in less than fifteen hours. It had been almost three months since he tried to see his wife and son on Christmas Eve. Sharon never did return his call. He continued to pen letters he wished Sharon could open, but the likelihood that they would be returned to sender made the alternate address on the envelope necessary. They'd be available when she was ready to read them.

After several weeks of leg work, Bill finished all the needed changes to present the proposal in his hand. He knew the competition was intense, but the cyber-attack protection components would likely push his company to the top of the list. He stepped into the elevator and headed up to the conference room, tapping the file with his fingertips. This meeting would make or break months of preparation.

Several hours later, Bill left the meeting with a sense that things weren't progressing in his favor. An argument broke out between a government official and a member on the selection committee. The company president seemed to have insulted an official, who stormed out of the room in disgust, and then the conference continued on as if the man was only a nuisance. The translator sat next to him, wide-eyed and silent, until her manager instructed her to continue. The argument was not translated.

The Beijing infrastructure proposal had been in the works for months, and he knew no other contractor could provide the quality of components that Davis Engineering could at a lower cost. There was always the chance that they would entertain value-engineered products, but the liability would be a gamble not worth taking. The president of the Chinese company installing the voltage regulators and security software knew Bill's firm provided compatible and safety-tested components, but the bid would be considerably higher than a value-engineered bid.

After popping a few antacid tablets, Bill pulled his suit coat on and straightened his tie. This evening's dinner, with several representatives from the selection committee, would be his last chance to secure the contract. He was the third of three qualifying bids, and his prototype simulation had clearly impressed them. He stepped into the elevator and pressed the button that would take him to the restaurant on the sixty-sixth floor. Mulling over the friction he detected in the meeting four hours earlier, Bill hoped a change in atmosphere, a gourmet meal, and a few drinks might help him allay any apprehension on their part.

The private table, reserved a half hour early, allowed him plenty of time to mentally prepare before the others arrived. He needed to exude confidence and respect, and he hoped the communication barrier would not pose any unforeseen problems. When his dinner guests arrived early, he was relieved that all three of them spoke fluent English. He would need to remember that his propensity toward jokes and sarcasm would not be an advantage in this country and would only get him blank stares and misunderstanding if he tried to employ them.

Bill stood and greeted the two middle-aged men he recognized as the president and vice president of the Beijing company he was courting, but he hesitated when greeting the woman with them. He was hardly to blame for his forgetfulness. The woman's modest black business suit and tightly coiffed hair had been exchanged for a barely there red silk cocktail dress, and her flowing, ebony hair reached several feet down her bare back. He forced himself not to stare. To think the almond-eyed beauty stunning would have been an understatement.

"Lynn," she offered, appearing pleased that her appearance caught him off guard. "Lynn Song."

"Lynn—yes, of course," Bill responded apologetically, keeping his gaze away from her plunging neckline.

A half hour and a few drinks into the dinner, Bill was embarrassed to notice Lynn leaning forward during their conversation, offering a clear view of her finest assets. Looking to the men that accompanied her, he expected they would tactfully remedy the situation. Surely, they were aware of their colleague's exposure, or maybe their impeccable manners enabled them to appear oblivious to the accidental display. Bill determined that water would be his beverage of choice for the remainder of the dinner, and an hour later, his choice would prove to be a wise one.

The two men were uncommonly agreeable, and Lynn Song, he determined, was fully aware of her wardrobe malfunction. As the dinner progressed, Bill decided the company heads were aware as well. They excused themselves, leaving Lynn to *wrap things up.*

Bill's palms began to sweat as Lynn slid closer to him in the private booth. He tried to talk about his wife and son, but she ignored his attempt to stall her advance. She was a sly one as she continued to talk business while sliding her hand onto his upper thigh.

"Bill, you didn't hear this from me, but your bid is eighty million dollars higher than the other two contractors."

He was all ears, but she was all hands. It was a ridiculous situation. Would his 280 million dollar proposal and four months of hard work really be decided over a lewd encounter in a restaurant booth?

"If you can reduce your bid by eighty million dollars and send us untested components, I can see they get past customs and marked tested before they are installed. Surely you are aware that quality corporations do this all the time, Bill. The inspector gets a *bonus* of fifty thousand American dollars and then provides the required stamp of approval."

So that was it. They sent Lynn Song after him to get him to sign off on untested components. They wanted his company's name but his competitor's price and gamble with liability. It was never going to happen. Four months down the drain for a lousy design-build fee. After costs, he would be lucky to make minimum wage on this one.

"Just think about it, Bill. Maybe a few million dollars could find its way into your personal bank account, as a thank you, of course. Why don't we go back to your room and discuss the fine details?" She ran her long, scarlet nails over the thin silk strap on her dress as if it was threatening to slip off her ivory shoulder.

Bill looked around for a plan of escape. The sultry Lynn would be happy to assist him back to his room, and like the thin strap on her dress, his resolve to keep her out of it was beginning to slip. *You lost the contract anyways. Why not enjoy yourself tonight?* the voice inside his head tempted him. *Look at her . . . She wants you.*

He pushed the uninvited voice away from his conscience. "I'm sorry, Lynn. I need to go back to my room and call my wife. I'll be touching you later." He closed his eyes with embarrassment as a red blush made its way up his neck. "I meant to say, I'd be getting to touch . . . in touch with you later . . . you and your committee, that is." He needed to get out of there!

"I heard what you said, Bill," she cooed. "Why not go call your wife, and then I will come by your room in an hour or so to talk about those *details*." She winked at him and slid out of the booth before he could verbalize a response.

He tried not to notice her details as she walked away from the table. His eyes must have been playing tricks on him because Lynn seemed to turn luminescent as she passed by a sconce light on the wall.

After paying the check, Bill hurried out of the opulent restaurant as if an armed assassin lurked in every alcove and shadow. Anxious to reach his hotel room, he made his way down the hall toward the elevators. A group of young, well-dressed women were close behind him and followed him into the confined space before the doors closed. One of the women covered her mouth and giggled quietly. Another said something he couldn't understand, but he was certain he was the object of their conversation. As he stepped through them and off the elevator, he could hear the women carrying on as if he had done something terribly embarrassing yet entertaining. At this point, he didn't care what manner of faux pas he was guilty of. He just wanted to get to his room and lock the door.

He slid his key into the slot and waited for the green light to permit entry. Once inside, he turned on the lamp by the bed and stepped past the mirror to set his wallet and phone on the nightstand, noticing a faint glow on the back of his pants. A closer inspection revealed the explanation for both Lynn's luminescence and the giggles on the elevator. His rear was glowing with some kind of shimmer powder he had wiped off the booth seat, left behind by the she-tiger that had him caged in.

"Wonderful," he muttered as he pulled the sparkling pants off and placed them in a dry cleaning bag. He splashed some water on his face and removed his shirt, noticing his left sleeve was also shimmering. After tossing his shirt in the dry cleaning bag as well, Bill slid the chain lock into place on the door. If

Lynn was crafty enough to pay off inspectors and trim millions of dollars from government contracts, she could probably get a key to his room as well.

How could this be happening? He sat on the edge of the bed, rubbing his hands through his thick hair and over his tired scalp. He picked up his wallet and pulled two well-worn pictures from a leather sleeve. Heaviness tugged at his chest as he looked at the first picture: two people in love and in paradise on a Jamaican beach. How could he feel both heavy and empty at the same time?

"I'm so sorry, Sharon," he choked out, trying to straighten the frayed edges. "Can you ever forgive me?" Sharon smiled back from over seven years ago. She never would have married him if she knew what he would do to her and Stewart. He pulled the second picture forward, as worn as the first one: the three of them in Mexico, the perfect family.

Bill told Lynn he was going to call his wife, but it was a lie. He stared at his phone sitting on the nightstand next to his wallet. It had been months since he called her, and now his guilt would keep him from dialing what used to be his own phone number. He pressed the contact button on the screen and scrolled to *home*. It was 11:45 p.m. in Beijing, making it 11:45 a.m. in DC. Sharon and Stewart would probably be finishing up with lunch. One press and the call would go through, thousands of miles away.

Tap, Tap, Tap. "Bill, it's Lynn."

He froze in place. Maybe if he pretended he was asleep she would go away. The key card reader beeped, and he could hear the handle on the door turn. The door creaked, but the locked chain pulled tight across the narrow opening.

"Bill, unlock the door. I need to talk to you . . . Bill, can you hear me?"

He held his frozen pose as if a grizzly bear were considering him for a meal. Lynn mumbled an angry foreign phrase then stomped away, leaving the door ajar. After several long minutes, he walked over to the door and pushed it shut. His shoulders felt heavy as he sat slumped forward on the side of the bed. This contract would be a colossal fail, and his first loss, but that was not the failure dominating his thoughts. He stared at the phone in his hand. On the other end of the contact marked *home* was what really mattered. Bill sat there for ten minutes more, worried that another man would answer if he pressed the green button underneath his hovering thumb.

Call her.

The voice seemed audible. Bill glanced around before chiding himself, his tired mind rattling his emotions and producing a mental cocktail that had him questioning his sanity. Why not call her? The screen on his phone faded to black. He could feel his heart rate increase as he challenged himself to follow through this time. Maybe it wasn't too late, and why would he ever consider giving up on his wife and son?

This could be his one and only chance to talk to Sharon. She had resisted paying for caller ID on their landline, so chances were high she would answer the call. Before he could talk himself out of it, Bill pressed the green call icon. He would beg her to hear him out. The long distance call took a few seconds to connect. One . . . two . . . three rings and then a strange voice answered with an apology: "I'm sorry. The number you have called has been disconnected or is no longer in service."

It was after midnight. Bill sat on the side of the hotel bed, panic-stricken. Sharon disconnected the phone. She shut him out, and it was what he deserved for failing her and Stewart. A thought startled him, causing his pulse to race even faster. What if they moved? Or, worse yet, what if something terrible had happened? He quickly pulled his laptop from its case and entered a search for the airlines. It was time to go home. He would leave on the earliest flight available.

CHAPTER 13

It was almost ten in the morning. Several hundred people stood around the luggage carousel at Dulles International Airport, tired from the fourteen-hour flight. Bill's phone vibrated in his jacket pocket. He had to take this call. It was Dwayne Davis, his boss and the owner of Davis Engineering. The work in Beijing had been left unfinished, and Dwayne calling him meant he had words for Bill, not encouraging ones.

"Hello, Dwayne."

"Bill, where are you? You were supposed to be in a meeting five hours ago!" His boss's voice was more anger than concern.

"I'm sorry, Dwayne. I had to come home." Bill knew his explanation would not be taken well.

"Was there an emergency?"

"I need to check on my family," he replied, knowing his boss already witnessed the neglect he was guilty of. The reason Dwayne gave him the position in the first place was his assurance that family obligations wouldn't interfere with his ability to travel for lengthy periods of time.

"You what? Bill, is everything okay? This is not like you." Dwayne was, above all, a businessman, and Bill had been a valuable asset to the company, adept at writing proposals and securing contracts. He had never let Dwayne down before.

"We didn't get the contract in Beijing. They wanted value-engineered components, and I knew we couldn't go there."

"No, Bill, you're wrong this time. The president of the company called me and wanted to know where you were. You weren't answering your phone, so naturally I thought you had an accident or something. Please don't tell me you walked away from this contract because you just realized you're a lousy husband."

The comment stung, but it was true. Unfortunately, it had taken this long to finally do something about it. So long, in fact, that he may have missed his chance altogether.

"I haven't been able to reach my wife, and I need to make sure she and Stewart are all right. I just need one week."

"Dang, Bill, we're talking about 280 million dollars here! Why couldn't someone else check on your family? I would have flown over to Beijing myself if I thought you were going to get all domestic on me." Mr. Davis's anger was barely contained. "You have one week. I can stall them in Beijing, but you better be on a flight for China by Friday."

He watched his luggage ride around the carousel as he contemplated how to answer his boss.

"Bill, did you hear me?"

"Yes, Dwayne."

"Well, do I have your word, Bill? Will you be headed to China next Friday, or do I have to take care of this myself?"

"I'll be back in the air by Friday." Bill nearly choked on his promise, knowing he would regret making it, but he couldn't afford to lose his job.

"Good, then. Don't drop the ball on this one. We need this contract." Not waiting for a reply, Mr. Davis ended the call.

Bill collected his luggage and passed the car rental counter, deciding to take a taxi to his hotel instead. "Kellogg Hotel, please," he informed the driver.

"Is that at Gallaudet University, sir?"

"Yes." He tried to sound friendly but failed even at that.

"Are you here for business or travel?" the driver asked as they pulled away from the airport.

"I'm headed home." Bill knew the driver figured he was lying but wasn't in the mood to explain himself.

The driver looked at him in the rear view mirror. "That's nice." For the rest of the drive, they both remained silent.

* * *

"See you tomorrow, Stewart. Bye, Mrs. Webster." Stacey waved before Sharon closed the alley gate and locked it behind her. Sharon missed her normal

Friday visit with Nanna May, who had been feeling under the weather for the last few days. She also wished Stewart's friend could have played a little longer, but she was off to school. Sharon spent the hour and thirty minutes of nearly uninterrupted time getting a multitude of things done but had only pressed two shirts from the large pile of uniforms on the wooden chair.

"Come on in, Stewart. Let's make some lunch."

As Sharon set small strips of vegetables on a paper towel for her son to munch on, she warned herself that there was no way to keep this month from revealing the reality of her situation. It was nearly the end of April and the anniversary of her husband's year-long contract. As the days drew closer to the end of the month, she wondered if he would even let her know what he decided to do with his future. She reprimanded herself for revisiting the hopeless situation, not having heard from him in nearly four months' time. Did she really expect Bill to show up just to tell her he found someone else to spend the rest of his life with? Still, the unknown haunted her. When the month was past, she would call Davis Engineering to gather any information she could and then try to sort things out from there.

After Stewart finished his lunch, she read him a few books until his eyelids grew heavy. Sharon considered taking a nap with him, but the pressing wasn't going to get done by itself. She didn't loathe the task. There was a small measure of accomplishment when she completed the order, but the reality that she might have to look for a different job loomed over her. She couldn't stand the idea of leaving her son with someone else while she worked all day. Maybe she could take a night job and work while he slept. She tried to push the overwhelming thoughts aside, but they continued to irritate her, like cheatgrass lodged in a runner's sock.

* * *

Bill set his suitcase on the luggage rack in his hotel room, threw his jacket on the bed, and scrolled through the contacts on his phone. Finding the person he was looking for, he selected another number he hadn't called in a long time.

"Bill, are you phoning me from Beijing?" Steve asked, sounding surprised to see his name on the caller ID.

"Hi, Steve. No, I'm in DC."

"What? How are you in town? Could it have anything to do with Dwayne stomping around the office?"

"Yes, it could, and it's a long story. Listen, can you do me a favor? I'm sorry to impose."

"Happy to. What can I do for you?"

"I need a car for about a week. I'll understand if you can't swing it." Bill felt like he was taking advantage of a faithful friend, but he'd avoid getting a rental car if he could. Should he lose his job, a rental would be another expense he couldn't afford.

"You don't want to hire a car? Or did you break your leg again?" Steve teased.

"No broken leg this time, but I might suddenly be short on expendable income, so I'd like to borrow a car if you know of one. I don't have my truck anymore."

"You sound a bit off, mate. What's up?"

Bill grabbed a handful of hair on the top of his head. "I screwed up, but I don't have time to go into it right now."

"I'll do whatever I can to help you get sorted out," Steve offered. "Give me half an hour."

Bill told his friend where he was staying and thanked him for going out of his way to help him. Steve had always been his most reliable friend, even though the Brit had stolen a few of his previous potential girlfriends back when they were still in college.

While he waited for Steve to find a car, Bill pulled his computer out to arrange his flight back to China. He would fly into Beijing on Friday morning, make it to the meeting that evening, and get on a flight back to DC around midnight. That would put him back in DC about noon the following day. He had never cut things so close before and was aware he left no time for sleep over the three-day trip, other than flight time. The phone on the nightstand buzzed as Bill reluctantly purchased his ticket.

"Hi, Steve."

"I got a car for you. I'll be there straight away."

Glad to hear that one small detail was working in his favor, Bill thanked him.

"Wait until you see the car before you thank me. You might regret the offer," he teased before hanging up.

Bill walked out to the front of the hotel to watch for his friend. A yellow Hummer taxi drove toward the hotel entrance, followed by a hotel shuttle. He continued to scan the cars driving toward him on the narrow street.

"Bill?"

He startled and turned around to see his friend standing behind him. "I didn't see you drive up." Bill grabbed Steve's shoulder and gave him a hug. "It's good to see you, man."

"It's good to see you as well, mate, but you look like total crap."

"I feel worse than crap, but I have to do a few things before I can fill you in, okay?" Bill hated putting his good friend off, but he would have to for now.

"You got it, boss," Steve said, patting him on the shoulder. "Take a look at your ride—brilliant, eh?"

Bill was wondering how he missed him until he saw Steve pointing at the yellow Hummer. Of course! He should have known. It turned out their friend from college was still doing well with his taxi business. When Steve called to see if Bill could borrow one of the Hummers for a week, their friend didn't hesitate to loan it out.

"Don't forget to turn the off duty sign on, cabby," Steve said in his usual lighthearted way before jumping in the front passenger seat.

"Where to, sir?" Bill inspected the buttons and dials on the dashboard.

"I need to get back to work. We can catch up later, right?" Steve looked at him, concern evident in his tight smile.

"Yes, of course. Thanks again, bud."

It took a few blocks before Bill was comfortable driving the taxi. A few people reached for the passenger door at an intersection before seeing the off duty sign. Steve laughed and talked about old times, obviously trying to lighten the mood and not pry into his friend's current circumstances. Bill pulled into the entrance of Davis Engineering, and Steve stepped out of the taxi.

"Call me if you need anything else. You know, the Lord and I, we both have your back." Steve tapped the top of the cab.

He thanked his friend and promised to call him. Steve always had a strong faith, but Bill didn't think God would give him the time of day, let alone have his back. He wondered if he could still pray and ask God for help, but that line, he was afraid, had been disconnected as well. There was always the chance God was listening, so Bill sent up a desperate plea as he drove toward home.

"Anything, Lord, I'll do anything to have my family back."

It was going to be hard to drive by the house incognito in a yellow Hummer. Making his way through the familiar neighborhood, Bill felt like a coward as he drove past the house, checking to see if the man that had taken his place might have a car parked in front of the house. But as he drove by, it was difficult to tell if anyone was home. The only way to know for sure would be to drive down the alley to see if Stewart was in the yard or if Sharon was in the kitchen—or he could get out of the car and knock on the door like a man. His heart was beating so hard the pocket on his shirt was pulsing as he stepped out of the taxi and walked up to knock on his own front door.

CHAPTER 14

Sharon pulled a plastic garment bag over a shirt and hung it by the front door. Stewart would probably nap for another fifteen minutes, giving her enough time to make a sizable dent in the pile of uniforms. She placed the next shirt on the steam rack before hearing a knock on the front door. Maybe if she ignored them, they would go away. She repositioned the shirt. There had been a lot of solicitors lately, some looking for donations and others selling things she didn't need. She always felt bad when turning them down, knowing they didn't look forward to asking people if they would like to buy a set of knives or try a vacuum cleaner that cost as much as a used car. However, in the off chance it was one of her friends from down the street, she set her steamer aside and answered the door.

Frozen in shocked silence, she stared at her husband, willing herself to speak. "Bill . . . what are you . . . I didn't know you were coming." She tried to say *home,* but the word refused to form in her mouth. This house had not been his home for the better part of a year. She stood there, stunned and nervous, until she could put a few coherent words together. "Come in. Why are you in town?" She forced a smile in an effort to mask her discomfort and stepped back into the house.

Shifting his feet in the small entryway, Bill seemed as if he were an uninvited guest, if not an intruder, in what used to be *their* home. Sharon was assaulted with a thousand questions, all bearing unwanted answers.

"I need to talk to you, Sharon." Bill looked at the hanging uniforms, his face etched with worry. "Where is Stewart?"

"He's taking a nap in the living room." She felt a protective surge come over her. "Why do you want to see him now?"

Startled by her question, Bill looked briefly at her with a pained expression and then stared at the floor. As intended, her word choice surely stung—*now*—as in, why not a year ago or months ago? If he hadn't presented her with visible guilt, she would have asked him to leave.

"I need to tell you that I'm sorry and—can we sit down?"

A step ahead of him, Sharon led the way into the kitchen, her chest tightening when he glanced into the living room at the sleeping figure on the couch. She removed the bag of shirts draped over the wooden chair and set them on the steam rack. He glanced at the uniforms for a few seconds. She thought he was going to ask her about them, but instead, he released a heavy sigh and pulled the chair closer to the table, his six-foot-four frame filling the small space. She'd been expecting this for some time, but the reality of it assaulted her. Her husband would hand her divorce papers and be out of their lives forever.

Was the woman Bill had gone to Brazil with still with him? This wasn't happening! Her throat burned as she resisted the urge to cry. The questions that bombarded her when she first opened the door started their second wave of attack: How will you care for your son? Will you have to sell the house? Where will you go? It was too much. Withdrawal from this battle was her only option.

"Sharon, I want to tell you I'm sorry for leaving. It was never because I didn't love you or Stewart. I was selfish." Bill's voice wavered with emotion. He clasped his large hands together on the table as if they needed restraining.

Sitting across from and painfully close to her husband, she struggled to respond, trying to keep herself from blurting out the first thing that came to mind—ugly, angry, hasty words, irretrievable once said. She considered the attractive man with the same blond, curly hair as her son and decided he at least deserved, if nothing else, an honest response.

"Bill . . . you don't love me." She kept her voice barely above a whisper. "That's guilt you're feeling, and maybe pity, but not love. People *show* someone they love them, so, no, Bill, you don't love me, and you don't love Stewart, or you wouldn't have stayed away so long. So, now, why are you suddenly here? Do you have papers you want me to sign? If you do, please skip the apologies, and let's get it over with."

"Papers?" he replied in whispered shock. "Do you think I'm here to have you sign divorce papers? No—Sharon!"

The sound of shuffling feet and impatient moans ramped up the nervous tension between them. Stewart stood at the table, rubbing his tired eyes until he realized that someone besides his mother was sitting there. He looked briefly at Bill, shifted his gaze toward her, and then looked out the window, his confusion soothed by rocking side to side.

"Hello, Stewart," his father said, glancing at her as if she might offer him some sort of direction or cue on how to respond.

Sharon nervously watched her son as he considered the man in the chair. He didn't seem overly concerned with Bill's presence, just confused. Did he want him there? Not sure of the reason for Bill's return, she would choose her words carefully

"Honey, do you remember . . . Daddy?" she asked, sounding like a bad actress.

Bill's eyes traveled back and forth from his hands on the table to his son. His nervousness was apparent as he tried to figure out how to respond to his own child. Reaching out, he cupped his son's small shoulder in his large hand for a brief few seconds, not unfamiliar with Stewart's sensitivity to the unexpected.

Stewart laughed and jumped around the kitchen, just as he did when the rainbows reflected on the wall. He walked over to his father and, looking past him, put a small hand on the Bill's large shoulder and then returned to his celebratory laughing and jumping. Bill appeared pleased with his son's reaction, a look of tender regret in his eyes. There was no questioning Stewart's thoughts. He was thrilled to have him there.

A fresh wave of conflict bombarded her: Stewart needs a father. I can't raise him alone. What if Bill leaves again? Why is he even here? Sharon had to create some distance between her and Bill. Two parents enjoying a moment with their son should be a welcomed occasion in the life of any happy couple, but the charade needed to end, or she would lose her sanity. They were not a happy couple.

Turning away from the table, Sharon poured a few inches of juice into a plastic cup and handed it to Stewart. "It looks like a nice afternoon." She glanced out the window at nothing. "Why don't we go outside?" The kitchen walls felt as if they were closing in on her, making her desperate to leave the confined space.

Bill almost jumped out of his chair. "Good idea. Come on, Stewart. Do you have toys in your sandbox?"

Sharon noticed Bill's quick agreement to go outside, likely as uneasy as she was and fighting internal battles of his own, only his would be full of regret. His own childhood had included lengthy separations from his parents, but being privy to this information had not made his absence any easier on her.

* * *

The only son of parents that would swear undying love for him, Bill had spent a good share of his early years with his grandmother while his parents globetrotted their way around the world. Based on his collection of pictures, Sharon figured he had become the third member in their traveling party around the age of twelve.

Bill never complained to her about the separation from his parents. She heard it, though, veiled in hints of disappointment when he shared the story behind some of his most prized possessions, gifts his parents had brought back from exotic destinations: an ornate brass frog purchased from Bedouin traders in the Negev Desert; a blown-glass miniature pirate ship from the Island of Gozo; and an intricately carved pair of playing bear cubs from Bavaria. Sharon noticed a phrase often tucked into his commentary: *I wish I could have been there.*

* * *

If Bill wasn't her husband, she might not have harbored such a ready defense against him, but it would stay firmly in place until she knew the extent of his regrets. She handed him a glass of iced tea, careful not to touch his hand when he took it.

He pushed the screen door open, holding it for her and Stewart before walking through himself. Bill's long reach provided ample room for Sharon to move past him unhindered, but his closeness still affected her—his familiar scent, warm and clean like fresh-cut oak washed in cloves. She noticed his distraction with the door's squeaky spring, moving it back and forth a few times as if the source of the grating sound wasn't obvious. She turned in time to see him set his drink back on the counter before the door closed between them and could hear through the screen that he was opening cupboard doors and shuffling through them.

The sounds offended her as if he were a stranger going through her things. The screen door opened again, accompanied by its usual high-pitched complaint. Bill squirted a few sprays from a can that must have been in an upper kitchen cupboard. He moved the door a few swings, sprayed it again, and then put the can away. When he came back through the door, the attention he'd shown it rewarded him with agreeable silence.

Assault number three fired off in her mind: *Leave things alone, Bill. You are not going to reenter smoothly into our lives.* Did he think his arrival alone was all she needed to repair all things broken? She focused on Stewart in an attempt to reset her thoughts. Her son was busy playing in the sandbox, just as content with Bill's presence as the screen door. Sharon struggled to maintain an appropriate level of discomfort. Forgiveness was not going to come easily for her, if that was even what he wanted.

They sat in awkward silence watching Stewart scoop sand with the wire strainer, attentive only to the sifting grains cascading over his fingers.

"Bill, are you going to tell me why you came back?" Sharon focused on the ground at his feet, looking toward him but not at him.

He instinctually found the same safe zone to gaze at, clearly ashamed, and chewed his lower lip. A few moments of heavy silence passed before he formed a response.

"I shouldn't have left you, Sharon. When Stewart was diagnosed and I couldn't do anything to help him, I felt cheated. I saw a future of endless limitations and a life of cloistered suffocation. Somehow, I pictured us retreating into solitude to accommodate our son's well-being and thought it would become easier to stay away from the public eye, rather than be a distraction or even a source of discomfort to people around us. In other words, I was selfish."

Sharon listened but said nothing, her jaw unable to camouflage tightly clenched teeth. When Bill chanced a glance at her, she refused to look at him; her attempt to appear unaffected beginning to fray.

He continued, "I struggled to find a quality of life I thought I was entitled to while still providing for you and Stewart. That's why I accepted the promotion. I'll be honest, Sharon, the first time I came home after securing the contract in the Seychelles Islands, I felt like my dilemma was solved. I thought I had everything figured out and all I ever wanted."

Sharon wanted to scream. How could he talk about getting what he was entitled to after leaving her home to fend for herself? *Everything he ever wanted?* Her thoughts goaded her, replaying his callous words and causing her to question where she and Stewart might fit into what he wanted. Her strength began to waver, barely resisting a verbal blast of razor-sharp accusations. She wanted to tell him he was a selfish coward who deserved a life of regret rather than her forgiveness, something she could not grant even if she wanted to. Furthermore, if anyone should feel cheated, it should be her. Where was he keeping his travel companion? Her own silent questions continued the attack but unexpectedly turned on her as she questioned how she could possibly love and hate him simultaneously.

Bill suddenly became her mother and father all over again. Both claimed to love her, but over time, she became dispensable to them, traded in for something more desirable yet, at the same time, never released from the relationship. Her stomach began to churn as she tried to resist an acidic assault slowly creeping its way up her throat.

"Sharon, for nearly a year I've neglected you and Stewart, and it has been the worst year of my life."

She looked at her husband, her armor-plated defenses determined to hold their place while she listened for any explanation that might help her see beyond her own inner conflict: a struggle that fought between both the need to hold him and the desire to hurt him.

"The first few months I was gone, I tried to justify my absence, but I knew what I was doing, and you did, too. I abandoned you and Stewart when I took the promotion. No excuse can make up for that. After a few months, I was so ashamed of myself but thought I could get the year over with and try to make it up to you. My job took me to places people dream of seeing, but what I thought would be freedom was complete emptiness. Sharon, I'll tell you why I'm here . . . I'm here to salvage any relationship that might be possible with you and Stewart. I should have been a husband to you and a father to Stewart. I know I've failed on both accounts, and I'm more than sorry. If I can't be those things, my life has no meaning. I don't expect us to pick up where we left off a year ago, but I'm begging you, Sharon, please try to forgive me. I know I'm asking a lot . . . maybe too much."

Sharon couldn't form a single word of response. She wanted to be angry but was afraid of regretting what she might say. She could feel a crack in her resolve to maintain her composure as a few tears rolled down her cheek. Capturing them quickly with the back of her hand, she hoped he didn't notice. If Bill had said the same thing six months earlier, her arms would be wrapped around him already.

Bill let out a long, heavy sigh and handed her a note with the name of the hotel and his cell phone number on it. "I'm staying at the university only a few blocks away. Would you feel comfortable giving me your number? I tried to call you before I came today, but the landline was disconnected. Did you get a new cell phone?" He looked away as if he'd asked her for private information.

Sharon winced, remembering the very moment she let her phone fall to the step and shatter. She took the note from him. "We don't have a phone. It was one more expense I really didn't need. Every time it rang, someone either wanted to sell me something or answer a survey, so I disconnected it." She could tell the comment stung.

"If it's okay with you, I'll drop off a cell phone for you tomorrow."

Sharon looked away and didn't answer.

"What's a good time for you?" Bill asked.

She knew he would wait patiently for a response but also recognized his offer as an attempt to see her again. Pushing aside her right to deny him, she considered her son and his need of a father. If she kept Bill away, the person that stood to lose the most was Stewart—not only *her* son, but *their* son.

"How about late morning, maybe nine or ten o'clock?" he offered.

"Ten is fine." She stood up and offered to take his empty glass.

"I got it."

Bill held the door open again. Sharon missed the squeak she'd grown accustomed to and wished he'd left it alone. Stewart followed them into the kitchen. It wasn't like him to leave his sandbox without being asked to, unless something was bothering him. Sharon watched with concern, wondering what he was thinking. Did he want Bill to stay? Once they were back in the kitchen, which seemed crowded with the three of them, Stewart pushed his father.

"What's wrong, Stewart?" Bill passed a questioning look to Sharon.

Stewart didn't seem agitated, just determined.

"Do you want something?" his father asked, bending down to make himself smaller.

Sharon watched with concern as Stewart pushed him again. Bill moved as best he could in the direction Stewart wanted him to go. After a few steps toward the table, there wasn't any room left to move.

"Buddy, I'm stuck. The chair is in my way."

Rocking back and forth Stewart looked past him, then stepped around his father and slapped his hands on the large wooden chair. It was more than obvious he wanted his father to stay. Except for the shirts waiting to be pressed, his chair had sat empty for nearly a year.

Sharon noticed Bill trying to swipe a tear away before it trailed down his face.

"Okay, son," he said as he took a seat.

As soon as Bill sat in the chair, Stewart ran to the living room. Bill looked at Sharon. She shrugged her shoulders, and they remained uncomfortably silent until Stewart ran back into the kitchen and threw a puzzle on the table, chanted a few urgent guttural sounds, and shook his hands back and forth at his armpits.

"Uhn, uuuuhn, uhn!"

"Sharon . . . can I stay for just a few minutes?" His expression revealed a mix of relief and sorrow, his eyes wet with emotion.

111

"Yes, of course." She felt one brick fall from her wall of angry protection as she watched her son slap his chest with his hands, then return to play with his father.

After ten minutes of frenzied introduction to a pile of Stewart's toys, Bill helped him put them back in the basket in the living room, but it was clear Stewart didn't want him to leave.

"I'll see you tomorrow, Stewart. Maybe we can do another puzzle when I come back, okay?" Bill shifted his eyes between Stewart and Sharon, eyes that begged her to help him understand his son. Sharon tried to calm him as Bill headed toward the front door, but Stewart pushed her and ran past his father, slapping the door and releasing an ear-splitting scream. Bill's discomfort was apparent as Sharon tried to pull their frantic boy away from the door.

"Can I show him my car?" he asked.

Sharon held on to Stewart's shoulders so Bill could step out the door. "Your what?" she asked, unable to hear him.

"Can he take a look at my car? Just for a minute?"

She nodded her head in apprehensive agreement, certain the diversionary tactic would merely prolong the problem.

Stewart continued to struggle with his mother until Bill bent down and asked him if he would like to go outside and see his car. With surprisingly instant compliance, he grabbed his father's arm and pulled him toward the door, ready to go.

Sharon followed them outside, but when she saw the car Bill was referring to, she covered her mouth with both hands. He pulled the passenger door open and Stewart jumped in as if he had just arrived at an amusement park, inspecting all the buttons and knobs. Bill turned back and looked at her as if needing approval for Stewart's enthusiasm.

"What's wrong?" Bill asked.

She felt sick. "Why did you drive that here?" Was she supposed to be charmed into remembering the good ol' days?

Bill looked back at the car as if he was as surprised as she was to see a Hummer taxi parked at the curb. "I'm sorry, Sharon. There's no insinuation here. I needed a car, and this one was available. That's all; I promise."

"Dun, dun, dun . . . dun, dun, dun." Stewart chanted a happy cadence that broke through the awkward exchange outside the cab.

Sharon looked around Bill as Stewart adjusted every knob and button, distracting her from her initial shock. "Should he be doing that?"

Bill slid in next to Stewart. "He can't hurt anything. It'll only take a few seconds to reset things."

HONK—HONK—HONK—Stewart jumped with shock and then covered his ears, laughing when he realized he was responsible for the loud sounds. *HONK—HONK.*

"Okay, Stewart," Bill said firmly but gently. "You can't do that anymore; it's too loud."

Stewart complied and continued to laugh, reaching for another compartment not yet inspected. Bill showed him a few interesting buttons and switches as he returned the dials to their original positions. Sharon was ready for Stewart to get out of the car. She needed Bill to leave.

"Come on, buddy; it's time to go back inside," Bill said, tapping him on the arm.

Sharon stepped closer to the cab, thinking Stewart would repeat the same tantrum he pitched when Bill first tried to leave.

"If it's all right with Mom, you can see the car again tomorrow if you listen now and go back inside."

Stewart looked at him for a second and then stared past him toward the house before climbing out of the Hummer.

"Dun dun, dun . . . dun, dun, dun." Stewart rolled his hands in circles in front of his chest.

Sharon moved toward the house and waved, a gesture that said *goodbye* as much as it said *you need to go now.*

He started the car before they reached the front door. The windshield wipers squeaked across the dry window, and the radio blasted a hip-hop beat, vibrating the entire vehicle. Bill smiled as he adjusted a few more dials and turned off the radio.

* * *

As he pulled away from the house and headed back to the hotel, Bill prayed in desperation. "Please, Lord, I need a miracle here, and I know I don't deserve one." Some of the questions that had dominated his worries were now satisfied. His wife and son were still there, and the *other man* was a figment of his imagination. His conscience had given him a sharp stab when he saw the pile of uniforms waiting to be pressed, his hasty suppositions on Christmas Eve kicked in the teeth. Why had I been so quick to think another man had taken my place? *You invited the possibility with the void you left behind,* his conscience reminded him.

With the major worry out of the way, his mind was now freed up to dwell on those that remained. He would relive and ruminate on every word spoken and gesture made during the short twenty minutes with his wife and son. First on his list was the fact that Sharon was not happy to see him, expecting divorce papers rather than apologies. *Why do you want to see Stewart now?* Her first question shamed him to the core. Did she really think he was there to discuss custody of their son?

"Oh, God, what have I done?" He parked the car outside the hotel. "I'm so sorry." The thought of it squeezed the air out of his chest and restricted his throat. She wouldn't even touch him—something he noticed when she handed him his glass of tea, as if the feel of his skin on hers would be loathsome. Bill pounded the steering wheel with the palm of his hand, setting off the car's alarm. Quickly pressing the panic button on the keychain, he silenced the loud, pulsing horn and stepped out of the taxi, lucky that the airbag didn't deploy and break his nose. What am I going to do until tomorrow morning? He trudged to the hotel entrance.

"The cell phone." Bill spun around and hurried back to the taxi. By the time he returned to the house in the morning, Sharon would have a new phone complete with everything she and Stewart could ever use or want.

* * *

Awake before five, Bill agonized as he watched the clock for nearly five hours. At 9:45 a.m., he grabbed the new phone and drove back to the house. The initial fear over the disconnected phone line was behind him, but he knew he had turned up the heat on an already boiling pot of emotions. If he couldn't find a way to enable some steam to escape, things were going to quickly head in the wrong direction.

"Good morning, Bill." Sharon's greeting seemed halfhearted at best as she backed away from the front door so he could enter.

He noticed she looked tired and was sure he was to blame for the sleep-depriving anxiety he'd introduced into her troubled thoughts.

"I have a phone for you. If you have a minute, I can show you the apps I added. There's something on it for Stewart I think you'll like." He wanted to tell her about his quick trip back to Beijing but didn't think he could bring it up without serious repercussions.

Sharon was attentive to his tutorial on the workings of the new cell phone, but he could sense her discomfort with his presence. He put together a few puzzles with Stewart and showed him the app he loaded for him. They inspected the dials and buttons in the cab again, and after being there for less than a half hour, Bill left but not because he wanted to. He could tell Sharon needed him to leave.

Three agonizing days later, Sharon's silence had solidified his worst fears. She didn't want him back.

CHAPTER 15

Stewart woke up Wednesday morning to a quiet house. He walked into his mother's bedroom and watched her for a moment while she continued to sleep soundly and then returned to his own bedroom. After emptying the clothes from every drawer in his dresser, he sifted through the pile on the floor and pulled on a loose shirt and a pair of knit pants, both easy for him to maneuver without any buttons or snaps, and then made his way into the kitchen. Not seeing his milk-less cereal waiting for him on the kitchen table, he returned to his sleeping mother's bedside, stood silent for a few seconds, and then tromped back into the kitchen.

Most of the food in the pantry was out of his reach, so he opened the refrigerator, pulled plastic wrap off an opened package of cheese, and took a few bites from the two-inch stack of slices. The second bite included unpalatable bits of waxed paper, so he placed the unwrapped block of cheddar slices back in the refrigerator and closed the door. After checking on his mother one more time, he tried the door to the backyard. It was locked. He then tried the front door—it opened.

Stewart stepped through the open door and stood on the front steps looking up and down the quiet street. Familiar things lined the sidewalk that led to Stacey's house. He stepped back inside and slipped on his elastic-strapped sandals and a navy-blue hat that Earl had just given him. After checking on his sleeping mother one more time, he walked back outside, glanced up and down the street, closed the door behind him, and walked toward Stacey's house. A boy on a skateboard careened toward him on the sidewalk.

"Get out of the way!" he yelled, one part bossy and three parts warning.

Stewart ran across the street. A car honked at him, having to slow down to the speed limit to keep from hitting him. Anxiety and disorientation became his failed compass as he ran several blocks north before reaching a main thoroughfare. Half a block away, cars came to a stop and then took off again at a busy intersection. He stood there for a minute, observing his surroundings. Nothing looked familiar.

People busily tapping on their phones passed around him and crossed the street at the light. Several older boys with backpacks signed back and forth with their hands. Stewart followed them as their conversation continued, swift gestures of communication passing from one to the other. Still behind them as they crossed the street, he spotted a cat sunning itself on the sidewalk and lost interest in the boys. The cat darted away when he reached out to pet it, so he walked north for another ten minutes and chose a bench outside a nearby grocery store as an acceptable place to rest. Just as he reached the bench, a man yelled down the sidewalk to someone walking out of a store, and then thunderous chaos broke out all around him.

* * *

Exhaustion caused by the emotional turmoil of her husband's unexpected return had afforded Sharon little rest over the past few days. Tuesday night turned into Wednesday morning before sleep finally claimed her sometime after three o'clock. Five hours later, she opened tired eyes and tried to focus on the clock next to her bed. It was eight thirty. She leapt out of bed as a surge of adrenaline assaulted her body, only one thing on her mind—Stewart!

She had always been a light sleeper, waking to the slightest of sounds. Her son would wake up between seven thirty and eight, a good hour later than she would, except for today. She ran to his room across the hall and found only crumpled covers on an empty bed and clothes dumped from the dresser drawers on the floor. Before panic overtook her, she ran through the house and tried the back door. It was still locked. Maybe he was hiding from her. She checked the bathroom and his favorite hiding spots.

"Stewart, honey, where are you?" she called. "Help me, God! Please help me!" she cried as she swiped the lock over on the front door. The door wouldn't budge. It hadn't been locked the night before, and she had just locked it in her confusion. "No! No! No!" she cried as she ran back to her room and threw on a pair of pants and a T-shirt, grabbed her shoes and phone, and headed for the front door.

"How could you forget to lock the door?" she screamed as she yanked the door open and ran outside, frantically looking up and down the sidewalk. Sharon called out as she hurried toward the Clarks' house, "Stewart! . . . Stewart! . . . Stewart!" She tried to sound calm, but it was impossible. If he thought he was in trouble, he might hide from her. She hoped he had only gone to visit Stacey, but they would have called if he had been there for more than a few minutes. "Please! God, please let him be there!" Sharon pleaded as she ran down the sidewalk and pounded on the Clarks' front door.

Earl opened the door within seconds. "Sharon, what's wrong?"

"Is Stewart here?" Panicked and pale, she squeezed her hands together. One simple word would fix everything.

"He's not, Sharon. Come in here." He grabbed on to her arm and told her to take a few breaths before telling him what happened.

She started to cry. "He's gone! I woke up late, and he wasn't there!"

Earl grabbed his phone and dialed 911. "You call Bill . . . right now," he said with an authoritative tone she had never heard before.

She jabbed at her phone with shaking hands, thankful for the phone Bill had just given her, and found his number listed in her contacts. He was staying a few blocks away at a hotel on the Gallaudet University campus, and she could barely punch the contact button, let alone search for a hotel number.

As soon as she heard the phone pick up, she felt a fresh surge of panic. "Bill . . . Stewart is gone! I woke up late this morning, and he's gone!" Salty tears ran down her face and lips and dripped off her chin.

"Where are you?" Bill's voice sounded urgent but steady.

"I'm at the Clarks'. Earl is calling the police. Bill . . . we have to find him right now!" Sharon nervously ran the palm of her free hand up and down her thigh, trying to subdue the involuntary jerks and twitches overwhelming her legs.

"I'll be at the house in five minutes. You walk around the block and meet me back at the house. We'll find him, Sharon. He couldn't have gone too far."

It took Nanna May a few minutes to throw her robe on and make her way into the living room. "Is it Stewart?" she whispered, her fingertips hovering over her top lip.

Struggling to calm herself, Sharon nodded a reply. As soon as Earl hung up the phone, Nanna May asked him what she could do.

"You call Pastor and get a few people over here to help us look for him. He's probably not more than a few blocks away. Then call Anna at work and let her know what's goin' on. She'll see the messages flying back and forth and needs to know that Stacey is with us." Earl tapped in their pastor's number for her and handed her the phone. "I'm goin' to walk with Sharon around the block and wait at her house for Bill and the police."

Earl and Sharon made a loop around the block, calling for Stewart. When they reached the house, Bill was already there, talking to a police officer whom Earl said was one of their new neighbors. Bill appeared calm from a distance, but when Sharon walked closer, she could see a visible beat in the pulsing veins on his neck and beads of sweat collecting on his forehead.

"Hello, Mrs. Webster, I'm officer Stevens. I'd like you to give me some information so we can find your son."

"Yes, of course," she replied, wringing her hands.

"What time was it when you first noticed that your son was missing?" The officer held a pen and notepad, ready for her answer.

"Eight thirty . . . eight thirty this morning."

The officer looked at Bill as if to see if he agreed with his wife.

"I wasn't there when he left." Bill looked at the ground and pulled on the back of his neck.

As the officer recorded the time Stewart went missing, he calmly asked Sharon the next important question. "Can you tell me what your son was wearing?"

She panicked. "I don't even know! He emptied his dresser . . . I don't even know what he's wearing!" Sharon buried her fingers into the hair at her temples and pulled. She was losing control.

Bill stood by her, silent, nervous, and unable to help.

"That's all right, Mrs. Webster. Do you have a recent picture of him?"

"I don't know . . ." She hadn't used the camera on her phone yet, and the most recent picture she had was on a memory disk in a drawer. Or was it in her desk?

"Here, I have one," Bill offered, punching a few buttons on his cell phone. "Will this work?" He showed it to the officer and then sent it to the number the man gave him.

Having what he needed, the officer called in the information and left. Earl offered to stay at the house so Bill and Sharon could search for their son. Someone needed to be at the house in case Stewart found his way back home.

Bill punched a contact on his phone as he pulled the car into the street. "Steve—I need your help."

Sharon stared out the passenger window, willing Stewart to be hiding behind every passing tree. *Where is he, Jesus? Please help us find him, and keep him safe,* she prayed as they slowly circled the block again. Bill's voice blended in with the traffic sounds as he asked his friend to search the southeast area of Brentwood for their son. Sharon winced when she heard Bill inform his friend that he didn't know what Stewart was wearing.

* * *

POP! . . . POP! POP! POP! POP! Gunfire erupted, blowing out the back window of a car a few feet down the sidewalk. Two men ran toward Stewart and disappeared around the corner. Another man cried out in pain and tried to run, falling to the ground in a small park across the street. Stewart screamed, but his cry of panic would only blend in with the cacophony of yelling and brakes screeching all around him. He ran behind a deli and hid, lodging himself between a concrete wall and greasy dumpster. Within seconds, the high pitch of multiple sirens and flashing lights closed in on him. He covered his ears and screamed again, his cry for help lost in the chaos.

* * *

As Bill ended his call with Steve, a distant siren made its way toward them and then stopped about six blocks away. Then another siren sounded, and another, then several more, all headed in their direction.

"Bill?" All color left Sharon's face.

He turned away from their neighborhood, both of them anxious to rule out the worst-case scenario. They sped toward the mechanical screams until forced to stop at a police blockade engulfed in a manic strobe of flashing lights. Nearly a dozen police cars and emergency vehicles surrounded a small shopping center thirty yards down the street, enclosed with yellow caution tape. They were stuck in traffic. Bill jumped out of the car and tried to approach an impatient officer that waved for him to get back in his car immediately.

"My son's lost," he yelled, hoping the officer would allow him to approach.

The officer waved him over. Only a minute later, Bill got back in the car and explained the situation to Sharon. A man had been shot leaving a liquor store. The shooter, or shooters, hadn't been caught and could still be nearby. They wouldn't be able to search the area, but the police would keep an eye out for anyone matching Stewart's description. Bill had given the officer his cell phone number, and as soon as the traffic started moving, they turned back toward the house.

* * *

Nanna May noticed the little girl bundled in her pink blanket, scared eyes wide and full of questions as she sat huddled on the couch.

"What happened to Stewart?" Stacey asked with teary eyes and protruding lower lip.

"Come here, baby girl."

Stacey moved to the comfort of Nanna May's ample lap.

"It looks like Stewart got up this mornin' before his mamma and went for a walk without her knowin' it. He might have tried to walk to our house but got himself all turned around or somethin', so we're gonna hurry up and try to find him."

Stacey sniffed and wiped the back of her purple pajama sleeve under her nose. "How can we help him? He's probably super scared."

"Why don't we ask Jesus to send Stewart a helper right now, honey, so he'll be safe and not so scared, okay?" She brushed tangled red hair away from worried, sky-blue eyes.

"Okay." Stacy sniffed again as a tear trailed down the side of her nose.

Nanna May wiped it away with her thumb. "Our precious Lord and Savior, we ask of you a hand of protection on little Stewart and plead with you to provide him the comfort of your Spirit. We know you love him even more than we do and ask in Jesus' name that you would protect him and guide him safely back home to us."

Nanna May hugged Stacey close to her and asked, "Do you want to pray, too?"

"Yes . . . I'm not sure what to say though." She looked up at her as if she were the source of appropriate prayer recipes.

"You can just talk to Jesus like he's one of your best friends sittin' right here with you."

"But the preacher says big words I don't know, like *sancrified* and *gloryness*."

"God don't care none about big words, Stacey, honey. You can use your own words and tell him exactly what you're thinkin'. God likes them kind of prayers best."

"Okay." With eyes tightly shut and hands clasped beneath her chin, she prayed, "Dear Jesus . . ." She peeked up with one eye barely open. "That's how Mrs. Diller prays at Sunday school." Nanna May nodded her approval. "That's fine; you go ahead now."

Apparently satisfied that she was properly prepared, Stacey continued, "Dear Jesus, please help my best-ever friend, Stewart, to not be afraid cause he's lost, and help him come home, amen . . . Wait, one more thing, and please give him a special friend since I can't be with him. Amen." She held tight to Nanna May's arm. "Who will Jesus send to help Stewart?"

"Sometimes he sends people that have angels all around them, helpin' them do what they need to do. Now, show me how to find the other phone numbers on this here phone."

Stacey hit the back button and found the contacts for Nanna May. "You just scroll down like this, and then when you find the right picture, you can touch it."

"Thank you, I see now. You stay right there and help me, okay?"

They called the pastor and a few other friends from church who took over the task of spreading the word.

"Do you see our neighbors on here?"

Stacey reached over and pushed the contacts icon.

"Here's one, Stacey. Call this one, hon."

Stacey tapped the screen for her. Nanna May called four of the contacts, and three were still home. They all offered to look for Stewart and call other neighbors living within a few blocks.

"Well, Stacey, I think that's all the neighbors we can call."

"That was our story," Stacey replied.

"What was your story?"

"Mrs. Diller told us a neighbor is somebody that helps people, even if they aren't best friends."

"Mrs. Diller is right." Nanna May collected Stacey's hair in her hands and wound it around her fingers.

"Yep. And she makes really good cookies, too."

"What?" Nanna may exaggerated her surprise. "You've been eatin' cookies at Sunday school all along? No wonder you ain't been hungry for lunch on Sundays." She tickled the little girl's tummy.

Stacey giggled, a sliver of relief on a morning tense with worry.

CHAPTER 16

The sirens finally stopped, but flashing lights continued to swirl all around, reflecting off windows and cars. Stewart moaned in anguished tones as he crouched behind the dumpster, tucking his head over bent knees to shield his eyes from the glaring colors. Something wet slid across his arm. He jerked his head up, dropping his hat behind him. A young black and white Border Collie jumped with its own startled reaction.

They looked at each other for a frozen second until Stewart reached out his hand and rubbed the dog's soft ear. The little collie moved in cautiously with tail tucked in and head down but open to the possibility of a tender introduction. A few more gentle strokes across the top of the soft, furry head sealed the friendship, and licks on an easily accessible face distracted Stewart from the flashing lights.

Stewart slid out from behind the dumpster and picked up the leash trailing behind his new acquaintance. The puppy wagged its tail and stared at him, waiting for the boy with the leash to determine the next move. Running his hand curiously over the dog's red halter, Stewart inspected the patches bearing letters and pictures. Several tags hanging from the dog's collar, jingling when the puppy moved to lick his fingers, caught his attention.

A man suddenly appeared from around the corner and yelled at them. "You get out of here! Nobody is supposed to be back here. Can't you see the yellow tape?"

Both Stewart and the dog stood still until the loud man stepped toward them.

"Move it, kid!"

The puppy lurched backward, and Stewart, willing to let his new friend lead the way, held on tightly to the leash in his hand. They crossed a multi-lane street blocked off with police barricades. The officers were securing the area and didn't notice the young boy and the small dog slip through the parked cars and cross the street.

* * *

Six Houses Down

Over the next few hours, Nanna May's phone rang continuously. It was Stacey's job to swipe the screen and hand it to her. Most of the calls were people checking in, wondering if she had any new information. One of their neighbors, living several blocks north of the Clark residence, called a few minutes before noon. On the way to work, they had seen a young blond boy walking toward the grocery store just past Rhode Island Avenue NE on Brentwood. It was around 8:45 in the morning and they would not have noticed, but they thought the boy looked too young to be walking to the store by himself. They were sorry they didn't get a better look at him, but they did remember he was wearing a blue baseball hat and maybe blue sweatpants.

"This is something. Quick, Stacey, help me find Mrs. Webster's number on this thing."

"It's the button that looks like people," Stacey reminded her.

"Good, I got it, and the green button calls . . . thank you." Nanna May passed the new information on to Sharon and Bill.

Sharon told Nanna May about the shooting and that the police officer wouldn't let them search the area. That had been almost two hours ago. Nanna May set the phone down. Stacey checked the screen and tapped the red button to hang it up.

"Mm, mm . . . poor thing, he might have been right there."

"What's wrong?" Stacey's eyes were wide, her expression anxious.

Nanna May didn't have an answer for Stacey this time. There was only one thing she could promise the worried little girl beside her. "Nothin' the Lord can't handle, sweet pea."

* * *

Pulled along by his new friend, Stewart covered seven blocks in a brisk walk and continued north through a residential neighborhood. The farther they walked, the less congested the streets became. The houses, with large manicured lawns, grew farther apart, and hundred-year-old oak and maple canopies shaded the roadways. Magnolia trees, heavy with pink blooms, scented the air with a sweet lemon fragrance. The puppy stopped to nibble on a blossom, rejected it, and moved on.

A man working in his yard close to the sidewalk spied the new friends walking up the street.

"Good morning. That's a nice dog you have there," he said as he moved slowly toward them.

Stewart pulled on the leash with both hands, nervously looking past the unfamiliar man. The puppy cautiously wagged her tail, staying beside the boy with the leash.

"Where are you two headed?" The man took a few steps closer, close enough to realize Stewart wouldn't be talking with him. "Is it all right if I pet your dog?" He bent down, reaching for the tags around the dog's collar.

The puppy squirmed, resisting his inspection.

"Come on now; hold still so I can see where you two belong." He tried to trap the puppy between his knees, but there would be no cooperation.

The little collie jumped and pulled hard on the leash. Stewart and the dog took off and turned west, determined to get away from the encroaching stranger.

"Rats!" the man muttered. He didn't want to scare the boy by chasing him down, and he was uncertain whether the two were supposed to be off on their own, but to be sure, he would call the police.

The operator, who took the man's call, sounded harried when she realized the emergency was only an inquiry into a possible problem. With the recent shooting in the area, the lines had been ringing off the hook. The man left a brief description, telling the operator the boy was handicapped and had a service dog. After briefly going over the details, the operator assured him an officer would drive through the neighborhood and do a welfare check and thanked him for his concern.

* * *

At ten thirty, Bill's phone rang. Seeing the caller ID, he quickly swiped the screen. "It's the police," he said, his expression a combination of nerves and hope as he tapped the speaker button so Sharon could hear the call. Her senses instantly tuned out everything around her and focused solely on the voice on the phone.

The officer identified himself, asked them a few questions to be sure he had the right case, and then continued, "Does your son have a service dog, Mr. Webster?"

"A service dog? No, he doesn't," Bill answered, his response telegraphing frustration. "We've received a call on a young boy walking with a service dog, but it was a quite a ways north of your neighborhood."

Sharon felt the demon of disappointment threatening her sanity. "Did the boy have a blue hat on?" she asked, needing the child to be Stewart.

"I'm sorry; he didn't. It doesn't sound like the boy was your son. We'll keep looking until we find him." The officer gave them the number and location of the call and hung up the phone. Since the missing boy didn't have a service dog, the welfare check was placed on the bottom of the priority list.

Bill and Sharon drove north toward the area the call had originated from just in case it was Stewart, even though it didn't seem likely. As far as they were concerned, any call about a young boy could be a call about their son. A few children were playing by the street, and others were working in their yard, but no one had seen Stewart. They called the phone number of the man that had reported the boy with the dog, but to their disappointment, no one answered.

* * *

The sidewalks grew wider as Stewart and the Border Collie continued west. Cars and trucks rumbled overhead as they walked under a noisy overpass. In front of them, large commercial buildings lined the sidewalks, and the number of people swelled around them as they worked their way up the busy street. The pair moved several blocks amongst the shops and businesses, carried along by the crowd.

A cafe on the corner with outdoor seating tempted passersby with the aroma of grilled sandwiches and freshly roasted coffee. Stewart stepped around the fence and planter boxes and took a seat away from the crowded sidewalk, ready for something to eat. A friendly young waitress in a black apron came to the table.

"Hi there, my name is Abbey. Are you waiting for your mother?" She set a cup of water in front of him and quickly realized the boy was probably non-verbal. She admired the little black and white dog in the red harness. "Is it okay if I pet your puppy?" She bent down, waiting for the young boy to grant her a gesture of permission.

Stewart smiled and touched the collie's soft ear. The little dog wagged its tail, danced its front paws back and forth, and sniffed the pockets of her apron.

"You're a little cutie, aren't you?" she said as she rubbed both sides of the dog's head underneath her ears. Abbey looked at the nametag. "Looks like your name is Angel."

The little dog wagged her tail and whined.

"I'll be right back, Angel. You wait here." She returned with a plastic bowl and poured a cup of water into it. Angel eagerly lapped up the contents and checked back with the young girl, apparently ready for the next course.

"Water isn't the only thing you're hoping for, is it, little girl?"

The waitress looked down the sidewalk both ways, wondering who deposited these two here by themselves. The boy was too young to be left alone, and since he was a special needs child, she couldn't believe the nerve of whomever was in charge of him. She checked back every few minutes, her agitation over the neglected boy increasing.

"Come on, people," she grumbled. "It doesn't take that long to use the loo." She pictured herself giving someone a piece of her mind, since they seemed to have lost theirs.

Abbey checked the time. The boy had been sitting there for twelve minutes, watching her with expectation each time she delivered food to a nearby table. She brought out two pieces of ham for the puppy and a cup with cubes of cheese and meat for Stewart. They both devoured the offering, clearly famished.

"I'll be right back." She purchased a cookie out of the bakery case, handing a dollar from the tips in her pocket to the girl at the register. When she went back outside, the boy and the puppy were gone.

Six Houses Down

Enough food in both of their stomachs to be comfortable, Stewart and Angel worked their way up the busy street. They crossed at the lights with others waiting, appearing as if they belonged to one of the many adults in the river of people. The buildings changed as they moved along, and the farther they walked, the less crowded the sidewalks became. Block castles lined both sides of the street, and a giant church with a bright-blue dome rose above them like a mountain. A large bell sounded the hour: *Bong . . . Bong.* Angel moved close to Stewart's leg as he stopped and listened to the ringing fill the space around them and echo back. Across the street, a long row of buses waited for passengers to board.

Standing on the sidewalk, the traveling pair seemed to be deciding if a change of direction was in order, until Stewart spotted the tour buses and urged the collie to cross the street. He moved slowly along the curb, peering through the open doors as if looking for a familiar face. A large group of tourists gathered around him and boarded one of the buses. Stepping up through the open door, Stewart and Angel followed the stream of people. The driver stopped him and asked for his ticket and then awkwardly realized the young boy was not able to respond to him. Figuring his parents were headed to the top seats already and pressed into a decision by the passengers stacking up behind the waiting pair, the driver let Stewart board.

The tour bus passed the Capitol and circled around the Washington Monument before parking in front of a museum. Stewart and the puppy followed the flow of people up the stone steps until he was stopped inside the museum entrance. A woman waved him over to her line, trying to keep the visitors moving along. She took a quick look at the service dog, waved a wand over his harness, and shuttled them through, calling for the next person.

Excited children shuffled from room to room, pointing at the extraordinary creatures in frozen poses. Stewart moved slowly as he and Angel made their way through the exhibits. Tourists, taking note of the service dog, were careful not to bump into him, giving him ample space to move about. A display of cats captured Stewart's attention. Angel tucked her tail and growled at a snarling tiger. They wandered into the museum's rotunda and considered an impressive elephant dominating the middle of the room. Satisfied with his lengthy inspection of the pachyderm, Stewart took off with puppy in tow.

CHAPTER 17

Earl stayed at the Webster house for several hours until Bill dropped Sharon off and went back out to continue searching. The elderly Mr. Clark went back home and returned a few minutes later with something for Sharon to eat. She thanked him and set the food aside, promising she would try it when she was hungry. Earl encouraged her to eat what she could and reminded her that she needed the fuel to stay strong.

"You hang in there." He gave her a hug and headed for the door.

The effects of her exhaustion were apparent to him, even though she struggled to present a facade of strength. He glanced back into the kitchen, knowing the few bites consumed by his grief-stricken friend were taken only to please him and that she would push the plate aside the second he closed the door.

When Earl returned home, he had something quick to eat, hugged Maybeline and Stacey, and reluctantly drove to work after trying for an hour to find someone to cover for him. Sickness and vacation had left the museum short-staffed. He had to cover his shift.

"Gracious heavenly Father," he prayed as he made his way into the heart of DC, "please lay your hand of protection and care upon that boy and bring him home safely."

When he arrived at work, Earl buttoned his green vest, straightened his nametag, and made his way through the rotunda at the museum. He caught a glimpse of a young boy with blond hair that looked like Stewart heading into a hall across the crowded room and quickly moved toward him.

"Stewart? . . . Stewart, wait." He finally reached him and tapped him on the shoulder.

The young boy turned to face Earl as if he were in trouble. It wasn't Stewart.

"Sorry, son. I thought you were someone else."

As he walked back to the rotunda, Earl thought he saw Stewart again. He followed another young boy through the crowded hallway, determined not to lose sight of him. Thirty feet ahead, the blond boy wove in and out of the crowd.

As Earl got closer, he could see the boy had a small service dog. Earl stopped for a second. The boy couldn't be Stewart, he told himself; he was just seeing things because he wanted to. It didn't matter; he would make sure the boy wasn't Stewart before giving up. Earl followed the hallway back into the rotunda, but the boy with the dog was gone. His stress over his missing little friend would have him seeing many Stewarts that afternoon.

* * *

Stewart and Angel stepped out of the elevator, left the museum, and followed the flow of traffic along the grassy mall toward Union Station. A few people looked at the dog and then back at Stewart, sure that he was with someone nearby. An elderly woman, with thick, white hair mushrooming atop a red, white, and blue visor, became irritated after traveling several blocks behind Stewart and the young Border Collie.

"Somebody should be holding that boy's hand when he crosses the street," she complained to her husband, speaking loudly enough for everyone around them to hear.

"He has a service dog, dear," her husband assured her, obviously trying to diffuse the uncomfortable situation.

"That's not a service dog . . . That's a puppy!" the woman scolded, shaking her head in disgust.

"Marge, it has a vest on," the elderly man in the matching visor replied.

"Don't argue with me, Walter."

The elderly couple walked halfway up the block and boarded a tour bus.

It was nearly five o'clock in the evening when Stewart and Angel walked into Union Station. The smell of food had both boy and dog considering their empty stomachs. Just inside the west entrance, they rode the escalator to the lower floor. Having been there before, Stewart pulled Angel along, making a beeline to the restaurants on the lower level of the station. He stopped in front of a glass case displaying cupcakes of all flavors and sizes.

"Can I help you?" a friendly sales girl asked before realizing Stewart would not be talking to her.

He looked at the giant cupcakes and smiled at her.

"Those look good, don't they? But, if you ate one of those all by yourself, you might get sick." The sales girl offered him a mini cupcake to sample.

He took it and ate it instantly, waiting for another to follow. Angel whined, apparently hopeful that a snack was coming her way as well.

"I'm sorry; I can only give you one sample. You have a good day."

Angel pulled on the leash, wanting to move toward the tables filled with people and food smells. Stewart saw the doors with the pictures of men and women on them and pulled angel into the bathroom. When they returned to the food court, he sat down at one of the tables toward the back wall, as far away from people as possible. The crowded area and loud noises began to overwhelm him. Crossing his arms on the table and resting his head on his forearms, he attempted to shield his eyes from the flurry of moving people and the bright lights. The leash, which had been around his hand most of the day, fell from his lap onto the floor, and the little dog slipped away into the crowd.

* * *

Anna, in a hurry to get home after a busy day at work, needed something quick to eat. Nanna May had told her not to buy any dinner because they were overflowing with food at home, but she was not going to make it that long. She picked up juice and a muffin from the store in the food court and headed toward the parking garage, almost tripping on a puppy that had slipped away from its owner. She was anxious to know if there was any new information on Stewart. Earl had gone to work hours earlier, so her constant updates had stalled. Nanna May was not fond of texting, so she would have to wait until she got home to get the latest on their young missing friend. Anna planned a quick stop at home before heading to the Websters' house to stay with Sharon while Bill continued to search for their son. Everyone thought he would have been found by now, so with the arrival of darkness, the *what ifs* that haunt a parent's mind in situations like this would surely begin their relentless taunting.

* * *

Stewart woke from his short nap with a bump to his leg. He opened tired eyes to the puppy pawing at him and wagging her tail. She had a chicken strip in her mouth, which Stewart was quick to accept and eat immediately. The little dog's belly bulged from her previous binge of discarded and unattended food.

A man across the room seemed angry. He had just returned to his table with a container of ketchup.

"Come on, man! Who steals chicken strips?"

A couple of teenagers laughed and looked over toward Stewart and the thief they witnessed absconding with the missing strips. The man scowled at the nearby teens, not seeing the humor in the situation.

"What? We didn't touch no food," one of the teens protested.

The angered man didn't believe them, cursed, and stomped away.

The three young men quickly chronicled the event, texting their friends on their cell phones. One of them had taken a picture of Angel stealing the food and posted it online.

It was 5:55 p.m., and Stewart was desperate to escape the crush of people coming and going in the station. He and Angel rode the escalator up to the mezzanine and walked through the hallways, peering into the various shops. There were few people on this level of the station, the lights and sounds subdued as shops began to close their doors for the evening.

A store with a tent display caught Stewart's attention. He and Angel slipped into the small pup tent as the storeowner turned off the lights. The loud clanking of a gridded-metal gate sliding shut and locking into place frightened Stewart. He pulled the puppy onto his lap and stroked her soft black and white fur coat, comforted by her companionship. Angel licked his face and then peeked outside the tent, eager to inspect the new surroundings.

Six Houses Down

Stewart followed the puppy around the dimly lit store and pulled on the locked gate blocking the exit. At his side, Angel whined and then walked behind a counter, returning after a few seconds and content to continue their investigation. A sleeping bag displayed with a variety of camping equipment in front of a large poster with snow-covered mountains caught Stewart's attention. After some struggle, he unrolled the bag in the back of the store and pulled it inside the tent. Once he had it positioned to his satisfaction, he climbed in. Angel sniffed the new bedding choice, sized up her options, and snuggled up next to Stewart on top of the thick padding. Both exhausted fugitives slept soundly, lulled to sleep by the constant humming on the floors beneath them.

* * *

Earl waited for the light to change, his heart heavy and mind distressed for Sharon and Bill. He'd been certain they would find Stewart, maybe wandering a few blocks from home, but the truth was unsettling; there was no sign of him. The early morning sighting of a young boy walking near a grocery store had given them hope, but a shooting kept them from searching the area for several hours. Sharon and Bill drove through a neighborhood north of the shooting, based on a call for a welfare check on a young boy—but, again, no sign of their son anywhere. Those had been their only leads, and the hours of silence since then compounded their desperate need to find him.

A song, familiar to Earl as a child, surfaced from the recesses of his memory. He sang the melody softly, his deep, bass voice drowning out the traffic sounds as he followed a long line of cars down the busy street: "A pilgrim was I and a wand'rin', in the cold night of sin I did roam, when Jesus the kind shepherd found me, and now I am on my way home."

* * *

The sky grew darker as the last sliver of sunlight disappeared behind the western skyline. When Bill left the house, Anna was with Sharon, trying to coerce his emotionally and physically exhausted wife into allowing herself a few hours of sleep. He continued to search for their son, hoping for the best but fearing the worst. Before Earl left them earlier in the day to go to work, he prayed with them. The older man's faith and his request for the blessing of a safe return of their son was a comfort at the time. Now, Earl's prayer replayed in Bill's thoughts as he drove through the dark neighborhood streets, retracing the same route a dozen times. His tired mind started to taunt him. Why would God offer him anything, especially the blessings that Earl prayed over them? In fact, maybe he was getting exactly what he deserved.

If you hadn't shown up, Stewart wouldn't be lost. The voice seemed audible, coming from the seat behind him.

He looked in the rear-view mirror and then rolled his eyes at his gullible response. "Pull yourself together." Determined to remedy his sleep-deprived imagination, he drove a few blocks to a gas station and picked up an extra-large coffee to keep him alert for the next several hours. He would drink five more before returning to the hotel late the next morning for a quick shower and a change of clothes.

The cold water felt good as it flooded over his face and tired body. He would need another coffee to beat back a headache reaching migraine pain levels. The pressure pushing on the back of his eyes made him nauseous. Bill wanted to call Sharon, but he decided against it, not wanting to wake her just to let her down with nothing to offer.

That's what you've always had for her, isn't it? Nothing to offer, the taunting voice whispered.

Bill blasted his face again with ice-cold water. Fatigue and anxiety were leaving him vulnerable to phantom perceptions.

CHAPTER 18

In the dark, rear corner of the store, Stewart and Angel dove back into the pup tent when they heard someone turning a key in the gated entrance. They had spent eight hours locked inside the shop and had slept well but were anxious to escape. Before the employee turned on the lights, the two slipped out of the opened door and made their way to the escalator. As they were ferried down to the food court, the clerk could be heard complaining loudly about something on the floor.

Cautiously weaving through the busy morning crowd, Stewart worked his way toward the same vantage point he had chosen the day before. The empty food court tables were wiped clean, and long lines at the busy retail counters kept him away from possible samples or offerings of kindness. They waited and watched passersby quickly consume their muffin or sandwich as they hurried to board trains and buses. Angel whined and pawed Stewart's leg. The two famished campers had little to choose from.

* * *

Anna found Sharon sitting in a lawn chair in the backyard and handed her a cup of coffee.

"Thank you, Anna." Sharon took a few sips of the hot liquid and stared blankly at Stewart's empty sandbox.

Wishing she could offer at least a fragment of hope to Stewart's mother, Anna pulled the other lawn chair over and sat with her hurting friend in silence. Everyone assumed Stewart would be found within hours of his escape, but with the passing of the night and still no clues to his whereabouts, an inner foreboding began to threaten the bleakest of outcomes.

Help me, Lord, Anna prayed before gaining the courage to speak to the grieving mother, only a few years older than herself. Anna wouldn't offer her friend empty promises that would do nothing for the heart of a mother that knows better. "Sharon . . . can I pray for you?" Fidgeting with one of her earrings, Anna waited for her reply, not sure she should have offered.

"That would be all right."

"Jesus . . ." Anna paused and pleaded silently for the Lord to help her: *Pray for me since I don't have words of my own to offer.* She could feel Sharon looking at her. "Jesus, Sharon is a wife and mother of a sorrowful spirit. She has poured out her soul before you and is struggling to trust that her son continues to be in your care. Please, Lord, answer her in her time of grief with your hand of love and mercy . . . Amen."

"Thank you, Anna, that means a lot. I think I'll go in and lie down for a few minutes." Sharon stood up and moved as if she were on autopilot; her labored steps into the house made her appear to be in slow motion.

Anna followed her to Stewart's room. "Can I take your cup?" The last twenty-six hours had offered her friend little respite.

Sharon looked at the cup still in her hand. "Oh . . . thank you."

Minutes later, Anna quietly peeked into the bedroom, making sure Sharon was all right. Seeing her asleep, she hurried to the kitchen and switched the cell phone to vibrate so it wouldn't disturb her.

* * *

"Look at that little boy over there," a middle-aged woman said to her son sitting next to her.

"What about him?" he replied, tapping away on his phone.

"He's been by himself for at least ten minutes. Something's not right." She continued watching Stewart, concern growing stronger with each passing minute that he sat alone in the food court with his dog.

"Mom . . . stop staring at that kid. You look like a stalker," her son grumbled, not looking up from the game he was playing.

"I'm going over there to see if he's all right. Maybe he's hungry." She stood up, determined to ease her mind.

"Mom, what're you doing? Sit down. We have to get on the train in twelve minutes. You're not going to save all the children of the world in a few minutes."

"I'll be right back."

"Whatever. Why don't you get me a drink? I'm your child, too, remember?"

"What would you like?" she asked him, anxious to check on the young boy.

"Get me a twenty-four ounce iced mocha with three shots. And tell them only one pump of chocolate. They always make it too sweet. Remember, I want it iced. Thanks, mommy dearest," he said with a sarcastic whine and continued playing his game.

* * *

A security guard stood at the top of the escalator and scanned the food court below. He pushed the button on the radio at his shoulder. "Bob here. I'm gonna check on a little guy sitting at the lower level. Looks like he has a service dog, but he's been by himself for a while. Let me know if someone here is missin' a kid." Riding down the escalator, the guard made his way toward the food court, keeping an eye on the two young travelers.

* * *

The middle-aged woman set two sausage breakfast sandwiches and a cup of juice on the table before sitting down across from the small boy. She could see he was nervous to have her sit there but more interested in the sandwiches.

"Look here; I have two of these. I probably can't eat two . . . Maybe you would like to have one?" She acted as if her indecision was nothing out of the ordinary, set one of the two sandwiches in front of him and unwrapped one for herself. Looking over the crowd for an approaching parent, she briefly caught the eye of a security guard as he walked past.

"Who's this here?" she said, petting the puppy under the table.

The puppy whined and licked her hand. When she returned her attention to the small boy across from her, she startled.

"Oh, sweetie—slow down now, or you'll choke." She opened an orange juice and set it next to him, her panic relieved after he took a few throat-clearing gulps.

"Can I give your dog a bite of my sandwich?"

The boy set the juice cup down and looked at the puppy under the table. Before the woman could stop him, he threw the rest of his sandwich on the floor, and the little dog quickly snatched it up.

Realizing the young man would not be able to talk to her, she checked her watch and stood to leave.

"I have to hurry and get on the train now. Maybe you would like to have this sandwich since I don't want to take it with me." She smiled at him, quickly made her way to the train, and boarded with only seconds to spare.

"Nice, Mom, you almost missed the train. Where's my drink?"

"I'm sorry; I didn't have time to get you one."

"Figures," he mumbled, returning to the annihilation of confections on his phone.

The woman prayed a silent prayer as the train pulled away from the station: *Lord, please provide for that little boy.* She tapped her phone. "Hello, I'm calling about a special needs boy at Union Station . . . That's right . . . Well, he's been sitting alone for some time and was really hungry. I was wondering if there was a report of a missing boy." She talked to the operator for a few moments, her eyes growing wider. She was sitting up straighter when the operator transferred the call, connecting her with a police officer. She ended the call after giving the officer a detailed description of the young boy and the dog and an account of her interaction with him.

"There *was* a missing boy," she told her son.

"What . . . Really?" He slipped his phone into his backpack. "What did they say?" he asked his mother as the train rumbled away.

* * *

The security guard made his way back through the food court and was surprised to see Stewart and the dog alone again. He pressed the button on his radio. "I'm going to check on the boy with the dog. He's by himself again. Looks like the dog has an ID tag on his vest . . . Yep . . . I'll see what I can find out." The man moved slowly toward the boy in question. When he reached the table, he knelt down beside the dog. "This is a cute puppy you have here." The guard petted the collie's head, but the puppy reacted with suspicion.

Dialing the number on the tag, the guard identified himself when a man answered, asking the owner of the dog if he could provide any information on the young boy.

"You say your dog got away yesterday? . . . Yes, she's a young Border Collie . . . Let's see here . . . Yes, it does. Her collar tag has the name Angel on it, but you don't know anything about the five- or six-year-old little boy that's with your dog?"

The owner of the dog would be coming down to the station. His service dog in training had run away when his friend was picking her up from the groomers. He told the security guard that a number of emergency vehicles were responding to a shooting, and the dog became scared and bolted, but he knew nothing about the little boy.

The guard carefully reached for the dog's leash, but the boy didn't want to let go of it. "Hey, buddy, why don't you come with me? You hold the end of the leash, and I'll carry the puppy, okay?"

When the guard stood and picked up Angel, Stewart panicked. Angel barked and tried to wiggle free from the man's grasp, but he had a firm hold on the puppy's collar. He tried to take Stewart by the hand, but the gesture frightened him.

"It's all right, son; I want to help you. Do you understand?"

Dropping the leash, Stewart raced for the escalator. The security guard tried to carry the restless dog and chase him, but Stewart could maneuver through the thick crowd much faster. Stewart ran up the escalator and turned toward the main entrance before circling back and running behind the escalator leading to the mezzanine. The guard tried to talk into the radio on his shoulder and hold the squirming dog at the same time: "10-78. Five- to six-year-old white male . . . ran toward main entrance. The boy is wearing a dark-green T-shirt and blue sweat pants. He's scared and special needs, likely unable to speak . . . Don't yell at him." The guard ran up the escalator, asking people to move aside, and turned toward the street-level entrance.

Stewart remained hidden at the bottom of the escalator carrying people up to the mezzanine. One floor up led to the retail shops and the bus terminals. Two more security guards jogged through the corridor toward the main entrance. A group of people gathered at the end of the hallway, but seeing no spectacle worth their attention, they quickly dispersed and continued on their way. While Stewart watched from his hiding place, he noticed a young man with a backpack stepping onto the escalator beside him.

Two younger boys followed close behind the man with the pack. Stewart watched with interest as the trio rode the steps up, signing back and forth in unspoken conversation. He stepped onto the escalator and followed behind them, compelled by the college-aged man with the same fiery red hair as Stacey. Stewart slipped in behind the trio as they walked into a parking area and boarded a shuttle.

* * *

Hi, Shane, are these boys with you? the driver signed. Without turning to see who was behind him, Shane agreed and took a seat. Stewart followed Shane and the two boys onto the shuttle and sat in an empty seat in the back. The driver recognized Stewart, having seen him at the church with Shane's sister following the Christmas Eve service.

Several people boarded the shuttle bus behind Stewart, filling the last empty seats. The driver pulled away from Union Station and wove through the busy downtown streets, making a few stops along the way before parking the small bus in front of the hotel on the university campus. Everyone on board stood up and shuffled forward. Stewart stepped down onto the sidewalk behind the boys with Shane. A small group of people made their way down the sidewalk, most of them turning into the hotel. Shane stopped to converse with the groundskeeper. His two young charges stood on either side of him as the two men signed back and forth. The older of the two boys also signed as Stewart stood and watched from a short distance away. The youngest boy laughed and shook his hands in the air before the three of them continued on.

* * *

The phone on the nightstand buzzed, the incoming call sent to voice mail. Bill stepped out of the shower and pulled clean clothes from his suitcase. A note, reminding him to view a rental, was on the nightstand. The appointment needed to be cancelled. He slipped on his socks and reached for his phone. A missed call flashed on the screen. Bill retrieved the message, recognizing the voice immediately. A surge of adrenaline pulsed through his body as he listened to the voice mail: "This is Officer Stevens. I have a message for Bill Webster."

Bill quickly tapped speed dial and had the officer on the line.

"Yes, hello, Bill. We received information that someone has identified a young boy at Union Station fitting your son's description. We're calling the station now. I'll call you back as soon as I have more information."

He pulled his shoes on, grabbed his wallet and keys, and bolted down the hallway past the elevator. He ran down the stairs, taking four steps at a time. People and luggage crowded the lobby, forcing him to slow down to keep from plowing them over. His chest pounded like a bass drum, and he could feel blood pumping in his neck as a group of tourists slowly pulled their suitcases through the door in front of him. He reached in his pocket for his cell phone to call Sharon before realizing he had left it on the nightstand in his room.

"You idiot!" he said aloud, causing a few people to send reprimanding glances his way. Not having the time to apologize or explain his rudeness, he spun around and maneuvered back through the crowded lobby and up the stairs. "Come on," he growled as he slid his key card in the door for the third time. Throwing the door open, he rushed toward the nightstand, grabbed his phone, and willed himself to calm down before hitting the call button below Sharon's name. Bill ran back down the hallway as the phone rang in his ear.

* * *

The phone in front of Anna flashed and buzzed on the kitchen counter. She closed her book, grabbed the phone, and swiped her finger across the screen. "Hello," she said quietly, not wanting to wake Sharon if she didn't have to.

"Sharon?"

"This is Anna. Sharon is sleeping. Should I wake her up?"

"Anna, it's Bill. I'm coming to get Sharon. Stewart could be at Union Station."

"At Union Station? Dear Lord . . . I'll get her for you!" Anna said as she ran to the bedroom.

"Just wake her up. I'll talk to her when I get there. I'm only a few minutes away."

"Sharon . . . Sharon, wake up!"

* * *

Pulled suddenly from a deep sleep, Sharon took a few seconds to gain her bearings. She sat up quickly, knowing Anna wouldn't wake her if it wasn't important. "Did someone call?"

"Bill is on his way to get you—Stewart might be at Union Station!"

Sharon jumped off Stewart's bed and peppered Anna with questions she couldn't answer. "Union Station? Was someone trying to take him?"

"I'm sorry," Anna said. "Bill didn't have time to tell me anything, but he'll be here right away."

By the time Sharon had her shoes on, Bill pulled up in front of the house.

* * *

The few people left walking on the campus filtered off into classrooms, dormitories, and offices, leaving only Shane and a young elementary student on the sidewalk. Shane turned and looked at the boy, recognizing his impairment and that he was too young to be out of class alone. Shane signed a few simple greetings. The boy rocked back and forth for a few seconds, briefly looked at him, and then gazed over his shoulder. The student then took a few steps closer and cupped his hands together in front of his chest. Shane recognized the sign immediately.

Help, Shane signed back, making sure he understood him.

The student nodded one exaggerated nod and repeated the cupped hand sign for help.

Shane searched for a way to communicate with him. It was evident he knew a few signs but didn't understand when he tried to ask him who he was. Motioning for the boy to follow him to the office, Shane took a few steps away, but the young boy hesitated.

With open hands flashed in front of his body, the boy signed *afraid*.

Thinking the student left the grade school on campus and lost his way, Shane pulled his phone out to text the office for assistance. The young boy eagerly waved a hand toward Shane's phone, making it obvious he wanted to see it. Stepping closer, Shane switched the screen and held it out for him. Maybe the student knew how to call a familiar number.

When the phone was in front of him, the boy seemed to be unsure what to do next. Shane tapped a few images but took a quick step back when the little guy startled him by throwing his hands up and hopping in place. The student leaned toward the phone and pointed at the picture icon, then resumed hopping and flapping his hands. A collection of photos filled the screen. Reaching for the phone until Shane relinquished it, the boy swiped at the screen until; he apparently saw what he was looking for. Shane looked at the picture, curious how it could provide the reason for the young boy's excitement. It was just a picture of Stacey and Anna. The language barrier aggravating, Shane snapped a quick picture of him and sent it to his sister, asking her if she knew who he was.

* * *

A text notice came across Anna's phone as she got ready for work. She was anxious to arrive early and see if Stewart was, in fact, there. Bill had taken Sharon to Union Station to look for Stewart, and she hoped to soon receive a call saying they had found him, but the message was from her brother. She considered retrieving it later but didn't want to make him wait, so she checked the text.

Do you know who this is?

"No way!" She slid her fingers over the screen to enlarge the picture. With hands trembling, she fired back a reply: *Keep him with you! That's Stewart . . . He's lost! I need to call his mother!* "Oh, my Lord! Thank you, Jesus!" she shouted as she tried to hold still enough to call Sharon.

* * *

The car tires screeched on the pavement in the parking garage as Bill turned up the ramp. Hitting the brakes, he slammed the car into park and threw the door open. Staying a few steps behind Sharon as they ran toward the station entrance, he heard Sharon's phone ring. They slowed to a fast walk while she yanked it out of her pocket, but then she shoved it back in without taking the call.

"It's just Anna."

Two seconds later, Bill's phone rang. He answered it in a hurried voice. "What is it, Anna?"

"Bill . . . Stewart is with my brother at the university!" she yelled.

"Anna, the police just told us he's here, at Union Station. Thanks for calling, but I think Stewart is here."

"No . . . Bill, listen to me! He's with my brother right now!"

Bill kept jogging behind Sharon. "Where?"

"Gallaudet University. He's there, Bill. I promise."

"What? How do you know it's him?"

"My brother sent me a picture. It's him!"

"Sharon—wait!" Bill grabbed her arm as they hurried through the parking lot.

"For what? I'm not waiting. I'm going to find Stewart!" She jerked her arm free and ran ahead of him.

146

"Sharon, Stewart is with Anna's brother at the university!" Bill hoped he was right. If they left the station and the boy wasn't Stewart, it would be on him, and Sharon would never trust him again.

"That doesn't make any sense! Stewart doesn't even *know* Anna's brother." She turned away and started running again.

"Sharon, stop! He's there. Anna is sure it's him."

"We can't leave!" With wild eyes, Sharon threw her hands up. "What if it's not?"

"It is." He caught up to her and took her by the arm, gently pulling her back toward the car.

"No! . . . I do not want to go with you!" she screamed, gaining the attention of a few people, including a nearby security guard scanning the parking lot.

"Sir, is there a problem here?" the guard said with a warning tone as he walked with a determined step toward them.

Bill tried his best to quickly explain the situation. The guard was in the lot looking for a missing boy. He radioed to see if anyone had spotted him. They hadn't.

"I'm leaving, Sharon. Are you coming with me?" Bill took several steps back, away from the station.

For several seconds, Sharon stood still, her face pained with indecision. "Yes . . . wait!" She turned toward him, and they both ran back to the car.

Ignoring the honks from offended drivers, Bill sped out of the garage and turned toward the university. Sharon didn't say a single word during the long ten minutes it took to reach the school. He didn't try to talk to her. The tension filling the car left no room for words. She needed to get to their son.

CHAPTER 19

Bill parked the car near the hotel, but before he could cut the engine, Sharon jumped out. On their way over, Anna sent Bill a text saying that Shane would meet them by the hotel entrance. Starting to feel light-headed as she frantically scanned the area, Sharon realized she was holding her breath.

"There he is!"

Sitting on a bench with a young man that looked a lot like Anna, Stewart's attention appeared to be trained on a cell phone. She sucked in a deep breath as she jogged toward them, trying to maintain her composure and not wanting to startle her son.

"Stewart . . ." She struggled to push calm words through a throat constricted with emotion. "I'm so happy to see you." She dried tear-filled eyes on her sleeve and reached for him, so badly wanting to catch him up in her arms and hold him forever, but she restrained herself.

Stewart jumped up and leaned his head on her side. Sobbing with released anxiety, she bent down and rubbed her trembling hand slowly along the length of his small arm.

"You look good, honey," she said as she wove her other hand through his tangled curls and kissed his forehead, breathing in the smell of him. Scanning the length of her son several times, Sharon took a mother's inventory of a potentially devastated son. Other than messy hair and slightly dirty clothes, he didn't appear overly traumatized, at least not physically.

Breaking out in a happy dance, Stewart rolled his hands in front of his chest and circled around her, then stopped suddenly, put his hand on his shoulder, and touched hers as well, the gesture familiar as his way of hugging.

Bill stood back, tears flowing freely down his face and dripping onto his shirt. He bent down when Stewart skipped up to him and shared the same shoulder-to-shoulder gesture with him. Bill smiled and gently placed his large hand on his son's thin shoulder. Stewart resumed his happy dance, Bill and Sharon sharing in his joy with claps and laughter. Her son was not only all right, he was happy, and at that moment, nothing in the world mattered more to her.

A familiar faded-gray sedan pulled up to the hotel and lurched to a stop in the middle of the road. Anna threw the door open and ran over to join everyone, her face a mess of tears and smiles. She hugged her brother, and they rapidly signed back and forth. Anna patted Stewart who seemed compelled to jump around again in celebration of the new familiar face joining the fun. Sharon and Bill briefly thanked Shane, using Anna for an interpreter. In the brief exchange, it seemed likely that Stewart had followed Shane and several young boys onto the shuttle at Union Station. Shane hugged them both and apologized that he needed to leave, already late for a class he was supposed to be teaching. Wanting to ease everyone's worries, Anna called Earl and Nanna May.

When the Clarks heard the good news, Anna pulled her phone away from her ear to lessen the volume of rapturous joy blasting through the speaker. She passed the phone to Sharon, who couldn't express her gratitude without crying again as she thanked her elderly friends for their help. Bill called Officer Stevens, who would meet them back at the house soon, and then sent another text to his friend Steve, letting him know that Stewart had been found.

The three weary but happy Websters got in the car and headed for home.

Sharon sat in the back seat next to her son, wanting to ask him so many questions, but they would all remain unanswered except one. "Stewart, would you like something to eat?"

"How about a cheeseburger?" Bill offered.

Stewart laughed and nodded his one exaggerated nod.

"There's a lot of food at the house," she reminded Bill.

"If I was six, I would want a greasy cheeseburger. Is that okay with Mom?"

"Sure, why not?"

Stewart chanted happy guttural sounds as they ordered at a drive-through.

"Can I get something for you?" he asked Sharon.

"No, thank you, I'm fine." Eating had not crossed her mind for hours or maybe days.

"I'm going to get you something, in case you change your mind, okay?"

"All right." Now that Stewart was with her, she would agree to anything.

The smell of the burgers in the car made it abundantly clear that all three passengers were ravenous. When they reached the house, Sharon invited Officer Stevens to sit and fill out his report while the three of them devoured the best cheeseburgers ever made.

* * *

Stewart slept soundly in his bed while Bill made a list of locks and alarms to be placed on the exterior doors and backyard gate. Needing to give Sharon privacy to recover from the ordeal, he reluctantly decided to head back to his hotel. Although exhausted himself, he'd much rather be at the house with his wife and son, but he knew it wasn't an option. If only she'd ask him to stay. As he opened the door, Sharon stood behind him, looking as if she had something she wanted to say.

"Bill . . . I, uh . . . I can't thank you enough."

"That was one good cheeseburger, wasn't it?" he replied with a silly, tired grin.

She rolled her eyes in mock disgust, her gaze on him for a fleeting second before shifting to his hand on the door.

"You're welcome, Sharon. Thank *you* for not letting them arrest me at the station." He smiled again and moved to step outside.

"I'm sorry I yelled at you." She touched the edge of the door, her voice serious and her expression timid.

"Sharon, don't worry about anything." He bit the inside of his lip, aching to wrap his arms around her and comfort her. "Everything is going to be all right. You get some rest. I'll call you this evening, okay?"

She nodded in agreement and closed the door behind him.

* * *

Six Houses Down

Bill could barely keep his eyes open as he drove the few minutes back to his hotel. When he reached his room, he slid his shoes off and collapsed face down on the bed. Sleep could have come easily if not for the hotel phone flashing and beeping. Without opening his eyes, he felt around for the extra pillow and pulled it over the back of his head, but the incessant beeping seemed to get louder. Pushing up on an elbow, he reached a heavy hand over to punch the button and retrieve the messages. The calls were from his office. They could wait, so he dropped his head back on the pillow and, seconds later, was sound asleep.

At one thirty in the afternoon, Bill's cell phone buzzed across the nightstand. Three minutes later, it buzzed again, but Bill was dead to the world until the hotel phone assaulted his senses, waking him from much-needed rest.

"Hello?" he answered, his voice groggy.

"Bill, Dwayne here. Something's wrong with your phone. I've been calling you for two days! Where have you been?"

"I had an emergency. Look, Dwayne, I can't come into the office."

"That's right, your son took off. Thanks for pulling Steve away from his desk, by the way. Your family emergency really cost me this week. Anyways, you're not going to back out on me at the last minute, are you? I need to know you've got things together enough to be on that plane headed to Beijing tomorrow morning."

"I'll be on the plane." Bill wouldn't waste any time arguing with his boss. Even if he wanted to, he didn't have the energy.

"You'd better be." Dwayne hung up without waiting for a reply. Bill laid his tired head back on the pillow, his thoughts plaguing him as he considered how he might tell Sharon he had to leave again. She might not believe him if he tried to explain the situation. It would sound like a repeat of the last ten times he called and promised to come home soon.

"Dang it!" he yelled, throwing a pillow across the room. He had to finish this project and go to Beijing or lose his job. If he quit now, it would cost him over half of his paycheck for not fulfilling the agreement he made when he was promoted a year ago. If he lost his job, he wouldn't be able to provide for Sharon and Stewart, never mind the separate living arrangements he'd now have to have for himself. He was stuck. *How is this happening?*

Lie to her. She doesn't need to know where you're going.

"No," Bill said aloud to his conflicting thoughts. "I'll tell her the truth. She'll never trust me if I lie to her now." Bill rubbed his eyes and picked up his phone.

Sharon answered on the first ring. "Hello?"

"I need to talk to you. Can I come over . . . right now? I know you're exhausted, but it will only take a few minutes and—"

"Bill, just come over." She sounded serious but not disappointed.

"Thank you, Sharon. I'll be there in a few minutes." Bill rolled off the bed and walked over to retrieve the shoes he had kicked off a couple hours ago. Something caught his foot. Hopping forward to catch his balance, he tripped and smacked his head on the TV with a solid thud.

"Really? Unbelievable!" He ran his hand over the fresh sting on his forehead and looked for the offensive object that caused his fall. Stupid Pillow. Moisture started to build beneath his hand as he made his way to the bathroom to assess the damage. A one-inch gash on his forehead began to spill out a steady stream of bright-red blood. With a washcloth pressed into the cut, he grabbed his keys, wallet, and phone and made his way to the lobby before the blood soaked completely through the rolled-up cloth.

The young girl at the front desk stared at him in shock. "Sir, are you okay? Do you need an ambulance?"

"No, I'm fine. I need a decent bandage, though. It's not that big of a cut really, just a lot of blood."

The desk clerk got the attention of her manager, who tried to talk him into a trip to the on-site clinic.

"I'm sorry; I have to be somewhere. It's really important that I get some gauze and tape. Anything will do. I don't want to bleed all over."

The manager quickly produced a first-aid kit with a collection of bandages. Bill grabbed several and thanked the man before stepping into the lobby bathroom and taping a thick layer of gauze to his forehead. Pulling on a pair of latex gloves, the manager followed him and swiftly collected the blood-soaked washcloth and bandage wrappers. The man tried once again to get him to consider a few stitches, but Bill assured the concerned manager he would be able to take care of it and thanked him for his help.

Within minutes, he was at the house but didn't remember driving there.

CHAPTER 20

"Bill . . . What happened?!" Sharon pulled him into the kitchen and had him sit at the table.

"I just bumped my head in the hotel room. Is Stewart asleep?"

"Yes, he's in his room. Um . . . I think we should do something about your forehead." She stared at him with wide eyes.

"It'll be okay." Bill was embarrassed that his clumsiness was so apparent.

"No, Bill, it's not okay. You have blood all over your face."

"What?" He ran a hand below the bandage and felt sticky moisture matting the hair above his ear. With blood-covered fingers, he jumped up and hurried to the bathroom.

A quick look in the mirror proved her right. The gauze had done little to stop the flow of blood. He could hear Sharon calling the Clarks. It seemed as if Earl was beside him in the bathroom before Sharon hung up the phone.

"I'm gonna take you down to Medstar and get you stitched up. All right with you, Bill?" Earl had a hand on his arm. It wasn't really a question.

"Wait . . . Sharon, I can't go. I need to talk to you."

"You need to go with Earl. I'll still be here when you're done." She pointed to the door.

"No, you don't understand. I have to go to Beijing, but I don't want to. "

Sharon looked at Earl. "We'd better get him in the car."

"No, please, Sharon, trust me this time. I'm coming home in a few days."

"It's okay, Bill. You just got back from Beijing. Earl is going to get you checked out. I'll see you in a little while."

Earl helped Bill get into the car. The towel Bill held on his head impaired his vision, and he felt like he might pass out.

"Earl?"

"Right here, Bill."

"I really screwed things up."

"There's nothin' broke here that can't be fixed."

"I hope you're right, Earl; I really hope you're right. Thanks for doing this."

"You just relax, son. You've been through it these past few days, and you aren't gonna solve all the world's problems this afternoon. You need to trust that God is in charge of things right now. All you have to concern yourself with is lettin' him know you're listenin' to what he's got to say."

"I appreciate the advice, but I don't think God wants to talk to me anymore."

"Are you still breathin'?"

"Well . . . yes."

"Then it ain't too late." Earl looked briefly at him with a raised brow then shifted his attention back to the traffic in front of them. "There's the clinic up ahead."

Within the hour, Bill had five stitches on his forehead, and they were driving back to the house. He thanked Earl, who insisted he see him to the door before going back home.

Stewart was awake when Bill returned and clearly aware of the injury on his forehead. His son glanced at the bandage with a faraway look of concern, stroked his mother's arm, and then sat down on the couch beside him, rocking back and forth and gesturing at the bandage.

"It's okay, Stewart," Bill patted his son on the leg. "I got a little cut, but now it's all better."

His son nervously ran his hand back and forth along the edge of the brown velour couch and continued to stare at the blood-tinged mound of tape and cotton.

"This will be all gone in a day or two," Bill assured him, lightly tapping the gauze on his forehead.

Stewart seemed satisfied with the explanation and switched his attention to a lighted box plugged into the wall, as if nothing out of the ordinary had happened over the last two days.

The words echoed in Bill's tired mind: *in a day or two*. In less than a day, *he* would be gone again, flying back to Beijing and proving to Sharon that, despite his best intentions and promises, he would continue to be an absent father and husband.

Sharon set a glass of iced tea on the coffee table in front of him. He thanked her and sat silent for a few moments. Even if Stewart wasn't tired, both he and Sharon were feeling the exhaustion of the two-day ordeal.

Wanting to get said what he came to say, Bill tried to craft a few coherent sentences. "Sharon, I know you're beyond tired, so I'll keep this short."

He looked at his wife, but she continued to watch her son press orange and green pegs into a lit paper grid. Any energy left in his body seemed to be consumed with the function of his vital organs. Reaching for the tea on the table, Bill almost knocked it over, his perfect vision apparently not so perfect under the present circumstances. He took a drink, held the cool liquid in his mouth for a second before letting it slowly slide down his dry throat, and forced the words needing to be said through heavy lips.

"Sharon . . . I'm flying home in a few days. Can I see you on . . . Monday, or if I get home late Monday, can I see you on Tuesday?" Bill looked at her, praying she'd understand.

Not avoiding his eyes, Sharon stared right at him with an expression of questioning concern. "Bill, do you know where you are?" She watched him as he looked around the room, his brow furrowed as he tried to process what she just asked him.

"Yes," he answered simply, not sure if he had missed a deeper meaning to her question.

"Can you tell me *where* you are?" Sharon asked.

Running his fingers through his hair, Bill rubbed over the bandage on his forehead and winced at the painful reminder of its location. His son didn't miss his reaction to the forgotten injury and climbed up on the couch next to him, leaning his head on his shoulder and wrapping both hands around his forearm.

Bill swallowed hard, trying not to let the moment overwhelm him. "You're a good boy, aren't you, Stewart?"

"I'll be right back," Sharon said as she headed to her bedroom.

* * *

Returning with a pillow, Sharon set it next to him on the arm of the couch. "Why don't you lie down and rest for a few minutes? We can talk when you wake up. Besides, I don't think you should be driving in your condition." She turned away and walked into the kitchen as if her offer was purely reasonable and nothing else. She heard him say he should let her rest for a few more hours and come back another time, but she ignored him, sensing indecision in his voice.

Waiting only a few minutes, she peeked in on them in time to see Stewart trying to cover Bill with his favorite blanket. A wave of conflicting emotions washed over her as she watched her son care for his father. She wished she could join them, lay her husband's injured, tired head down on her lap, and brush her fingers through his hair, coaxing away the pain of flesh and conscience. Bill seemed to be considering his options and then gave in to the pillow and his son's generosity. Within seconds, he was sound asleep.

Sharon walked quietly into the living room and waved for Stewart to follow her back into the kitchen, but he set his chin and crossed his arms in defiance as if he'd decided it was his job to stand guard over his sleeping father.

"Honey," she whispered, "why don't we go outside to play so Daddy can sleep?"

Making his intentions clear, he aggressively thrust his palms toward her, then covered his lips with two fingers. He wasn't going anywhere, at least not without a fight. To keep him quiet and occupied while Bill slept, she set a basket of toys beside the coffee table, but she couldn't stay in there with him. Seeing Bill asleep on the couch made her uncomfortable.

Isn't this what she wanted, the three of them together again? No—it wasn't. She shook her head to dislodge the thought. Bill's presence made her feel vulnerable, as if her insecurities were now to blame for their failed relationship instead of his unfaithfulness. Needing a distraction, she went back to the kitchen. There was always the pile of uniforms on the steam rack, and being two days behind, she filled the steamer with water and turned it on. Bill had apologized for neglecting her and Stewart, but he didn't know she knew about the other woman and apparently had no plans to admit it. Until he told her the truth, she wouldn't have room for him in either heart or home.

After finishing the first shirt, she quietly peeked around the corner. More than just asleep, Bill appeared to be in a coma with his feet on the floor and his long legs bent at an uncomfortable angle, far too long to fit on the six-foot sofa. Content to inspect a sticker book, Stewart sat on his knees, swayed side to side, and then leaned closer to look at the images holding his attention.

Surprised when she realized she'd pressed a dozen shirts in what seemed like minutes, she looked back at the clock in disbelief. Stewart had remained occupied and quiet in the living room, so much so that she turned off the steamer. Worried that her son's uncommon silence might be an expression of his trauma from being lost and alone, she tiptoed back to the living room. Stewart's silence had nothing to do with trauma.

Bill, sporting nearly a hundred stickers placed randomly from head to foot, continued to slumber, unaware of his recent embellishment. Familiar with the concept of guilt, Stewart jumped to his feet and chuckled. Bill stirred at the sound of Stewart's laugh, swiped at a cow sticker stuck to end of his nose, then drifted back into the depths of sleep.

Clamping a hand over her mouth, Sharon stifled a laugh. She would let Bill continue to sleep, adorned with a colorful variety of farm animals dancing across their lanky landscape.

* * *

It was nearly eight o'clock at night, and Bill showed no signs of waking. Sharon made Stewart a quick dinner of reheated casserole, and when the microwave beeped, the sound of it had no effect on their snoozing houseguest. After Stewart's bath, she helped him into his pajamas. Her son rubbed his tired eyes and walked into the kitchen for his bedtime ritual of milk and graham crackers. Before brushing his teeth, he stopped at the couch to inspect his sleeping father and grabbed the corner of his blanket. Sharon thought her son might decide that his father's turn with the blanket was over, but he left it in place and headed to the bathroom. Before long, Stewart was asleep as well.

For her sanity's sake and Bill's well-being, it was time to wake him up. If he slept much longer in that twisted position, he would surely have multiple aches and pains to deal with. She hoped the few hours he was able to sleep would render him coherent enough to drive home and tapped him gently on the shoulder.

"Bill . . . Bill."

He began to stir and feel for foreign objects on his chin and ear. "Sharon, I'm sorry. What time is it?"

"It's just past eight." She waited for his sleep fog to clear before offering him something to eat.

"After eight? I'm so sorry." With a hand on the arm of the couch, he set Stewart's blanket aside and stood to his feet. "I didn't mean to camp out. I'd better go." Reaching for the keys in his pocket, he noticed the array of stickers covering the right side of his body.

"You were playing with Stewart while you slept." She put a hand over her mouth to cover a smile. "As you can see, he was quite entertained."

Bill chuckled and peeled a pig off his neck.

"There're a few stickers on your head, too."

He reached up and pulled a group of chickens out of his hair, but his expression turned serious. "Sharon, I have to fly back to Beijing tomorrow morning." He watched her reaction, but she remained guarded. "That's what I wanted to tell you before I cracked myself on the head. I thought I'd lost a contract there and left before the job was finished. I needed to see you and make sure you and Stewart were all right. Now, I have to go back for a few days, but then I am coming home—to stay, Sharon. Can I see you and Stewart when I get back?"

Sharon looked at the floor as if her response was written there. "Your son needs you, Bill. Please don't stay away too long this time."

"I won't, Sharon. I won't. Not this time."

* * *

As Bill drove back to the hotel, he wished he could tell her that things were different, that she could trust him and he loved her and would promise to make it up to her and Stewart, but his promises had failed her before. He would have to come back and prove it.

In the hotel lobby, he purchased a few protein bars and a water bottle at the front counter before heading up to his room and noticed the young lady that took his money avoided making eye contact with him. He also caught several people staring at him in the elevator. Apparently, it was not in style to wear farm stickers all over oneself, especially not with a bandaged head.

Lying in bed in the dimly lit room, Bill checked the clock on the nightstand for the third time. It was eleven o'clock. He replayed Sharon's response over and over in his mind: *your son needs you.* Only Stewart needed him—not her. He prayed the damage he had done was not permanent.

* * *

The long return flight from Beijing to DC finally touched down at nine o'clock Monday evening. Bill collected his suitcase and tried to avoid the rain as he hurried to the next available cab. His face was unshaven, and his eyelids felt as if they harbored a fine layer of sandpaper with every blink. Water dripped off his hair, reminding him he was past due for a haircut, the long curls at the nape of his neck funneling rain inside his jacket and soaking the back of his shirt.

"Where to, sir?" the taxi driver asked, looking at him as if he was giving a ride to a serial killer.

"Gallaudet University." Bill bent down to slide into the cab, noticing an ache in his neck making its way up the back of his head and across his shoulders. Somehow, the few minutes of sleep he had managed to get on the airplane were just enough to leave him with a knot at the base of his skull.

"Are you staying at the hotel there?"

"I am," he replied, staring out the window at the rain-blurred lights of the city.

Six Houses Down

As the taxi moved along the busy downtown streets of DC, the Capitol Building came into view. The grandeur of it never ceased to amaze him, the dome alone constructed with nearly nine million pounds of cast iron. That's an accomplishment to be proud of. The bid he just secured for Davis Engineering was his most lucrative project to date, and Dwayne Davis would be full of attaboys and accolades, at least for a few weeks.

There was, however, only one thing that continued to command Bill's attention, and he hoped his window of opportunity remained open. Like the tempered iron in the Capitol's dome, the structural integrity of his marriage had been put to the test. His own failure to love his family as a husband and father should threatened to push Sharon beyond the critical point and make her fracture, like iron too long in the fire.

Please, Lord—I have not been who I promised to be. I cared for myself above my wife and son. Please forgive me and help me strengthen anything remaining, any love Sharon may still hold for me . . . please, Lord . . . please.

Bill's cell phone vibrated in his chest pocket. He had sent a text telling Sharon his plane had landed, and he desperately wanted her to call him back. If she even hinted that she wanted to see him, he'd go straight to the house.

"You are the man!" Dwayne yelled. "I knew you could do it. You'll have a fat paycheck from this one, pal. Why don't you meet me at the bar right down from the office? We can comb over a few details."

"Thanks, Dwayne, but I'm spent. I really need to get some sleep." Bill's stomach grumbled, reminding him it had been hours since he had eaten anything.

"Of course, of course . . . you get in a quick nap and then get on down to the bar. I'll meet you there, say . . . ten thirty?"

"I can't, Dwayne. I'm going to pass on the offer and go pass out for about eight hours. I'll see you tomorrow at the office." No way was he interested in profit-induced camaraderie with his fickle boss.

"All right, but be ready first thing in the morning. We've got to get at it. I have some major possibilities coming down the pike, and I'm gonna need my golden child to work his magic."

"Sure. See you tomorrow, Dwayne."

The taxi splashed through a few more intersections before pulling onto the university campus. As he wrestled his suitcase from the trunk of the cab, rain poured over his back. Apparently, the driver wasn't interested in braving the storm for a few extra dollars in tips. He paid the fare as water drained down along the curb, filling his shoes.

Bill sloshed through the entrance toward the front desk, leaving murky splotches on the clean marble floor. While he waited for his room key, he checked his phone again. Sharon hadn't called him over the last three days, but he didn't expect her to. He'd sent her and Stewart a few pictures of strange food items and crowded markets while he was in Beijing, wanting to show her he was thinking of them.

The time already pushing ten o'clock, he slipped off his rain-soaked shoes and placed the contents of his pockets on the nightstand. He considered calling Sharon one more time, but she and Stewart would already be asleep. Bill turned the shower handle to extra hot, peeled off his soggy clothes, and stepped into the steaming stream, mulling over how he might navigate the next few days. Somehow, he would try to reenter lives adjusted to managing without him. Sharon had needed him desperately when Stewart was lost, or maybe she was just willing to exhaust any resource to find her son. Now that Stewart was safe, she was free to loathe her absentee husband again. Bill warned himself not to fixate on the things he couldn't change, mistakes already made. He would call Sharon in the morning and try to fix any repairable damage.

CHAPTER 21

Bill's phone rang as he waited in the hotel lobby. His rental car had arrived. As he drove to work, he checked the time. The second he parked the car at the office, he tapped the green icon on the screen and waited for Sharon to answer. If she saw the caller ID and answered her phone, then she was at least willing to talk to him. He waited . . . four rings . . . five rings. "Come on, pick up." She didn't answer.

Bill's hands started to sweat as he left a quick message. "Hi, Sharon, I wanted to let you know I'm at the office. I'd like to come by for a few minutes and see you and Stewart, if you're not too busy, maybe this afternoon. I'll call back later." He checked the time, 9:15 a.m. An uncomfortable heaviness settled in his stomach as he walked to his office and shut the door. Why didn't she answer?

Dwayne burst into the room without warning. "There's the man of the hour," he crowed like a rooster that had risen far too early.

"Morning, Dwayne," Bill said, feeling the effects of both jet and heart lag.

"Look at this profit projection, pal." Dwayne tossed a graph on his desk. "That's all you, big guy." Dwayne stood too close to him with his hands on his hips before pounding his thick palm on Bill's back.

Over the next five minutes, his boss droned on about an opportunity in Sri Lanka. One minute into the conversation, all Bill could hear was Charlie Brown's teacher.

"Wau, wau, wau . . . wau, wau . . . Bill, what do you think?" His boss leaned forward, his mouth hanging open as if he expected him to react with fist-pumping excitement.

Not sure what Dwayne was asking, but fairly certain it had something to do with him going to Sri Lanka, he needed to enlighten him, the sooner, the better. "I'm not going."

"What do you mean, you're not going?" His boss looked dumbfounded. "This will be twice the paycheck that Beijing was. You have to take this one!" Several drops of spit landed on Bill's face.

"I'm not, Dwayne. I gave you a one-year commitment when you promoted me, and Beijing was the last proposal on my time clock. Traveling is not going to work for me anymore." He'd made up his mind, and this time, there was no room for manipulation.

"Are you insane? You're just tired because you've been burning the candle at both ends. Be reasonable. You know you have a gift for this type of work. When you open your paycheck from this last project, the fog in your head will clear up." Dwayne smiled at him, forcing lines on his face that his skin wasn't accustomed to. "You think about it for a couple weeks before you go making any hasty decisions. I have faith in you, Bill."

Dwayne finally left his office. He wasn't an easy one to deny, but it didn't matter this time. No paycheck would be big enough to coerce him away from his family.

Pulling a note with several numbers out of his briefcase, Bill wondered if the five-day-old list was already obsolete. There was one number in particular he wanted to check before starting his search all over again.

"Hello, I'm calling about the house you listed for rent. Is it still available? . . . Yes, I have references. The lease is $2,300 a month, right? I can be there at noon today . . . okay, thank you."

Things were looking up. The owner of the house had been out of town until this morning and was inundated with messages about the rental. If Bill could meet the owner at noon, the rental was his. He hoped Sharon would approve. The house was located in an area where most people purchased rather than rented, across the street from the Clarks, and only six houses down from Sharon and Stewart.

Steve tapped on the door and poked his head into Bill's new office. "How's it going, *big guy?*"

Bill rolled his eyes. "You heard that, huh?"

"Everybody heard it. What are you going to do?" Steve's expression suggested warning, his head tilted forward and eyes narrowed.

"I'm not leaving again, and I don't care if he demotes me. It's not worth it anymore. You're not married yet. Since Dwayne is your cousin, why don't you take a stab at being his *big guy?*"

"Not going to happen, mate," Steve replied without hesitation. "I'm not obligated to stay on here, and I don't fancy being a traveling engineer."

"Why not? I thought you liked to travel." They had taken several trips together in their college days. Traveling abroad had been one of their common interests.

"Climbing Mt. McKinley is my idea of traveling, Bill, not chasing contracts all over the world. Besides, there's something else I would rather be chasing." Steve leaned against the doorjamb of Bill's office, clearly waiting for his reaction.

"So, you're already bored with miss . . . wherever she was princess of? You've only been seeing her for a few months. What did I miss in the three days I was gone?"

"Her name was Vanessa, and, no, I'm not seeing her anymore. Her prince from a few years ago came back from Neverland, and the duffer claimed she was his one true love. She fell for his rubbish, and they rode off into the sunset together." Steve didn't appear to be upset about the rejection.

"Sorry, bud." Bill wondered if his friend was more disappointed than he let on.

"It's all right. Before she dumped me, she managed to shed a few crocodile tears. Listen, I need to talk to you, away from ears and interruptions. Can you get away for lunch?"

"I hate to put you off," Bill replied, "but I have to check on a rental at lunch time. How about burgers tonight?"

"Sounds good," Steve replied as he left Bill's office.

* * *

It was almost noon, and Sharon still had not returned his call. Bill was hesitant to lease the house without talking it over with her first, but time was running out. He drove over and parked outside the rental, scanning the sidewalk behind him for any sign of Sharon or Stewart. A black Mercedes pulled up behind him, and a middle-aged man stepped out of the car.

"Xavier," the man said, offering Bill a hurried handshake.

"Bill. Nice to meet you." He followed the impeccably dressed man into the rental. The place was perfect.

"I'll need a year-long lease. Is that going to work for you?" the owner asked him.

Bill hesitated. "Would you be interested in a six-month lease? I could be here longer, but I'd prefer committing to six months if I can."

The man released a heavy sigh and looked over the references Bill had faxed before the appointment. "It's just you, right? No girlfriend, kids, or pets?"

Bill shifted to his other foot and looked out the window toward the Clarks' house. The front door opened, and he could see Earl holding the door for someone. Bill continued to watch the movement across the street as he answered. "No, just me—What?" Bill moved closer to the window and saw Sharon and Stewart step out of the house. Sharon said something to Earl, who gave her a hug and waved at Stewart before they walked down the sidewalk toward home.

"Did you have a question?" The man had the rental agreement on the table ready to sign and checked his watch impatiently.

"No, sorry," Bill replied, realizing Sharon might not have known he called earlier because she didn't have her phone with her. He reached for the pen to sign the agreement when the cell phone in his coat pocket vibrated against his chest. Thinking it could be Sharon, he apologized to the man, who didn't seem thrilled to be put off.

"Hello." Bill answered without checking the caller ID.

"Bill, don't rent that house."

"Steve—what the heck?"

"Don't sign the lease, Bill. I'll explain later. Trust me on this one. See if you can get back to them, but don't sign anything. Don't do it, mate."

"Did something happen at work? What's going on? This place is perfect." Bill wanted to hear a good reason why he should pass up what seemed like a gift from God.

"I have to go—really, don't sign anything." Steve hung up, leaving Bill completely in the dark with decisions needing to be made.

"I'm sorry," Bill said, hoping he was not going to regret this. "I have to wait for something before I can sign the lease."

"I'm not holding it for you. Take it now or forget it. I don't have time to be left hanging. There are twelve messages on my answering machine at work, all people desperate to have this place, and two that will pay more than I'm asking. You were lucky enough to call before I had a chance to play phone tag."

"I'm sorry, then." Bill showed himself out.

The owner locked up the house and sped away before Bill started his car. He looked at the clock on the car's dashboard: fifteen minutes before he had to be back at work for a meeting, not enough time to eat anything. He pulled a U-turn. He could say he was in the area. It was a chance worth taking. Bill pulled up in front of the house and hurried to the door. He would have to make this quick.

"Bill?" Sharon clearly wasn't expecting him.

"I was in the area and had a few minutes before I needed to be back to work. I really wanted to see you and Stewart and say hi . . . really quickly." He watched her expression, trying to sense a positive reaction to his presence. Her eyes looked tired, and she was hard to read, but she surprised him.

"Come on in." Her reply seemed friendly enough, maybe even warm, as if she were happy to see him. "Stewart is in the kitchen."

Bill covered the short distance from door to kitchen in several long strides and noticed Sharon's cell phone sitting on the counter. A missed call flashed on the screen. Stewart, obviously happy to see him, jumped around before settling back in his chair in front of a small bowl of ice cream.

He pulled a chair out and sat next to his son. "Hi, buddy, how is Stewart today?"

Stewart hopped out of his chair again, grabbed the cell phone off the counter, and held it out, impatient for him to take it.

Not sure what he wanted, Bill took the phone and looked at Sharon, hoping she could tell him what Stewart wanted.

"Un-un-un-un." Their son clapped with expectation.

"He wants to see the picture of the bugs on the sticks. The ones in the food market. And he really likes the close-ups of the people eating the scorpions and the grasshoppers."

"You liked those, huh?" Bill searched Sharon's phone for his texts. "Look, Stewart, you just slide your finger up or down on the screen to move it." Bill handed the phone to him so he could try it, sensing a new, fresh warmth replacing the earlier worries that had lodged in his gut. Sharon and Stewart had looked at the pictures he sent while he was gone and likely talked about him and where he was. That small thread of connection did more to encourage him than Sharon could ever know.

Bill tried to watch Sharon as he interacted with their son, assessing every movement and expression without making his inspection obvious. She was hard to read and was perhaps evaluating him as well. He noticed her distraction with refracted light passing through a glass bird in the window, casting rainbows of color on the kitchen wall. Stewart continued to slide through the pictures on Bill's phone, reacting with giggles when he found one of himself and then resuming his search for scary food.

"There it is. Slide down a bit." Bill took the phone and spread the picture of a skewered scorpion across the small screen. "Would you like to eat one of those?"

His son laughed and clapped his hands before covering his mouth.

"You don't want that thing in your mouth, do you?" Bill laughed at his son's antics and noticed Sharon laughing along with them.

"I have to go, okay? You hold on to Mom's phone, and I'll send you another picture right away." Bill stood up to leave. "Thank you. It's so good to see both of you. I'll call you after work?"

Sharon smiled and nodded. "Did you get a chance to eat lunch?"

"Thanks, but I'm good . . . and late for a meeting," he walked toward the door.

"Here." She grabbed something out of the refrigerator and wrapped it in a napkin. "Take this with you."

Resisting a strong urge to kiss her goodbye like he'd done so many times before, he accepted the wrapped item and closed the door behind him. The clock on the car's dashboard reminded him he was already five minutes late for the meeting. Reaching for the napkin, he unwrapped the mystery food as he sped back to the office. The offering was half of a crust-less ham and cheese sandwich. Bill took a big bite. The sauce-free sandwich was so dry it stuck to his teeth like glue. While he waited at an intersection, he snapped a quick picture. The sandwich had to be Stewart's leftover lunch, and he loved every bite of it.

The phone in his pocket buzzed. He ignored the call. It was his boss wondering where he was. When he reached the elevator and headed up to the meeting, Bill searched for the picture he had taken for Stewart on the drive back to work. His phone buzzed again. It was Dwayne.

"I'm on my way," he said, hanging up before his boss had a chance to say anything. Finding the picture of himself grinning with cheese and bread stuck to his teeth, he sent it to Sharon's phone and tapped in a message: *Thanks for the sandwich—It was my favorite.*

An instant response: *You're welcome.*

Taking a chance, Bill sent a text offering to put up the new fence around the backyard on Saturday. She returned a simple text agreeing with his plan, but that was it for the rest of the day. It was a start, and that was all Bill could hope for.

* * *

If he hadn't been Steve Davis's friend in college, Bill knew he wouldn't have been given the job he had, right out of school. Steve was Bill's connection at Davis Engineering, and his friendship with the boss's cousin had granted him a slide to the top of a long interview list and a subsequent position he was lucky to have. Unfortunately, the affinity he had for his job began to wane months ago. As he left the company meeting, Bill was more annoyed than ever with his boss. The meeting turned out to be a grand presentation of his wages, complete with manipulation and flattery. Dwayne made a big show of Bill's $200,000 commission check, as if it was a gift from the company. He then promised everyone a probable raise because of the success Bill would likely bring to the firm when he accepted the project in Sri Lanka.

Steve followed him into the elevator, "I feel absolutely jilted," he joked. "I don't get a party every time I get my paycheck. Dwayne is really quite persistent, isn't he?"

"I'd say something, but this elevator is probably bugged," Bill shoved his hands in his pockets.

"I wouldn't doubt it. Did you sign the lease?" Steve seemed beyond eager to tell him something.

"No, I didn't, and you'd better have a darn good reason why I shouldn't have." Bill trusted him, but Steve couldn't understand how convenient living so close to his wife and son would have been.

Steve put a finger to his lips. "Shhh, not here. Burgers—seven o'clock?"

"That'll work."

Whatever reason Steve had for interfering, it would have to wait until later.

* * *

A roll of thunder threatened the release of a heavy spring rain. Stacey had come over to play after school, and the dark sky kept the children inside for the afternoon. Stewart reached for the cell phone on the kitchen table and handed it to his friend.

"What is on his teeth?" Stacey said, her face dramatically portraying a bad case of picture-induced nausea.

Stewart laughed and hopped with excitement, reaching for her to return the phone.

"That's his father's sandwich, stuck in his teeth," Sharon informed her, entertained by the exaggerated show of disgust.

"That is so gross," Stacey shivered and pretended to gag. Stewart slid the screen back until he found the picture of the scorpion on a stick. Surprised to see that he'd remembered how to manipulate the pictures on her phone, Sharon continued to watch their interaction with rapt attention. He'd been shown only once how to find the pictures. Stacey saw the offensive images earlier in the week, the day they were sent, and gifted Stewart with frantic terror. He clearly hoped to duplicate her initial reaction. She did not disappoint him.

"Get it away!" she yelled as she ran down the hall.

Stewart laughed and chased after her, taunting her with the menacing picture. Soon the phone lost its potential to frighten, and the two children played with puzzles in the living room.

Sharon retrieved her phone, recalling how it held Stewart's attention more than the rainbows reflecting on the kitchen wall. She knew it wasn't the phone commanding his interest; it was his father. She had witnessed the exchange between father and son with conflicting emotions. A twinge of jealousy tried to seed itself in her thoughts, but she wouldn't allow it to take root.

* * *

Anna stood at the front door with an umbrella, ready to retrieve her daughter, but Sharon asked her to come inside while the kids picked up the toys.

"What happened to all the stickers in this book, Mrs. Webster?" Stacey asked, pointing to the pages of missing farm animals from the book she'd brought over several weeks earlier.

Sharon smiled as a picture of Bill with chickens stuck in his hair came to mind. "Stewart had a lot of fun with those, but I'm sorry they're all gone."

"I'm glad he liked them, but he should learn to share more." She pursed her lips and put a hand on her cocked hip.

"Stacey, you don't talk to Mrs. Webster like that. It's disrespectful," Anna said sternly. "What do you say?"

"I'm sorry, Mrs. Webster, for being disrespectful," she mumbled, her eyes half-open.

Sharon tried not to laugh and thanked her for bringing him the book. "I didn't know he liked stickers until you brought them over."

Stacey's humbled demeanor changed instantly. "I have lots of stickers, and I can bring lots more over if Stewart wants some."

"Maybe a few would be nice," Sharon agreed as they stepped toward the front door.

Anna turned back quickly as if she'd forgotten something. "Would you mind watching Stacey tomorrow afternoon at about three in the afternoon? Earl and Nanna May have a meeting at church. I could get off work a little early and be here by five."

"Sure. And there's no reason to leave early." Sharon didn't need any further explanation. "Bill will be here working on a new fence, so it will be nice if Stacey could be here to distract Stewart."

Anna seemed relieved. "The plan was for Stacey to hang out at the church, but she would be bored out of her mind, not to mention a handful for Earl to track down every ten minutes. Thank you." She stepped outside and pushed a large umbrella open over herself and Stacey as they walked away.

Sharon closed the door behind them. She couldn't keep from comparing her and Anna's predicaments. Would it be more difficult to be completely rejected from the beginning of a relationship or strung along for years, wondering if there was a possibility of reconciliation? Neither was the happily-ever-after that any woman hoped for.

* * *

Bill parked the car at Union Station and found Steve sitting at a table.

"Hey, you're here already." Bill was used to Steve being ten minutes late for everything, so he had taken his time to get there. The smell of frying bacon reminded him how hungry he was, and since Steve already had his food, Bill turned toward the counter.

"I ordered for both of us. Hope you want your usual." Steve scooted a tray across the table, looking more interested in talking than eating.

"Sure, thanks. I'll take whatever." He sat down and took the sandwich Steve pointed at. "What's going on?"

"Hear me out before you say anything because, at first, I'm going to sound off my rocker." Steve held his hands up as if he was protesting already. "When you went to Beijing, I interviewed with another firm in Washington state." Steve scanned the area to make sure no familiar faces were nearby.

Bill was both surprised and confused. "You what? Steve, I want you to tell me why I shouldn't sign that lease."

"Listen, Bill. You don't need a rental. You can lodge at my place for a few weeks until you have a chance to . . . well, you know, get sorted out."

"Steve, that's great of you to offer, but it might take more than a few weeks to get my life straightened out. Did you say you're moving to Washington state?"

"I did, now hear me out. I applied a few weeks ago, but I didn't want to bother you with it until I was certain I secured the position. This engineering firm," Steve continued, tapping on the envelope in his hand, "is in Pullman, Washington, and is on the cutting edge of protection systems—globally. Take a look at their expansion plans, including cyber-attack technologies, your specialty. I told them about you, and they are quite keen on giving you an interview if you're interested."

"What? Steve, you've got to be kidding. I'm not about to leave Sharon and Stewart to get a job all the way across the United States. What are you thinking?"

"I didn't say anything about you leaving your wife and son, mate. Listen . . . take them with you."

"What? I can't just . . . Sharon would never agree to it." Bill was questioning his own answer.

"You could use a change of scenery and so could your family. Here's the information. Ring them and set up an interview. Worst-case scenario, you don't accept the position if Sharon doesn't fancy a move west. What do you stand to lose?"

"Oh, man . . . Steve, what are you getting me into?" Bill shook his head, not wanting to process what Steve was asking.

"You need this. You could be the next groundbreaking designer of your own components. Ring them. I'm going to wait to tell Dwayne until I know if you're leaving or not. He is going to be gutted, to say the least."

"Why don't *you* look for another job here in DC?" Bill asked, wondering why the only option seemed to be in Washington state.

"I've been looking for a while now. This is the one; I can feel it."

Bill took the packet of information. "Tell me this isn't about some girl you met online."

Steve sat back in his chair and threw his hands up in mock offense. "Come on, mate, give me some credit."

"It's only an educated guess. You're not getting any younger, and now that you're single again, maybe you're getting desperate," Bill teased.

"Well, I might have taken a bit of a look around while I was there, but this is not about chasing a woman. Now, if you please, back to my point. You do not have to choose your job over your family, which will be a constant struggle if you stay with Davis. Like I said, ask Sharon. Tell her you won't consider going if she won't go with you."

"I'll think about it." Bill took the packet and thumbed through a few papers. "What's this?"

"You don't need that. It's nothing really, just a receipt." Steve reached for the slip of paper.

Bill pulled it away. "Looks like your server was really attentive: *Call me— Summer.* You have a waitress's phone number. You are getting desperate, aren't you?"

"No. I didn't intend to keep the receipt. She was attractive, but nearly ten years too young as well," Steve replied, somewhat frustrated with Bill's insinuation. He took the receipt and left it crumpled on the tray with their food wrappers.

Bill folded the manila envelope and put it in his jacket pocket. "I'm not promising anything, but I'll take a look at it."

The following day, Bill moved his few belongings over to Steve's apartment. The man-cave decor left him feeling as if he was back in college, but it was a nice place with a private bath in each of the bedrooms.

Throughout the week, Dwayne continued to press Bill for a decision on his position with the company. If he rejected the renewal of his previous agreement, he would be demoted several rungs down the ladder to feel the depths of Dwayne's disappointment. The pay would be livable, but the work environment would be tedious, especially with Steve gone. It was time to consider his options.

Six Houses Down

* * *

"I think I'll buy a car this week," Bill said as he searched the internet at Steve's apartment.

"Why would you buy a car if you might be moving?" Steve got up and opened the refrigerator, looking back at him when he didn't answer.

"I'm not sure I can ask Sharon to move. I might be regretting that I didn't lease that house. It was only six houses down from Sharon and Stewart."

"Bill, what are you on about? *Friends* live six houses down—not *husbands.*" Steve shook his head and set his drink on the table with a thud. "You need to know the truth. If you would have left your wife, I would have considered marrying her. That's right, mate—her over you any day. You really diddled your way out of all your responsibilities when you took off, didn't you?" Steve leaned against the kitchen counter and crossed his arms, meeting Bill's angry glare with steely eyes and set jaw.

Bill's blood turned to an instant boil. "You . . . you helped yourself to my wife while I was conveniently gone? Nice. What a friend!" Body tense, he would fly out of his chair and pound Steve if he took one step closer.

"Some husband you are . . . you barmy fool! One hug on Christmas morning hardly counts as an affair . . . so why don't you belt up. I did not set foot in *your* house or even spend a single day with *your* wife while you were gone. Why? Because if I did, I would have been tempted to fall in love with her. You prat! Sharon was completely alone thanks to you!"

Bill slumped down in his chair and buried his forehead in his hands, his heart thumping painfully hard in his chest. "I hate you right now."

"I hate how utterly stupid you are." Steve shot back. "Your marriage isn't going to mend itself. You have to make it work, Bill. It's not Sharon that needs to *come around.* Why do you insist on leaving the ball in her court every time?"

"What are you talking about? As if you're some kind of marriage expert. You don't know anything about being married."

"You've always been like that—Mr. Friendly, always with the funny thing to say, but when it comes right down to making a personal decision, you're never the one willing to take the risk." Steve's anger had come down a few notches, his voice still strained but not loud. "You don't seem to have any problem gaining the upper hand when securing a contract, but when it comes to Sharon . . . You're no ace, mate."

"You're wrong." Bill remained seated, frustrated by what his friend was accusing him of.

"You know I'm not," Steve countered. "You're blinkered. Who called whom on your first date with Sharon? Did you call her, or did you leave it up to her to call you, no skin off your teeth if she didn't want to go out with you?" He released a deep, perturbed sigh. "What really has you brassed off is that you know I'm right," Steve challenged.

"I'd never admit it, even if you were," Bill replied, less drained by the verbal sparring than the fact that his friend was making sense.

"Bill, think about it. Six houses down might as well be six miles or six states down. Or, when Dwayne finds out his *golden child* might leave, he'll fight like mad to keep you at the firm, and then you'll be six countries down." The steam had gone out of Steve's anger. "I'm not keen on having a row, but I don't fancy standing silent while you scrap what you have left of your marriage, then live the rest of your life with regret." Steve stared at the floor for a second as if in deep thought. "I'm taking a shower, and I plan on using all the hot water."

With his eyes closed, Bill dropped his head and ran a hand over the back of his neck. "I still hate you."

"No, you don't, mate; you hate that I'm right," Steve replied, before closing his bedroom door.

The words stung, but Bill knew they were true. Trying to focus on a solution rather than his anger, he got up, pulled a towel from the dryer, and headed to his bathroom. Steve had been his friend since their first year in college, and even the girlfriends Steve had stolen were probably his own fault. He hadn't pursued anything more than a friendship with several potential romantic interests. By the time he decided to be a committed boyfriend, they got tired of waiting for him to come around. Personal risks were his weakness, and his friend had called him out on it.

Six Houses Down

As hot water stripped the sticky sweat off his body in the glass-enclosed think tank, Bill sifted through a long list of *what ifs*, trying to formulate a plan. Steve was right, Sharon and Stewart were worth any risk he needed to take. His *waiting for things to work themselves out* plan was not going to cut it this time. Something Earl had said came to mind as he rinsed the shampoo out of his hair: *there's nothing broke here that can't be fixed.* It was time to do more than wait. Risks needed to be taken. He could fail, but not for lack of trying.

With a pair of shorts on, he ran a towel over his wet hair. He wasn't committing himself to anything by making a few inquiries. Bill pulled a clean T-shirt over his damp skin and set his computer case on the bed. It was six o'clock in DC. That would make it three in Pullman. He took out the manila envelope and paced the bedroom as he read through the job description several times. Why not give it a try? Bill picked up his phone and dialed the number for the engineering firm on the other side of the United States. Three minutes later, he had an online interview scheduled for the following Monday. It was only an interview, not a decision.

Now, there was a fence that needed mending—besides the one at the house. Bill found Steve sitting in the living room watching a game. "I'm sorry."

"I'm already over it; no groveling or hug required." Steve clicked the remote, surfing back and forth between two games.

"I called Pullman."

Steve hit the pause button and set the TV controller down. "Now what?"

"I have an email interview on Monday."

"A hiring team will probably give you a call by the end of the week. Don't be too shocked by the salary. Remember, the cost of living is about a third of what it is here. You won't regret it," Steve said as he returned to the game. "I told them I needed a few months before I could move over there."

"Are we really going to do this?" Bill asked as he grabbed a drink.

"There's nothing keeping me here. Whether you go or not is entirely up to you."

CHAPTER 22

With a determined pace, Anna headed up the sidewalk to retrieve her daughter, already fifteen minutes later than she said she'd be. As she drew near to the Webster house, she noticed a shiny black sports car slowing down as it passed her. Just what she needed after the day she'd had at work. It wasn't like men were hitting on her all the time, but this particular day happened to be a lousy one. It's my job to smile, be friendly, sell tickets. Why me? When the obnoxious stalker wouldn't leave her alone, her manager called security, and the man was forced to leave the station. The whole situation humiliated her. Seeing the black car pull over to the curb ahead of her, Anna's pulse quickened. What if that's the guy from the station?

Twenty feet ahead of her, the stalker stepped out of his pimp mobile. Probably a sex trafficker looking for an easy target. She noticed the stranger was on the tall side and had wavy, dark hair, but she was careful not to make eye contact with him. That's definitely not the same guy.

"Hello," the stalker said as she walked passed him.

"Hello yourself," she shot back without looking, mumbling that players were ruining her life.

"Bad day?" The guy asked, falling in behind her.

"Yes, *really* bad, and you're making it worse. I'm sorry; I'm usually a *really* nice person, but I am *really* not interested."

"Really? Interested in what?" the purp teased as she turned to walk up to the Websters' house. He stopped at the end of the walkway and watched her while she knocked on the front door.

"I'm *really* not interested in being *stalked* by some guy with a fake English accent," she said with a snarl, looking at him closely for the first time. Her eyebrows arched as heat spread across her face in an instant shade of blush red. That's a gorgeous pimp. She whipped around and faced the house, her nose only a few inches away from the door.

The pervert chuckled quietly and stood there for a few seconds without saying anything, clearly entertained by her frustration.

"Answer the door already, Sharon," she whispered, not wanting to face Mr. Handsome again.

"I'm sorry," he said. "I didn't catch that last bit, luv, or maybe you've spotted something on the door?"

Anna whipped back around to face him. "What do you want? Do I have a sign on me somewhere that says *desperate and single?*"

He squinted and took a few steps in her direction. "I don't see one. Are you, then?"

She couldn't think straight. "Am I what?"

"Desperate and single?" he asked with a conniving smirk.

Sharon finally opened the door. "I thought I heard someone out here. Sorry, Anna, I was in the backyard with the kids and didn't hear the door. Hi, Steve. It looks like you've met Stacey's mom. Anna, this is Steve Davis, Bill's friend."

Anna dropped her chin and covered her face with both hands.

Steve tried and failed to suppress a laugh, then introduced himself properly, "Hello, Anna, it's a pleasure to meet you."

She slowly slid her hands off her face and looked up, offering him an embarrassed, guilty grin. "Hi."

"You really *can* be a nice person. I'm headed to the garden. Have a brilliant day, Anna." He stepped around the frozen redhead and disappeared into the house.

Sharon looked confused. "What was that all about?"

"Me being humiliated," Anna replied. "Thank you for watching Stacey. I'll crawl back home now. Oh, before I forget, I wanted to tell you that Stacey has a doctor's appointment on Monday, so she won't come over to play that day."

"Is everything okay?" Sharon asked.

"Everything's fine. It's a routine check-up. She has one every six months." Anna looked into the house, "Um . . . would you mind getting Stacey for me?" She smiled as if to say, *please don't make me go in there.*

Sharon started to retrieve Stacey, paused in thought for a second, and sprouted a mischievous grin. She turned back toward the front door. "You know what, Anna? I'm pretty busy right now. Could you do me a huge favor and get Stacey yourself?"

Her face regained the rosy glow she'd just recuperated from. "You wouldn't dare!"

Sharon raised her eyebrows. "I would."

Anna huffed with exaggerated embarrassment. "I can't believe you're doing this to me." She stomped past her.

"Believe it," Sharon replied.

Anna sneaked into the tiny backyard, knowing there was no way to go unseen. "Stacey, we need to get going."

"Hi, Anna, how are you?" Bill greeted her from the corner of the backyard, a mere fifteen feet away.

"Hello, Bill," she answered, not looking at the two men working on the fence.

Steve had a smug grin on his face and tried unsuccessfully to suppress a laugh.

Bill looked confused. "Anna, have you met my friend Steve? Steve, this is Anna, Stacey's mom."

"Yes," Anna impatiently answered, "thank you very much, Bill, we've already met." She continued to keep her eyes trained on Stacey as she brushed the sand off her daughter's pants.

"Why is your face all red, Mom?" Stacey asked, loudly enough for everyone to hear.

Steve chuckled and set the drill he was holding on the ground. He closed the short distance between them with a few long strides. "Listen, Anna, don't worry about it. I hope you have a better day at work tomorrow." He held out his hand. "Truce?"

Anna couldn't keep an embarrassed smile from taking over her face, sure that it was a bright shade of I'm-an-idiot red. "Truce," she agreed and shook his hand, noticing he was careful to release hers the instant she pulled it away.

"May I stalk you home?" Steve teased.

"Thanks for the offer, but I think the ten girlfriends you already have are enough to keep you busy." Anna cocked her head, flashed a gotcha smile, and pulled Stacey through the kitchen door.

Bill released a sudden blast of laughter. "She pegged you, dude."

"What do you mean 'she pegged me'?" Steve acted as if he was greatly insulted. "Did she think I was merely chatting her up?"

"Are you kidding? You have *ladies' man* written all over you. Maybe that pretty face of yours is a curse after all." Bill laughed, clearly entertained by the exchange.

"Whatever. I guess it's my burden to bear. So . . . about Anna." Steve tried to change the subject.

"She's not going to be the next one on your list," Bill said. "She has too much on her plate to be toyed with."

"Toyed with? Since when have I ever pursued dodgy relationships? I'm truly interested. There's something about her I rather like."

"Of course you like her. You fall for every woman that rejects you," Bill continued to secure cedar slats in place.

"What are you on about?" Steve asked, sounding offended.

"Steve . . . you imprint on them like a baby duck."

"Simply not true." Steve tried to act insulted, but his curiosity got the best of him. "What is her story, all joking aside?"

Bill told him what he knew, not realizing that Sharon was eavesdropping on their conversation through the kitchen window while she washed the dishes.

* * *

Stacey stood in the alley behind the fence, ready to play as usual.

"Mrs. Webster," she called from the other side of the tall gate, "I can't remember the numbers to get in the yard."

A loud buzzer sounded when Sharon opened the gate and showed Stacey how to punch the numbers in and wait for the green light to flash before pulling on the lever.

"I see now. I did do it right, but I didn't wait long enough." She marched into the yard and joined Stewart in the sandbox. "Look what I brought for you." She pulled a small packet of stickers out of her pocket and handed them to him. "You can have those ones 'cause I already have lots of that kind. I got them at the doctor's yesterday when they were done taking pictures of my heart."

Sharon wanted to ask Stacey a list of questions, but she wouldn't burden their little friend with her worries. She would have to ask Nanna May or Anna if Stacey had something wrong with her heart. Trying to be careful not to jump to conclusions, Sharon figured if Stacey's health was compromised, Nanna May would have told her already.

Stewart took the stickers, inspecting the colorful animals through the clear plastic wrap. He smiled and waved them around before giving them a second look.

"You like those ones, don't you? Try not to use them all up at once because then you won't have any more again, just like the sticker book." Stacey placed her hands on her hips, appearing pleased with the reaction to her gift.

Sharon pulled a lawn chair over and sat next to the kids as they played. The yard seemed even smaller with the chain-link fence replaced by a solid cedar one. She scooted closer to the sandbox so she could be part of the lively exchange of gestures and monologue.

"I got those because my heart is flopped over," Stacey said, pointing to the stickers.

"Thank you for sharing them with Stewart." Sharon wanted to be careful how she responded to the privileged information but would let Stacey speak her mind.

"When I was a baby in my mommy's tummy, my heart flopped the wrong way. It's called a super big name . . . deck . . . dectru . . . I can't remember how to say it. Wait . . . it sounds like deck of cards or cardios. Anyways, my mom says I'm fine, but the doctor wants to take pictures of my heart so he can watch it while I get bigger, and I can do all the regular stuff that other kids can do, including clean up my room." She rolled her eyes.

Anna must have influenced that last comment. Stacey scooped a trail in the sand and dumped a bucket of plastic figurines on the wooden edge of the sandbox. "You want to know something else?" she asked, not waiting for Sharon's response. "You know the fat, little-boy angel that's naked, the one with the love arrows?"

"Cupid?" Sharon asked, a hand over her mouth to hide a wide grin.

"Yep, Cupid. Anyways, Mom says if he tries to shoot me with a fall-in-love arrow it won't work 'cause he won't know where my heart is, and I'll have to choose my own boyfriend . . . when I'm old, of course, and want one, like on Valentine's Day. Mom says we shouldn't tell Cupid my secret. She doesn't even know I'm too old to believe Cupid is real. I'll be ten in three years," Stacey said, cocking her head to the side and placing several plastic people along the freshly leveled sand street.

The precocious little girl's exaggeration of her age was entertaining since she had several months to go before she would turn seven. Apparently, those few months were inconsequential. Sharon would ask Anna or Nanna May about Stacey's flopped over heart, but according to Stacey, there wasn't any reason to worry.

Stewart seemed to be uncomfortable, rocking his fist in agitation.

"He has to go to the bathroom," Stacey said, continuing to place figurines in the sand city. "It's okay, Stewart. I won't take your people when you're gone. You better go or else you'll pee your pants."

"Come on. It'll only take a minute." Sharon helped him brush the sand off and hurry to the bathroom, wondering how Stacey could be so in tune to her son's needs.

Stewart panicked as Sharon helped him snap his pants. "You're okay. Stacey isn't leaving."

He calmed down and stopped resisting her help, quickly washing his hands, then running for the back door.

The kids played for another half hour before Sharon unlocked the gate for Stacey to return home. Bill had installed a lock requiring a person of adult height to open the latch from the inside. When Sharon pushed the gate open, a high-pitched buzzer sounded until the latch closed again. As annoying as it was freeing, the alarm served as a constant watchman while her son played in the yard.

"Do you want to come inside, Stewart?"

He remained engrossed in the arrangement of the plastic city stuck in the sand, so she asked him again.

An exaggerated *no* was offered in response, shaking his head as he righted a plastic tree. Sharon pulled a chair over and sat next to him, watching as he arranged then rearranged his sand toys. It didn't take long for images of Bill to wander into her thoughts: sleeping on the couch, covered with stickers; building a new fence; and showing Stewart how to find pictures on her cell phone. Along with the images, questions surfaced as well.

Why was it so difficult to let her husband know how much she loved him? Not long ago, she thought she lost him. When he suddenly returned, she wished he hadn't. Stewart needed his father. She needed him as well, but he'd been unfaithful. There was something else, something she couldn't identify triggering her involuntary protective instincts. No answer pulled from her degree in psychology and counseling satisfied her. Self-preservation and fear of rejection were likely contributors, but somehow her struggles went much deeper than textbook explanations.

CHAPTER 23

Three weeks had passed since Stewart scared everyone with his self-guided trip to Union Station. Sharon couldn't deny that Bill helped her throughout the ordeal and helped her recover from it as well. He also told her the truth before leaving for Beijing. He said he was coming home, and he did. After his return, Bill worked most afternoons at the house, securing doors and building a fence, but it was still *her* home—not *their* home.

* * *

Having a few rare moments to herself, Sharon called Nanna May to see if she and Earl were up for a quick visit. She wasn't accustomed to going anywhere without her son, but Bill wanted to take Stewart back to Union Station, a place that could hold a continued fear for him unless he returned without a reason to be afraid. It was good for Stewart to spend time with his father, and for reasons she didn't understand, their son appeared to be more at ease in new places with Bill than with her.

A twinge of jealousy needled her. She was a good mother, and for the last year, she had been the only parent giving her son the love and care he needed. Suddenly, his father returns and his abrupt reintroduction into their lives moved her down to second fiddle within a few weeks' time. She was embarrassed by her own thoughts. A boy needs his father, and if Stewart was delighted with his father's return, she should appreciate that, at least for Stewart's sake. He needed to go places and see new things, especially now that he was getting older. The sandbox was too small of a world for a six-year-old boy.

The air was crisp as Sharon walked down the sidewalk toward the Clarks' residence. She took the time to admire the new leaves on the narrow strip of trees at the street's edge. When she reached the small row house, she tapped on the door and noticed the addition of clay pots with bright yellow tulips lining the steps. Maybe the pots had been there all along.

The door opened and a familiar smile greeted her. "Look who's here, Maybeline; we have us our own angel, sent straight from heaven's gate."

She hugged Earl's neck. "Wait, does that make me a fallen angel?"

Earl chuckled. "No, ma'am."

"Stop leavin' me out of the fun, you two, and get yourselves in here," Nanna May called from the living room.

Sharon stepped into the house and hugged her dear friend.

"I'm so glad you came to see us, sugar."

The warmth of this place made her feel as if she were visiting her own childhood home. Nanna May's rich, deep voice was a verbal hug, and Earl, with his aging face carved by decades of friendliness, never met a person he didn't like. Sharon couldn't think of a more welcoming place than this small row house. The three of them visited for a few minutes, laughing at the latest antics of Stewart and Stacey and drinking tea so sweet you could frost a cake with it.

Sharon rubbed her hands together when Earl asked about Bill. A heaviness came over her that she tried to conceal, not realizing the discerning couple had been waiting for the right time to help her with this burden. Sharon offered a few vague details about Bill's travels.

Earl excused himself. "Maybeline, can I get you anything before I tend to some neglected plants in the backyard?"

"You go on, babe; I don't need a thing." She smiled at her husband as if they were married yesterday and patted an overstuffed chair. "Sit here, honey."

Sharon moved closer, a bit nervous that her elderly friend might be able to read her mind.

The older woman took her hand and patted it. "Sugar, let me tell you a story about your ol' friends Earl and Nanna May."

Sharon was instantly drawn in, the worries on her mind pushed aside.

"Earl was a fine lookin' young man in his Navy uniform. His family went to the same ol' Baptist Church as mine, and I'd find any reason I could to get close to him any time he come home. Mm-mm, I chased that boy so long he finally gave up a runnin'. I never met a finer man, no, not ever. He had a way of meltin' your heart with one look of those dark, smilin' eyes—and such a gentleman.

Six Houses Down

All the young women in the church were pushed along by their mammas to do whatever they could to land that sailor." She chuckled again. "Poor young man. He was so polite and had to endure lots of bad cookin' from all them desperate she-wolves. He still says it was my home-baked vinegar pie loaded down heavy with sugar and eggs that slowed him up 'nough so I could catch him."

An engaging storyteller, Nanna May swooped her arms around, catching-a-man style. She amused herself as much as she did Sharon, and the two women laughed together at the charade. Then the eyes of her elderly friend grew somber.

"He nearly got away from me when he came back from fightin' in Vietnam. I wasn't so easy to shake, though. My Earl had an accident and things were real bad. There was an explosion and lots of shrapnel cut through him. Some of his dearest friends passed on, but he got better and came home to us. His injuries healed up and all, but something was still botherin' him terrible.

"When he was hurt, he was left unable to have children, but he didn't want to tell me. I asked him if he didn't love me no more. That made him cry, and he promised he loved me but said he'd decided not to get married. When I told him he owed me a reason for changin' his tune and tryin' to brush me off, he told me the truth. He was gonna stay single so I could find me a husband that could give me children of my own."

Sharon glanced over at the wall covered with pictures, remembering the first time she saw them and assumed they were Nanna May and Earl's children with a few pictures of friends added to the mix.

Nanna May followed Sharon's gaze and looked over the pictures for a few seconds before continuing on. "Earl knew how I'd always dreamed of havin' a big family. Oh, Lord, I prayed, how can you give me a love like this and take away my children? I cried me so many tears my well went plum dry for a couple months. I asked Jesus how I deserved this hurt. My daddy told me to trust the Lord. I didn't care to listen 'cause he was the preacher, and he told everybody to trust the Lord; it's what preachers are supposed t' say.

"'Maybeline,' he told me, 'Do you think you know what's best for you, or does God know?' I was honest with my daddy. I didn't think God cared much 'cause he put a love in my heart for two things and now I had to choose between

Earl or children. I told him I'd been a good person and asked him why God would make me choose. That's when he traded his preacher voice for his daddy voice, and he told me we don't get what we deserve in this life; in fact, we more often get what we don't deserve 'cause this world is an unfair place. He asked me to pray and let Jesus help me decide and then to trust the Lord to be in charge of the desires of my heart.

"I loved Earl too much to give him up. Three months later, we got married. It was hard goin' when all our friends started havin' babies. We never had our own." Nanna may reached over and tapped her hand. "You'll never guess what happened. We weren't married even a year before we held our first child in our arms, a beautiful baby boy. All we knew about him was that his daddy died in the war. We didn't know who his mother was neither, but she'd asked the hospital to call us. We hadn't even looked into adoptin'. The Lord works in mysterious ways. Not long after that, our house started to fill up with kids of all ages. There were so many people that needed carin'. Some stayed on for only a few days, some months, and some for many years, and now Stacey and her momma are with us."

Nanna May continued to survey the people smiling back at her from the living room wall. "Just look at all them sweet faces. Why, I got me a family so big we have to have Christmas dinner at the church to fit them all around the table."

Nanna May sat quietly for a few seconds, but Sharon knew her friend, wise with experience, had more to say.

"Sweetheart, do you want to share with me what's troublin' you?"

Sharon smiled at her friend, overflowing with care for the whole world and cheated out of the ability to have her own children. Not wanting to burden Nanna May with her worries, she considered keeping them to herself.

"Come now, child, you have a load on your shoulders that needs set down, so let's start unpacking those burdens. They don't need carried no more." Nanna May patted her hand gently, waiting for a response.

Suddenly the floodgates burst wide open, and a torrential flood of tears and sobs overtook Sharon. She was surprised at herself, wanting to gain control, but the beast of bottled emotions would have to empty itself before she could gain her composure.

Nanna May let her cry it out with few words. "That's right, sugar; you let it all go." She pulled a box of tissues off the table and set them next to her.

Composure back in place and empty of all reservations, Sharon shared her deepest pains. Bill was back and wanted to be a part of her and Stewart's life, but she was unable to forgive him. He didn't deserve it. He had treated her just as her parents had—still belonging to them but dispensable.

What pained her more was that Stewart needed a father and she didn't want to deprive her son just to spite Bill, but how could she ever trust him again? There was an uncommon gentleness to Bill that was apparent, and Sharon was certain Nanna May had sensed it the first time she met him, but that didn't make him any less guilty.

"Sugar, that's the thing about forgiveness; it's not given 'cause it's earned."

"What do you mean?" Sharon asked, wiping her face with a tissue.

"The good Lord told us to forgive, not for the sake of the one who done us wrong but to mend our own broken heart."

Sharon knew Nanna May and Earl had witnessed many difficult situations and respected the elderly woman's lovingly offered advice. "It's so hard to forgive," Sharon admitted.

"Yes, it is. It's hard to forgive, but you aren't on your own. Heart healin' is the Lord's doin'. If we tell him how hurt we are and that we want that hurt to go away, he tells us to forgive and trust him to help us see it through. He made you, and he knows a sound heart gives life to a body. If your heart is broken, so goes the rest of you. That's why we need to forgive, and when we do, that opens the way for those that wronged us to find their own peace."

"What if he can't handle being a husband and a father and leaves us again, even if I forgive him?"

Nanna May took her hand in hers. "I've seen my share of happy endings—and not so happy endings. That's the thing about forgiveness; it don't come with no guarantee that everything's gonna work out the way you want it to. You still love that man, don't you? In fact, you love him so much it hurts. I know what that feels like. Problem might be, you're afraid to show it. I think you're still all soldiered up for a battle that needs to be over. Lower that shield over your heart, sugar, or it just might turn to stone." She set her hand on the arm of the chair and gave it a pat.

"I don't know where to start," Sharon answered softly.

"Give Bill a chance, child. A broken heart needs more than a few days to mend. Now, things may never be perfect; fact is, they won't be, but for myself, forgiveness has never been the wrong thing to do." Nanna May gave Sharon a big hug and prayed that the Lord would give Sharon the ability to forgive her husband and show him she loved him.

"Now that I'm done meddlin' in your worries, sugar, I got a few questions. Who's this Steve character anyway?" She smiled and raised her eyebrows, ready for Sharon to satisfy her curiosity.

Sharon filled her in on Anna's embarrassing meeting with Steve at the house. Nanna May laughed so hard Sharon had to wait awhile for her to catch her breath and then couldn't resist laughing with her when she started back up again.

Her friend waved a tissue in front of her face. "Well, now you know where Stacey gets her gumption," she said, trying to arrest another wave of giggles, but they broke through and attacked Sharon as well.

"What's all this cacklin' goin' on in here?" Earl said as he walked into the room. "You women ain't mindin' your own business, are you?"

Nanna May couldn't wait to tell Earl about Anna meeting Steve. Her version of the story had them all laughing again before she could even get all of the facts out. Sharon didn't know what was funnier: Nanna May telling the story or the story itself.

Sharon thanked her dear friend, noticing for the first time that the elderly woman had stepped into a space that her own mother had left vacant. She said goodbye to Earl and felt unusually peaceful as she walked down the sidewalk toward home. She would give her husband a chance. Nanna May was right; her broken heart would never mend if she refused to forgive him. She was in danger of begrudging her husband love that would cost not only Bill but her and Stewart as well. She could forgive him and even love him—from a safe distance.

CHAPTER 24

When Sharon returned home, she noticed Bill's leased pickup parked outside, but the house was empty, and a large, pink bakery box sat on the kitchen counter. A quick look through the window answered the whereabouts of Bill and Stewart. They were setting up a small pup tent on the small patch of grass in the backyard. She stood and watched them, Stewart clearly thrilled with the new acquisition.

"How was your trip to Union Station?" she asked as she stepped through the door.

Bill smiled at her with eyes brighter than usual. "We had a great time, but listen to this. As soon as we got there, we had to ride the escalators up to the mezzanine. It was clear he was on a mission. I followed him to a store with this tent set up in one of their floor displays. It was obvious Stewart wanted it, and the manager agreed to sell it, even though it was part of a display and not something they stock. From the mezzanine, we were off again, and I am telling you, Sharon, he knew exactly where he was going. We beelined down several escalators to the food court. He was most interested in a cupcake counter displaying giant cupcakes, but he settled for a burger when I told him we could bring the cupcake home for later. I hope that's all right."

"Of course. So, he didn't seem upset at all to be there?"

"Not at all."

"It's a huge relief to think he might not be as traumatized as we were," Sharon said as she peeked in the tent.

"He did get nervous a few times when we had to press through crowded areas, but other than that, he seemed like a happy camper."

He was a happy camper indeed. Sharon watched with pleasure, matching Stewart's mood as he gleefully crawled in and out of the small tent. Bill pushed his hands in his pockets and smiled at her, shifted his gaze to Stewart, and then adjusted the side of the tent.

"I better get goin'."

For the first time, Sharon wanted Bill to stay longer but wasn't brave enough to tell him. Reluctant to see him go, she held Stewart's hand at the front door and waved goodbye as he drove away.

* * *

Sharon placed her son's dirty clothes from the day before in the washing machine, noticing dog hair on them again. This wasn't the first time she'd found short black and white hairs on his cloths, but she figured the rental car Bill was driving must have had a canine passenger at one time.

The cell phone on the kitchen counter buzzed, startling her. She recognized Nanna May and Earl's number. "Hello, this is Sharon."

"Hey, sugar, this is Nanna May. Can you hear me okay? . . . Earl, is this thing working? Are you there, Sharon?"

"I'm here." Sharon smiled. Her elderly friend was just as adept with technology as she was.

"I don't know why we had to get this silly toy thing. There was nothin' wrong with my big old phone with a decent-size earpiece. Anyways, I didn't call to complain to you about the phone. Can you hear me okay?"

"Yes, I can hear you." Sharon pulled the phone farther away from her ear.

"Good, then. Anna was wonderin' if she could visit with you this afternoon after she gets off work. It seems her brother, Shane—you remember him, right?"

"Yes. We met him at the university," she replied.

"Oh, yes, of course you met him. Well, Shane's been visitin' with Stacey some, and he thinks Stewart has been signing with her. He wants to come over with Anna and talk to you."

Sharon wondered if she heard Nanna May right. "Signing . . . with Stacey? Shane thinks Stewart was signing?" she asked again, not wanting to disappoint Anna's brother but certain he was mistaken. "We were told over a year ago that Stewart wasn't a candidate for communicating through sign language. He was in a program for a while, but they determined his limitations too severe to continue pressing him to sign and that it would only serve to aggravate him."

"Well," Nanna May continued, "Shane was curious about Stewart since he's studyin' and doin' research on that sort of thing. He says Stewart asked him for help. In the excitement of it all, Shane didn't get the chance to have Anna ask you who taught him to sign."

"What?" Sharon was not sure she understood. "He signed *help*?"

"That's what he told Anna. He says he signed *afraid*, too," Nanna May added.

"I wonder if it's just a coincidence." Sharon was careful not to get her hopes up, unsure how or when he would have learned to sign.

"He's all excited to see you. Apparently, Stacey has been teaching him. When Anna asked her about it, Stacey said he knows all kinds of signs. They weren't sure if she actually taught them to him or was just takin' the credit for it."

Sharon stood in shock. Was it even possible, and if so, how had she missed it?

Nanna May continued talking, not realizing how important her news was, "You never know with that child. She has more going on in that head of hers than opinions in the Capitol. Land sakes, that girl talks non-stop unless she's eatin' or sleepin' . . . Are you there, sugar? Earl, is this phone still on?"

Sharon could hear Earl assuring her that she was still connected.

"Can you hear me?" Nanna May asked again.

"I . . . yes, I can hear you . . . I don't know what to say. I would love to visit with Shane and Anna. Have them come over whenever they can."

"All right. I'll let them know. Anna gets off work around four, so I'd be expectin' them round about four-thirty or close to it. You have a good day. Bye now. Earl, how do you shut this thing off?"

Sharon set her phone back on the counter and went outside to check on her son. He had pulled his favorite blanket into the tent, choosing it as his preferred nap site, and was sound asleep. Surely she would have noticed if he was signing. She unfolded one of the lawn chairs and sat next to the tent, trying to recall if Stewart had been doing anything different since Stacey had been coming over. Maybe he had. There were a number of times he had touched his shoulder and then her shoulder. He started cupping his hands together when he wanted something. Was that signing?

Sharon needed to share her excitement with someone. She looked at the contacts on her phone, already knowing she wanted to call Bill. He would love to hear the news, but she had never called him just to talk since he had returned from Beijing. All of her previous phone calls had been strictly business: when to pick up Stewart or a reply to a text he'd sent. She tapped on his name, hesitated for a few seconds, and then hit the call button.

He answered instantly. "Sharon? Is everything all right?"

"Hi, Bill, everything is fine. Are you busy? I can call back if you are. I wanted to tell you something about Stewart."

"Hold on just one second," he said quickly.

Sharon rubbed her arm, worried that she'd interrupted something important. She could hear him asking his colleagues to excuse him.

"Sorry, Sharon. Did you say something was going on with Stewart?"

"Do you have a minute, Bill?"

"I've got all day, and I'm all ears."

Sharon smiled, remembering Bill's often-used pet phrase. She told him what Nanna May said and that Anna and Shane would be coming over when Anna got off work.

Bill was as excited as she was. She asked him if he would like to hear what they had to say and invited him to stay for dinner, if he wasn't too busy. Bill assured her he wouldn't miss it and thanked her for the dinner invitation, offering to pick up a few things for her on the way to the house.

＊ ＊ ＊

As soon as Bill hung up the phone, he rescheduled a meeting planned for later that afternoon. No way in the world would he miss the visit or dinner tonight with his wife and son. A litany of questions passed through his mind in rapid succession: What if Stewart was actually signing? Why didn't he respond to the therapist before? Had he been a typical, stubborn little boy that didn't feel like talking to a stranger? Did Stewart understand far more than he was given credit for when he was younger because he wasn't yet motivated to cooperate?

Another voice in his head forced its way to the front, taunting him with what ifs: *What if you would have stayed home and given him a reason to communicate? What if those months of being fatherless caused irreparable damage to his potential to learn?*

"Stop!" he said aloud, willing himself to move forward rather than obsess over things he couldn't change. There was much to celebrate. Stewart might be signing, and Sharon finally called him because she wanted to, rather than needed to. "Thank you, Lord, for bringing me home."

Bill left work early so he could go back to the apartment before heading over to the house. He felt like he was going on a first date. Don't get ahead of yourself. Rome wasn't built in a day. Forget Rome. He'd get it right this time. This was his second chance.

* * *

When Stewart woke up from his nap, Sharon resisted asking him her anxious questions, not wanting to overwhelm him before Anna and her brother arrived.

"Hello, sleepyhead. Did you like taking your nap in the tent?"

He laughed and patted his stomach with both hands. She couldn't help wondering if he was signing for something.

"Let's go inside and get a snack," Sharon held the tent flap open.

"Guess what? We're going to have visitors today. Won't that be fun? Stacey's mother is coming over and so is her Uncle Shane. Do you remember Shane?"

Stewart chuckled and then turned his attention to the cheese and apple slices set in front of him.

No longer able to resist, Sharon chanced an innocuous question. "Do you remember that Shane talks with his hands?"

Stewart was listening, but it was unclear if her inquiry was of any interest to him. That would be the end of her prodding. The waiting would test her patience, but she wanted to avoid coercing Stewart or causing him to be apprehensive when their visitors arrived.

Instead, she offered him news sure to please. "Daddy is coming over, too."

Steward hopped up and patted his stomach with his hands, tumbling them over and over, and jumped around the kitchen. There wasn't any guesswork when it came to how he felt about his father. She calmed him down so he could reserve some of his energy for later, letting him take a few of his favorite books out to his tent while she made a few preparations for dinner.

Realizing she had not had company over for a long time, Sharon began to fret as she searched through the cupboards. "Where are the serving bowls?" She opened upper cabinets and scanned stacks of unused dishes. "Oh, no. I don't have any napkins." Meals had been simple for the last few years, food dished up from pot to plate with paper towels replacing napkins.

* * *

The doorbell rang. Sharon fidgeted with her shirt. "Hello." She felt awkward with Bill continuing to be a guest in his own home.

"Thank you for calling," he said as he stepped inside. "I picked up a few things. I hope you don't mind." He carried an armload of groceries into the kitchen and set them on the counter.

"A few?" Sharon replied.

Bill smiled at her and shrugged his shoulders. "Looks like Stewart is still enjoying the tent." He stood for several seconds, looking out the window. "I should go out there."

"He'd like that."

Unfamiliar warmth settled deep within her as she watched Bill peek into the tent, followed by an eruption of excited squeals. She was grateful for the inner calmness, a welcome respite, even if it was temporary. Sharon emptied the groceries, noticing Bill had picked up several of her favorite things. That was just like him, no grand gesture but enough to show that she was on his mind. Fifteen minutes after Bill arrived, Anna and Shane Hayes were at the front door.

"Hello . . . come on in and have a seat." She wanted to say something friendly to Shane but wasn't sure how to, so she offered him a smile. Anna's brother was clearly cut from the same cloth as she was, with the same fair skin and brilliant red hair. Shane returned the smile and seemed at ease, signing a few quick gestures to his sister before sitting on the couch in the living room.

"We left Stacey with Nanna May and Earl so we would have a chance to talk without her interrupting," Anna said. "I hope Stewart won't be too disappointed."

"That's all right. If you'll excuse me for a second, I want to let Bill know you're here."

Sharon returned with glasses of iced tea, Stewart and Bill not far behind her. She pulled out a few baskets of toys for Stewart to play with while the four of them visited. Anna shared what she knew about her brother's work at the university and his interest in Stewart and Stacey's ability to communicate.

Sharon started to thank Shane and caught herself. "I'm sorry," she said, not knowing if she should talk to Shane or Anna.

"Don't worry about it," Anna said. "Shane can read lips fairly well, and if he misses something, he'll ask me to clarify. You can talk to him."

Shane had an easy smile as he gestured from his eyes to Sharon's mouth and made an OK sign with his hand. She appreciated him being so patient with her. Bill smiled at the exchange and nodded his head as Anna explained how to make things easier for everyone. It wasn't long before Sharon and Bill were able to comfortably communicate with Shane. Anna seemed to sense when her brother needed clarity, and their conversation began to flow naturally. They revisited the day Stewart was found, Shane again explaining when he first noticed Stewart needing help.

Bill shook his head. "I can't believe it. I was right there. I probably walked past the shuttle with him on it."

Shane was curious to know how Stewart happened to be at Union Station, one of the many questions that would remain unanswered. The details of their son's disappearance would forever remain a mystery.

Anna spoke for Shane as he signed, "That day at the station, I had several boys with me. He must have slipped in with them."

Small pieces of the puzzle began to come together. Sharon thanked Shane for his part in finding Stewart and apologized for waiting so long to tell him how much she appreciated him. He shook his head and waved a hand; the *don't worry about it* gesture didn't need to be interpreted. Shane signed rapidly, and Anna continued on as his mouthpiece: "Can you tell me how Stewart learned to sign?"

"We didn't know he could; that's just it. I was told by a therapist he wouldn't be able to. Are you sure he was signing?" Sharon asked, wanting to believe he could.

"Maybe we should ask him something now, or do you think he'll resist us, like he did with the therapist?" Bill asked, eager to know if his son had communication skills waiting to be developed.

"Stacey told me a while back that she was showing Stewart how she talks to her uncle with her hands," Anna said, "but I had no idea he understood her. I'm sorry, Sharon, for underestimating him." Anna looked at the floor and drew imaginary lines with her feet.

"No, Anna . . . please don't worry about it. I'm his mother, and I would have thought the same thing. In fact, I attributed several new gestures of his to Stacy's influence, but I never imagined he was signing."

"Well," Anna replied, "Stacey is adamant that your son's signing skills are a product of her skilled tutelage. I'll admit I didn't believe her."

"What if she's right?" Bill asked. "How can we figure this out?"

Sharon asked Stewart a few questions, but he simply smiled and continued playing.

"Is it possible he's only mimicking gestures without knowing what they mean?" Bill asked.

He could, but he clearly told me he needed help and that he was afraid, Shane signed to Anna.

Sharon could feel her pulse quicken.

"How do we get him to repeat the gestures?" Bill asked, tapping both feet on the carpet.

Shane threw his hands in the air, clearly excited.

"What?" his sister said as she signed, surprised by her brother's actions.

"*Help* and *afraid* weren't the only things he signed," Anna said as her brother quickly gestured. "He also signed *I love you.*"

"What?" Sharon gasped and covered her mouth with shaking hands. Instant tears began to stream down her face. "Are you sure—how?"

Bill reached over and took one of her hands, his own reaction visible in his tear-filled eyes. They took a few seconds to absorb the news, both reaching over and touching their son lightly on his arm. He smiled at them but continued playing.

A person unfamiliar with sign language would not have recognized the incomplete signs. Shane demonstrated how *love* is signed, with both hands crossed over the heart, and then proceeded to show them how Stewart expressed it, crossing one hand over his chest and touching his hand from his shoulder to their shoulder. Both Sharon and Bill instantly understood. Stewart had shared that very gesture with them, and at the time, they hadn't realized what he was saying.

Reaching over and running her hand over her son's loose, blond curls, Sharon whispered, "I love you too, son."

When Stewart looked up from his toy, he noticed his mother was crying. He stood up and patted her arm.

"It's okay, honey." Sharon wouldn't try to coerce him to perform the celebrated sign. She knew he'd shared it with both her and Bill and would tell them again that he loved them in his own time.

Anna and Shane cut their visit short, wanting to leave them to adjust to what they had just learned. Sharon and Bill thanked them both and invited them back, promising to answer any questions Shane had. After they left, Bill and Sharon sat and played with Stewart until it was time for dinner, soaking in the wonderful news they'd been given.

"I'm sorry. I forgot all about dinner," Sharon said as she hurried into the kitchen, pulling a pasta dish she had prepared earlier out of the refrigerator and checking the clock on the stove.

Bill and Stewart followed her into the kitchen. It would be another half hour before dinner was ready. Stewart wasn't going to be content with the wait.

"Thank you for bringing this," Sharon said as she pulled the lid off one of Bill's impulse purchases, soft cheese and dipping crackers.

Stewart didn't hesitate to help himself when she put the plate on the table.

"Do you like that?" Bill asked his son, watching every movement he made.

Stewart laughed and put a hand to his mouth and then dropped it down.

"Do you think that's a sign for something?" He looked at Sharon and pulled his phone out of his pocket. A quick search informed them their son knew the sign for *good*.

Bill checked the demonstration on his phone and repeated it back to his son. "It is *good*," he said, dropping his hand from his mouth to his open hand.

Stewart clapped his hands in agreement and returned to the crackers and cheese, keeping a close eye on the plate they were sharing, apparently concerned with supply and demand.

Bill found an app and loaded it onto his phone. "Look, Stewart, you can touch a picture to tell us what you would like." Bill pressed a button for food, and a boy's voice said, *I am hungry.*

Stewart waved his hands back and forth with excitement and reached for the phone.

"Let me show you one more thing before I give it to you. You touch the food picture and then you can choose one of the foods. Here, you try it."

Stewart took the phone and pressed the food button, delighted when it provided him with voice responses. He scrolled through all of the food items, skipping every one until he found a picture of a cookie. *I would like a cookie, I would like a cookie, I would like a cookie,* he played repeatedly.

"Well?" Bill asked, looking at Sharon.

"What?" Wrapped up in watching Stewart's reaction to the prompts, Sharon missed the obvious. "Oh . . . yes . . . you would like a cookie." She pulled a box from the cupboard and handed him an animal cookie.

Stewart clapped and returned to the picture, tapping it again: *I would like a cookie, I would like a cookie.*

"Only one more and then you need to save some room in your tummy for dinner. It's almost ready." Sharon handed him the cookie. "You better show him another group of pictures to select from. I think the cookie button is going to be a favorite."

Bill scrolled through a few more categories with him. "Sharon, look how quick he is with this app. He manipulates it better than the average adult."

"He's certainly better at it than I would be, but that's not saying much." She sat at the table with them and watched Stewart navigate the category options. "Goodness, honey, you can really work that thing." She looked at her husband with wide eyes. "Our son appears to be full of surprises."

Bill grinned at her as if he'd won the lottery.

"What?" She replayed what she just said, wondering if he might have misunderstood her. Of course he was pleased with Stewart's unearthed talent and ability to communicate, but his smile seemed to have originated for an altogether different reason.

"Our son is full of surprises," he agreed, his voice wavering and his eyes on his phone.

CHAPTER 25

Steve finished his lunch and walked down the hall to Bill's office, eager to see if he had any news on his interview. Leaning through the doorway, he looked at Bill with expectation without saying a word.

"I got it," Bill informed him.

Steve grinned and gave him a thumbs up before heading back to his office. They wouldn't discuss it until after work.

When Bill arrived at the apartment, he had a lot on his mind. He needed to give his notice, but before he could do that, he had to talk to Sharon.

"So, then," Steve said before Bill had a chance to sit down, "looks like your online interview was a success. What did you think?"

Bill hesitated before he answered him, not really sure what he thought. "The interview went well, but you know I'm not going to accept the position if Sharon doesn't want to leave DC."

"So, then ask her."

"I'm not sure yet." Bill filled a water bottle and set it on the counter. He was getting restless with the decision he knew needed to be made but became more and more unsettled as he thought about it. "I'll be back in an hour or so. I'm going on a run."

Bill pulled on a pair of sweatpants and a T-shirt, hoping a good run might help him formulate a plan. If he was honest with himself, he was afraid. What if Sharon wanted him to take the job but didn't want to go with him? No way would he leave without her, but if he pressed her into a decision, he risked damaging any progress made since his return from Beijing. For the first time since he'd been back, Sharon called Stewart *our son*. He'd taken a few steps forward, but he was a long way from where he should be. Reconnecting with his son had come easily, but gaining Sharon's trust had not. He knew she continued to harbor unasked questions.

Can you blame her? His heart pumped faster as he pushed himself up the jogging path. Bill welcomed the pain in his legs, the lactic acid burning as it spread across his thighs. It had been a month since his return, and in that time, he had come to realize how serious Sharon's anxiety had been over his neglect of her and Stewart. Within the last year, she parked the car and cancelled the insurance; disconnected the phone line and her cell phone; took a job pressing uniforms; and with the money he provided every month, she'd saved nearly every cent beyond the bare minimum, just in case he one day abandoned her completely.

Bill felt his face getting hot as he ran along the path in Rock Creek Park. He'd told Sharon how sorry he was and tried to show her and Stewart he loved them both, but because of his own shame, he had left their future together in her hands alone. *What am I doing?*

He left the park and ran back to the apartment. *Why would I ever let her think I wasn't desperate to have her back?*

You don't deserve her, the unwelcome, inner voice needled him. *Haven't you done enough damage already?*

Trying to push the negative thoughts away, Bill prayed for strength and committed himself to showing his wife what she and Stewart truly meant to him. He pulled his phone out of his pocket and dialed Sharon's number without really knowing what he was going to say.

She answered on the first ring. "Hello?"

"Hi . . . Sharon." Bill tried to catch his breath.

"Bill, are you all right? Where are you?"

"I'm fine," he replied after realizing he should have waited a few minutes to call her. "I was . . . on a run . . . and I really . . . wanted to call you." He bent over, sucked in a deep breath and rested a hand on his twitching thigh.

"Is everything okay? Did you hit your head again?" She sounded worried.

"No . . . I'm fine . . . just fine." He checked the time; it was only seven thirty. "Can I come by tonight for a few minutes?"

"Sure."

The caution and concern in her response was understandable. "I'll be there in twenty minutes." He hung up the phone and sprinted back to the apartment.

Steve looked up from his computer as Bill burst through the door. "Someone's in a bit of a hurry. Where's the fire?"

"I'm headed over to the house," Bill said, trying to suck in enough air to fill his empty lungs.

"I hope you're planning to shower first; I can smell you from here." Steve kept his attention on the screen in front of him.

"Yes, Mother, I'll even wash behind my ears."

"There's a good lad."

Bill took a quick shower, towel-dried his hair, and threw on jeans and a T-shirt. Grabbing his wallet and car keys, he took a few deep breaths and headed for the door.

"Take those with you," Steve said.

"What?" Bill asked impatiently.

"Those flowers on the counter." Steve nodded toward the kitchen. A dozen roses sat in a vase on the counter with a blank note card.

"Where did these come from?" Bill asked.

"Usually you get flowers from a florist, genius . . . Yes, I bought them and obviously I didn't buy them for you. I picked them up so you could give them to Sharon. I thought it likely you would be going there tonight, and on your way, you'd say to yourself, *man, I should have bought her flowers.* I told you I had your back. By the way, they cost sixty quid. You owe me."

Bill was grateful and surprised. "How did you know I'd need them?"

"You rarely go for a run unless you're getting ready to do something quite important. However, if you were going to talk to Dwayne, I would have advised skipping the flowers. Good luck, I'll be praying for you mate. Now get out of here."

Bill set the flowers carefully on the passenger seat, next to the box from the post office he'd picked up the day he returned from Beijing. He tried to think of what he would say to Sharon, but nothing seemed right.

"Please help me, Lord . . . Please help me," he prayed as he parked the car and grabbed the blank card out of the flowers and wrote, *Sharon, I love you—Bill.*

Six Houses Down

* * *

Sharon heard the light tap on the front door. "Hello—oh—what's this?"

Bill handed her the vase of beautiful red roses. "The truth, Steve picked these up. I hope you like them, but I should have been the one who bought them."

"I'm a little confused. Why did Steve buy me flowers?" she asked as she walked into the kitchen and placed the flowers on the counter.

"He was trying to help me out." Bill confessed as he followed her into the kitchen and took a seat at the table. "Is Stewart asleep already?"

"Yes, he went to bed early tonight. Shane had him and Stacey at the university for a couple hours this afternoon, so he was extra tired. Why did Steve buy these?" She straightened a few of the buds and reached for the card: *I love you—Bill.* "These are from you?" Her expression was full of questions.

"I didn't come here tonight to bring you flowers, Sharon. I came to ask you something." He ran his hands nervously down the sides of his legs and stood to his feet. "First of all, I want to tell you again that I'm so sorry for leaving you and Stewart alone. I was a coward . . . a selfish coward." He tried to look her in the eye, but her gaze shifted from her hands to the floor.

"It's nice to have you back, Bill. I hope you can stay this time," she replied, still guarded and nervous.

"That's just it. I haven't really been back, Sharon. I want you back, too." His throat tightened as his palms began to sweat. He noticed she was starting to panic, running a hand through the hair at the back of her neck. "I'm considering a move to Pullman, Washington, but I won't move there without you and Stewart. I will never leave you alone again. Please, come with me." He waited for a few seconds and repeated his plea, taking a small step closer. "Please, Sharon, come with me."

She looked confused. "Pullman?"

"Yes, I've been offered a job in Pullman, Washington, as in Washington state. But I won't even consider it unless you and Stewart go with me. I know it's a huge change, but it could be the fresh start we need. I love you so much . . . I'm sorry I ever took that promotion and left you and Stewart alone, and I'm begging you to forgive me and come with me . . . together, as a family. Before you say anything, there's something I have to show you." Bill stepped away and turned toward the front door. "I'll be right back."

He had her full attention now. Tears began to stream down her face, not knowing if she could give him the answer he wanted to hear. She wanted to go—to trust him and love him, but he had been able to live without her once before. It was too big of a chance to take. She could hear Bill returning to the kitchen as she dried her face with her sleeve.

"These are for you," he said, setting a cardboard box on the counter.

Sharon looked into the box, her jaw dropping open in surprise. "Bill, there's close to fifty letters in here. What are these?" She flipped through them, seeing her name but not their address on the mailed envelopes, postmarked by a variety of countries. "Why didn't you send them here?"

"I couldn't. None of them said what you needed to hear . . . that I was coming home to stay. I got the post office box and then waited for the right time to tell you they were there. Now seems like the right time, but I should have told you months ago." He reached for her, running a hand down the side of her arm. "Please, Sharon, I never stopped thinking about you, not even for a day. Can you forgive me? I've said a lot tonight, and I'll understand if you need some time before you can tell me what you're thinking, but I need you with me—every day—and I need you to need me like I need you." Bill nervously chewed his lower lip and gently pulled her toward him.

Sharon pulled back but not away from his hand on her arm. "What about the woman you took with you to Brazil? Where does she fit in all this?" She had to know and wouldn't allow herself to give in to him until he admitted to cheating on her.

"Sharon, I wasn't and never have been with another woman. What made you think I had?" He was clearly pained by her accusation.

"I called you a few days after you asked me to go with you to Brazil. I said some things I regretted and wanted to apologize. Bill, I would have given anything to see you, even if only for a few days, but when I called, a woman answered the phone and said you two were flying together to Sao Paulo and you weren't available." She'd finally said it. The affair was out in the open now, and she couldn't look him in the eye.

"No way!" Bill threw his head back and ran his hands through his hair. "No wonder you couldn't stand the sight of me. Sharon, please, you have to believe me!" He took a step away from her and turned in a circle, his hands laced together on the back of his neck. "I was bumped up to first class, and this woman sitting next to me, already hitting the free booze, needed her appeal validated, but I shut her down."

"Was she beautiful?"

"Beautiful?" Bill took a step toward her and looked directly in her eyes. "I'll admit she was attractive, but I was in no way interested."

"I believe you." She looked at his hand on the counter. "Do you remember her name?" She wouldn't hold it against him if he did, but if she was really going to believe him and let this go, she didn't want to obsess over possible names for the in-flight seductress.

"Her name?" He stared blankly at the ceiling. "I don't know . . . Maybe something like placenta. That's probably not it."

"Probably not."

Bill shook his head. "She made some lewd comment about things being unbuttoned. I'm pretty sure I ticked her off, so I excused myself and went to the restroom."

There it was, exactly what she needed to hear. "That's what she told me . . . You had a few things you needed to button up!"

"I'm such an idiot." His eyes brightened as if realizing something for the first time. "That's why she was so dang smug when I sat down! Sharon, I'm so sorry. What was I thinking? If I'd only taken my phone with me."

Bill took her hand in his and traced the back of it with his thumb.

"When I was in Mumbai, I finally cracked and couldn't stand to be away from you any longer, so I flew home to see you and Stewart on Christmas Eve, but you were gone. I made some assumptions myself. I'm afraid I allowed a few misunderstandings to wreak havoc on us. I'm so sorry, Sharon."

"Wait—what?" Sharon couldn't speak.

207

Bill looked at her with a sudden panicked expression. "I saw the uniforms by the front door and thought—"

Shaking her head, she interrupted him. "You were here?"

"Yes, on Christmas Eve. I left a present for you and Stewart in the house before going back to India. When you didn't return my calls, I nearly gave up."

"Bill, I thought . . . you didn't want . . ." Overwhelmed and speechless, Sharon realized how close she'd come to ending her marriage over assumptions. There wasn't another woman, and Bill had come home after all. The gifts, the shawl, it was from him. Even worse, her broken cell phone left him thinking she didn't care about him enough to return his call. She pulled her hand out of his and grabbed his shoulders. With her face buried in his chest, she sobbed uncontrollably. No longer hindered by fear, all of her protective measures peeled away, she was free to love him.

Bill kissed the top of her head and held her close, stroking his hand through her hair and down her back. "I love you, Sharon . . . I'm so sorry . . . I love you so much," he whispered over and over again until she stopped shaking.

"I'm sorry, too."

He smiling at her tear-stained face and brushed his thumb across her cheek. "I love you," he whispered again.

She could tell he was hurting and struggling to maintain his composure. Running her fingertips over his lips, she considered what she had wanted to do since he returned home but wouldn't allow herself to do it. "I can't reach your lips," she said timidly, inviting him to take back what belonged to him.

He softly caressed her lips with his, kissing her gently, pulling her closer to him, and wrapping an arm around her. With her head cradled in his hand, he kissed her again before burying his face in her hair. Sharon rested her hands on the back of his neck and stepped back to admire her husband. He looked as if he were in pain. "I forgive you. I love you, and I do need you. I'm sorry I thought you had someone else." She kissed his cheek, wet with salty tears. "It doesn't matter to me where we live as long as we're all together." She wrapped her arms tightly around his neck as if she would never let go.

Bill's chest heaved a few times as if he suddenly couldn't breathe.

"Bill?" Sharon lurched back.

He pulled her tight against his chest and sobbed into her hair, thanking her repeatedly. "I don't deserve you."

Sharon leaned back and traced the worried lines on her husband's face with fingertips that had longed to touch him since his return. He smiled at her—a pained smile that continued to plead for her forgiveness. "I'm so glad you're home, Bill," she said softly as she brushed his face with her hands.

"This is my home," he said, pulling her back to his chest. "You and Stewart are my home."

Sharon could feel anxiety leaving her husband's body as he held her close, the muscles in his arms quivering and his heart pumping enough blood to sustain a battlefield. All of the restrictions Sharon had placed on her love for him were now gone, weapons lowered and both emerging as victors. And, to the victor go the spoils. Her husband no longer needed alternate accommodations.

CHAPTER 26

"So, looks like you no longer need a place to lodge," Steve said as he leaned into Bill's office Monday morning. "Cracking weekend?"

Bill gave him a thumbs-up without saying a word.

"Are we going to go in and have a conversation with Dwayne now?" Steve asked, closing the door behind him. "Or, does Sharon need some time to consider the move?"

"Yes, we are going to talk to Dwayne. He's not going to like us much after this morning. I was going to give him a month. What do you think?" Bill asked.

"A month is ample. What did Sharon say about Pullman?" Steve pulled one of the office chairs closer to Bill's desk and sat down.

"It took a minute for her to process what I was really asking. Let's say she warmed up to the idea."

"Warmed up?" Steve asked with raised eyebrows.

"Anyways," Bill continued, "we talked about it over the weekend. She was a little worried about Stewart traveling and missing her friends but was sure she wanted to go. Steve . . . I need to thank you." Bill felt awkward, not wanting to expose his already raw emotions.

"We're good, mate; say no more." Steve reached over and straightened a chair across from Bill's desk that was already straight. "What about Anna and Stacey?"

"Why the interest?" Bill asked with a knowing grin.

"Don't hassle me, duffer. If it wasn't for those flowers I picked up, you'd still be at my apartment."

Bill crossed his arms and laughed. "I told her you bought them. She didn't care about the flowers." Feeling someone's eyes on him, Bill looked through the glass of his closed door and could see Dwayne staring at them from the windowed wall in his office.

"There are some things we still need to figure out, but Sharon and Stewart are coming with me to Washington. I'll have to tell you about Anna later. I can see your cousin knows we're up to something. It's time to let him have it."

Bill and Steve walked into Dwayne's office, ready to give him one month to replace the both of them, knowing he'd be none too happy about it.

"I see you two have a lot of time to shoot the breeze today," Dwayne said as he shifted in his leather office chair. "You are aware we have a design deadline in a couple weeks, right?"

"It'll get done," Bill said, "but there's something we need to discuss."

Steve and Bill had worked for Davis Engineering since they graduated from college ten years ago, and their boss, Steve's distant cousin, was used to them teaming up on him to ask for a raise or to work on a project together. Dwayne had been pleased with himself when he was finally able to separate them and send Bill abroad, bringing in contract after contract.

"So, is this best-friends-asking-for-a-raise day?" Dwayne grumped, shifting again and rolling himself closer to his mahogany desk so he could rest an elbow.

"That's not the half of it," Steve replied. "You have us for one more month. Enough time to complete the designs we are currently working on . . . and then we're done here."

Dwayne sat up in his chair. "What do you mean *done*?" he asked, pounding his hands on the desk. "Steve, you spoiled Brit, you have this job because you're family, and Bill, what the heck? I just promoted you a year ago and gave you a sweet raise. Are you really going to let your Brit buddy here call the shots? Isn't it about time for you to buck up?" Dwayne jumped up out of his chair, clearly fighting to control his temper. "Okay, what do you need to stay? You know you got me up against a wall here. I can't lose one of you, let alone both, and, furthermore, I don't appreciate this gang-up tactic." Dwayne sat down and grabbed a pen, ready to negotiate and record his hasty promises.

"There won't be any negotiations, Dwayne . . . One month and we're done. We've already accepted jobs with another firm," Bill said, feeling an uncommon strength in his resolve.

"That's not going to happen! I'll pay you ten percent more than anything they've offered. You want better benefits? Since you're squeezing me where it hurts, I'll add another few weeks of paid vacation to your contract. What's it going to take to keep you?" Dwayne tried to look burdened and beaten down, even friendly, but it wasn't working. "Steve, did you go over this with your father?"

"I make my own decisions," Steve replied coldly.

Their angry boss waved them out of his office without another word.

* * *

A few minutes before lunch, Dwayne pulled out Bill's expense account and looked it over. There wasn't a reason to question the charges, but if he could find anything out of place, he might hold it over Bill's head to keep him around. As everyone left for lunch, except the receptionist, it became abundantly clear that Bill had spent far less than his account allotted. A closer look revealed he'd chosen to fly coach rather than first class, something he didn't even do, and preferred less expensive meals when he dined alone. Bill spent a third less than had been budgeted for him, saving the company close to twenty thousand dollars.

CRASH! Dwayne kicked a metal trashcan, sending it flying through the air into one of the large picture windows in his office, littering the hallway with shattered glass. He grabbed the hair on his head with both fists, instantly regretting the ill-placed punt.

The receptionist ran through his door. "Is everything all right, Mr. Davis?"

"No . . . everything is not all right. My GQ cousin and his sidekick BFF are trying to ruin my company!" He scowled at the young woman. "Don't just stand there; call a glass company and get them over here to clean this mess up!" Slamming his chair into his desk, he stomped out, leaving the receptionist to take care of the broken window.

* * *

Steve took another bite of his sandwich before bringing Anna up again. "You were going to tell me about Anna and Stacey."

"I was?" Bill replied, annoying him on purpose.

"Come on, mate; stop messing with me. We only have ten minutes until we have to get back to work." Steve sat silent, ready to listen.

"Anna and Stacey . . . they aren't going to be in DC much longer—or not at the Clarks' at least. I'm not sure what their plans are once her brother Shane is done with his doctorate."

Steve asked him a few more questions he couldn't answer. Bill filled him in on what he knew about Stacey's father or lack thereof.

"As far as I know, Stacy's father wasn't interested in being a dad. I think he used Anna's deaf brother as an excuse, but that can't be all there is to it since her brother is more than able to take care of himself. Sharon mentioned that Stacey has a heart defect, but apparently, it's not a serious problem. She talked to Anna about it, and Anna said the only person affected by it is the uninformed radiologist, flipping the film over and thinking he has it backwards. Anna did say it could have been a lot worse and that she didn't really know what to expect until Stacey was born. She doesn't have a lot to say about Stacey's father, except the fact that he was out of the picture a few weeks after finding out about the heart defect. I don't know anything else about him. Sounds like a real jerk."

Steve set his sandwich down. "I'm interested in asking Anna out, but I'm afraid she'll think I'm trying to take advantage of her. She said as much, informing me that she was in no way the *desperate and single* type. She has her guard up, doesn't she?"

"She does," Bill replied. "Can you blame her?"

"Now I'm leaving in a month. I've dated women for fourteen years, having little in common with any of them, and when I find one to imprint on . . . like you said, she won't have anything to do with me. I need to try and change her mind straight away," Steve said, gathering his wrappers and empty cup.

They walked the short block back to the office, Bill silently trying to brainstorm a chance meeting with the temperamental redhead and her precocious mini-me.

"Why don't you sell your car?" Bill asked.

"What's wrong with my car?"

"She probably doesn't like it."

"You're off your rocker. Why wouldn't she like it?"

"It's too . . . egotistical for her. It's probably one of the reasons she thought you had ten girlfriends waiting at your beck and call. I know it's not an over-the-top expensive car, but she probably sees *ladies' man* written all over it. Besides, you're not going to drive it to Washington, are you?" Bill passed the elevator when they reached the office and headed for the stairs.

"No, I was going to sell it in a few weeks, but if you think I need to get rid of it for Anna's sake, I'd sell it in a tick." Steve fell in behind Bill on the stairs.

When they stepped through the door into the hallway, they were surprised to find a glass company fixing a missing window. The receptionist waved them over to her desk, clearly eager to fill them in.

"Steve, I think Dwayne is really mad at you guys, so I'd walk softly if I were you." She looked at them both with a tight-lipped smile.

Dwayne spent the next few weeks pleading and promising until he finally accepted the fact that they were both determined to leave. He wasn't interested in burning any bridges, hoping they might consider returning someday, so he had the receptionist plan a lavish farewell party for their last day.

CHAPTER 27

"We're getting our own house," Stacey announced as she skipped into the kitchen.

Sharon wondered if Stacey and her mother were actually moving or if the news that they were leaving had influenced an imaginary move of her own. "That's exciting. Do you know if you're staying in DC?"

"Yep . . . we're movin' across the street from Nanna May and Earl's house. Mom saved tons of money so we can get our own house, but we're not going to stay there forever 'cause it's still another guy's house; we only pay to stay there."

I would like a cookie, Stewart's new tablet informed his mother as he stepped into the kitchen.

"You need to pick something else, honey; you've already had a cookie."

I would like some juice, the app sounded, followed by, *I would like a cookie.*

"Stewart," his mother warned.

He laughed and slid through the pictures. *I am funny.*

"Yes, son," she said, touching the tip of his nose, "you are funny."

"That's a super cool thing, Stewart. Can I see how it works?" Stacey leaned into him and pointed to the tablet.

Sharon watched Stewart show his friend how to navigate the pictures. Her son was helping Stacey. Sharon marveled at the realization that this little girl had not dropped into their life by accident. She was a gift, sent in a spicy little package when God knew she and Stewart needed her the most.

"Is everything okay, Mrs. Webster?" Stacey asked.

"Yes, sweetie, everything is okay, but we sure are going to miss you when we leave. You're a very special little girl."

"Thank you, but I'm not really little anymore; I'm almost seven," she replied. "And Mom said we have one more week before we have to say goodbye, so we shouldn't be sad yet."

I am sad, Stewart's tablet informed them.

Stacey and Sharon both looked at him, surprised to have him join the conversation.

"Stewart . . . are you really sad?" Stacey asked him.

Sharon watched the interaction between her son and his friend, shocked that he understood what it meant to be sad, something she had once been told he was incapable of comprehending. Stewart blankly stared out the window.

Sharon rubbed her hand on his arm. "Honey, it's all right to be sad. We'll miss our friends, but you can send pictures to Stacey on the phone."

Stewart smiled and turned his attention to the list of responses on his tablet.

"You know, Stacey, I need to thank you for showing Stewart sign language. The signs you've taught him have helped us in a lot of ways."

"You're welcome, Mrs. Webster, but it's no big deal. It's just talking."

Just talking, Sharon thought, *if she only knew.* "Stewart, honey, do you want to tell Stacey thank you for being your friend?"

Stewart smiled and put a hand to his mouth, then lifted it up and away. He looked briefly at Stacey and then back out the window.

"You're welcome, Stewart," Stacey replied with a proud smile.

Apparently, it was a bigger deal than Stacey wanted to admit. Sharon's throat tightened as she witnessed her son *just talking* with his friend. Her son was there, deep inside a mind that struggled to make sense of everything, and was finally free to speak.

* * *

The apple trees were in full bloom, perfuming the air with a light, sweet scent. Thousands of pink petals swirled around their feet as Bill, Sharon, and Stewart took their time strolling along the pathway toward the Washington Monument. Sharon soaked in the pleasure of the moment, watching Stewart run ahead of them and flap his arms in his own organic choreography, the dance of the falling blossoms. Only months earlier, she would have thought this day impossible. She had been consumed with a foreboding sense of failure, certain that life had afforded her several brief, happy years only to taunt her with cruel fate, but she was wrong. Now, new memories were being made—the three of them on a perfect day.

Bill wrapped a hand around her shoulder and studied her for a moment. "What are you busy thinking and not saying?"

With a content grin, she wove her arm tight around his waist. "Just happy." Peace had taken up residency in her soul. "Not just happy . . . blessed . . . I feel blessed," she added.

"It's nice to hear you say that. We are blessed, aren't we? This feels so good," he said, planting a kiss on the top of her ear.

Sharon faced him. "You're something good."

"You only said that because you had to—because I said it first."

"What? How could you say that?" She poked his side.

Bill pulled her to a stop and kissed her. "Can we get together like this every day?" he teased.

"I'll check my schedule," she replied with a sly grin.

"Your schedule . . . I'll clear your schedule," he threatened, running fingers over her ribs.

"Stop—it's clear . . .my schedule is all clear!" she promised, laughing and soaking in the attention.

Stewart stopped a few steps ahead of them and waited to cross Independence Ave. Sharon tried to get her son to notice the monument up ahead, but something down the road captured his attention.

"What is it, Stewart?" she asked, looking down the busy sidewalk toward the Smithsonian museums. She didn't see anything out of the ordinary.

"Is there something down there you want to see, son?" his father asked.

"Bu, bu, bu," he said, pointing down the sidewalk.

Sharon instantly understood, "He wants to see the bugs . . . You want to see the bugs, don't you, honey?"

Bill appeared to be in disbelief. "Of course, son, we can go see the bugs." He looked at Sharon. "How did you know what he wanted, and how long has he been doing that?"

She told Bill about their trip to the Natural History Museum with Anna and Stacey, but at the time, she thought he was merely repeating the sound. Now there was no longer any doubt; Stewart was trying to talk.

After wading through the crowded entry, the three of them took the stairs to the second level, walking quickly past thousands of creeping things of all colors, shapes, and sizes. Stewart seemed to know exactly where he was going, not slowing down until he found a line of children waiting to hold an insect that looked like a stick. A few kids stared at him as he flapped his hands with anticipation, anxious for it to be his turn. The young girl in front of him lost her nerve and opted to defer her interaction with the insect.

Stewart held on to his wrist to still his outstretched hand as the man placed the long bug on his palm. The living stick slowly walked up his arm until Stewart gently moved it back to his palm.

Bill watched him closely and whispered, "Sharon, look. He's standing perfectly still . . . and focused on that insect . . . amazing."

"Yes, it is," she agreed.

Stewart reached over to switch the moving stick to his other hand.

Bill stepped forward, his hands cupped beneath the exchange. "Careful, son."

Sharon was having as much fun watching Bill's reaction to Stewart as she was with Stewart's captivated interest in the bug.

"Sharon . . . look at him. Can you believe this?" Bill said, not taking his eyes off his son.

The next child in line asked if she could hold it, clearly impatient for it to be her turn. Stewart reluctantly gave the bug back to the museum attendant and watched intently as it was placed on the older girl's hand. The three of them spent the next hour looking through the collections of beetles and butterflies before Stewart shocked them both again.

"Bug . . . bug-g-g-g . . . bug."

Bill and Sharon both froze as if they were imagining things. People passed around them, unaware of the miraculous event unfolding.

"He said it . . . he said *bug!*" Sharon's eyes were huge as she tried to maintain her composure. "Yes, honey, you're right. That is a bug."

"Actually, it is a Pheropsophus Verticalis, belonging to the phylum Arthropoda," a middle-aged man said, holding a magnifying glass and an expensive camera.

"I think I'm coming down with something," Bill announced as he coughed on the man's shoulder. "You might want to keep your distance."

The man instantly stepped backward with a horrified look on his face, pulled a bottle of hand sanitizer out of the pocket on his safari shorts, and disappeared into the crowd.

"What is this, Stewart?" Bill asked, pointing to a large beetle in a glass case.

"Bug," he said as he laughed and pointed, "Da . . . bug."

Two words now—another surprise. Sharon looked at Bill, trying to figure out what else their son might be saying.

She pressed Stewart carefully, "What's *da*, honey?"

Stewart looked at her as if he was unsure of her question and then patted his father on the arm. "Da."

Bill was visibly affected, "Yes, son, I'm Da . . . your *Daddy*," he said, touching him on the shoulder.

Sharon was tempted to be envious of their connection, but her love for the both of them vetoed any potential jealousy. Stewart didn't have any other words for them that day, no matter how hard they subtly tried to coerce him into speaking.

On the way home, they picked up a few things at the grocery store. Bill had declared that he and Stewart were in charge of dinner, and Sharon would get to relax while they took care of everything. She reluctantly agreed, trying several times to weasel her way into the kitchen, but Bill shuttled her back into the living room, telling her she would spoil the surprise if she didn't stay there.

"Now, do not come into the kitchen until I say, *Come on in, Mom*—okay? No matter what I say. Dinner's ready . . . Mom, let's eat . . . those are not the key words." Bill looked at her as if waiting for a promise of compliance.

"I got it . . . *Come on in, Mom*. What are you up to?"

"You'll see," he said as if something amazing was about to happen.

"That must be some dinner you two are making in there."

"Don't try to get any secret information out of me. Just remember the key words." Bill walked backward into the kitchen, pointing a you'd-better-mind finger at her.

Instant macaroni and cheese, peas, and French bread sat on the table. Everything was ready.

Bill whispered to Stewart, "We should call Mom so we can eat."

Stewart looked at him and appeared to understand what his father was saying to him.

"Dinner's ready, Mom," Bill called out.

Sharon sat on the couch, confused, but obediently waiting for the *key words*.

"Mom's not coming, Stewart. Do you want to call her?"

Stewart started to walk toward the living room, but his father gently stopped him. "I'll call her again. Mom, let's eat," he said, a little louder this time.

Stewart looked at him as if he wondered why his mother wasn't coming, looked toward the living room, then back at his father.

"Do you want to call Mom? Maybe she will hear you," Bill said quietly.

Stewart stood staring at his father for a second and then yelled, "Muh . . . muuuuuh."

A smile consumed Bill's face. "Come on in, Mom."

"Muuuuh," Stewart called out again.

Sharon walked into the kitchen with tear-filled eyes. "Here I am." Wiping her hand across her cheek, she joined them at the table and reached for Bill's hand. "Thank you," she said, another tear sliding down the side of her nose.

Macaroni and cheese had never tasted so good. Sharon took another bite of undercooked noodles and lumpy cheese. Bill smiled at her, an unspoken conversation of gratitude traveling between them.

Stewart, apparently hungry for attention, poked his father in the arm.

Bill poked him back. "You'd better eat now, son, or we're going to get in trouble with Mom."

Stewart smiled at her and started to giggle, which proved to be contagious. Without warning, Stewart landed a hard slap on the middle of Bill's chest, startling both of them but mostly Bill.

"Hey now," his father said, sending a knuckle into his young son's arm, hard enough for him to feel it but not so much that it would hurt him.

"Muuuh," Stewart said as he grabbed his arm, turned to his father, and began giggling again, not ready for the power exchange to end.

"Listen, boy," his father teased, "if you're going to poke me, I'm going to poke you back." Bill tickled his son's armpit.

Stewart screamed with delight and grabbed his armpit to shield it from further attack.

A memory was sparked as Sharon tried to persuade the two men in her life to calm down: Stewart holding his arm after Stacey had delivered the "slap of fairness." He was tattling on Stacey. He had yelled for her then; she had been *Muh* for months.

CHAPTER 28

"I sold my car," Steve announced, leaning into Bill's office. "They're picking it up around noon."

"That was quick. I hope you didn't give it away."

Steve listed his car online that morning, and it had sold within a few hours. Bill felt a twinge of guilt since a hastily spoken opinion had influenced the sale of Steve's only transportation. Steve had always been impulsive, a personality trait that paid off on occasion but cost him on others.

"No, I got a fair price, and you were right. I wouldn't bring it with me to Washington," he said half-heartedly.

Bill noticed Steve wasn't his usual self. "What is it? You're not thinking about your car, are you?" Bill pointed at an empty chair.

Steve stepped the rest of the way into Bill's office and shut the door before taking a seat across from him. "I'm a bit unsettled." He nervously tapped his fingertips together. "I'm worried that I've talked you into something I'm beginning to talk myself out of. Things are a bit off." Steve looked out the office window then turned to face him.

"Are you having second thoughts about moving?" Bill asked, surprised but not angry.

"I don't know. Can't quite put my finger on it. I was so sure of everything a month ago, and now I can't say I'm certain of anything. Sorry to be wonky, but I wanted to tell you, even if I couldn't explain myself." Steve put a hand on the desk as if he had something else to say, but he seemed to be at a loss. He drummed his fingers a few times and then stood up to leave.

"Hey, bud, don't worry about it. You're so used to being the man with the answers. Maybe you need to trust God on this one," Bill said. "You know, give God a chance to clear things up before you forge on with your own plan."

A smile spread across Steve's face. "Thanks, Pastor Bill."

"Hey, can Pastor Bill give you a ride home? You are a person in need," he offered.

"I am that. Sure, I'll take a ride home. If something comes up, though, I can hire a cab," Steve trudged back to his office.

Bill scanned the calendar on his desk. In two weeks, he'd be leaving DC and starting a new job on the other side of the United States, along with his family. However, it was far more than a new job; it was a fresh start. Steve had influenced him to apply for the job in Pullman, but it had been his own decision to go through with it. He was surprised when Sharon agreed to such a drastic change with little apprehension. The process would bring its challenges, but he felt as if he was finally traveling in the right direction.

* * *

The cell phone buzzed in Bill's jacket pocket as he and Steve walked through the parking lot to his car.

"Hello . . . no, I don't want you to show the house until we've moved out, like we talked about . . . I don't care if they have cash . . . yep, thanks."

"Sounds as if someone wants to buy your house," Steve said as he slid into the passenger seat. "That was quick."

"I listed our place with a realtor, but he didn't think I meant it when I said I wanted him to wait to show it until we were gone. Someone was probably waving cash in his face, so he figured it was worth a try."

Steve was unusually quiet, watching the traffic flow by without saying much.

"We're going to barbeque tonight. Why don't you come over for dinner?" Bill offered.

Steve ran his hand through his hair. "I don't know . . . thanks for asking. Maybe another time."

"Come on, bud, you'll be glad you did. What are your dinner plans? You don't have any, do you?" Bill interrogated him until he gave in and agreed to come over.

"I'm warning you; I'm not feeling like the life of the party, Bill. You're going to wish you had taken me home."

"It's only a burger. Besides, Sharon and Stewart won't hold it against you if you're not Mr. Funny this time." Bill turned toward the house.

"I didn't say I wasn't going to be Mr. Funny. There are some things I can't help," he replied with a weak grin.

"There's the ever-humble Steve, just a little slow in his game," Bill replied.

* * *

Opening the front door, Bill announced that they had company. They walked past the kids playing in the living room.

"Sharon, I hope it's okay I brought a stray home for dinner."

"Hi, Steve," Stacey's pixie-like voice greeted him louder than necessary. "Me and Stewart are looking at pictures."

"Sounds fun, luv," he whispered.

Anna sat at the yellow kitchen table with a deer-in-the-headlights look on her face.

"The more, the merrier," Sharon replied.

"Hi, Anna, how are you?" Bill asked as Steve walked in behind him.

"Good . . . I'm good, Bill," she replied, a nervous, forced smile on her face.

"Surprise," Steve blurted out. "Lucky you, luv. Guess who you get to have dinner with tonight?" He then attempted to lose his accent: "Big Steve is in the house."

Sharon reprimanded him with a shame-on-you slap on the shoulder and then gave him a hug. "I'm glad you're *in the house*, Steve, but you'd better behave yourself."

"I knew you were going to stifle my creativity. I promise to be a gentleman for the remainder of the evening." He turned to Anna and presented himself as if he were the most dignified English gent alive. "It is a pleasure to see you again, Anna. We parted too quickly when last we met, affording us far too little time to properly acquaint ourselves with one another."

Anna rolled her eyes. "Shut up, pride and prejudice," she shot back, trying to appear unaffected.

"If I kissed you now, luv, would it be too soon?" Steve teased, covering his heart with his hands.

"Is he a *registered* sex offender?" Anna asked Sharon, earning her a blast of laughter from both men.

"Come on, Steve, you'd better come outside and help me with the barbeque before Anna has you arrested for harassment," Bill warned as he carried a tray of burgers and hot dogs out the back door.

"I suppose I'd better," he said, as if in deep remorse. He turned to Anna as he stepped out the door. "Begging your forgiveness, ma'am."

Anna rolled her eyes again but couldn't hide the grin on her face or the fact that she didn't mind the attention.

"Not feeling like the life of the party, huh?" Bill asked quietly as he opened the grill.

"I couldn't help myself. You think I was a bit over the top?"

"When have you ever *not* been over the top? It's good to see you're back to your old self again and all, but remember what I said about Anna . . . Don't make sport of her," he replied, trying to sound as British as possible.

"Got it, Dad . . . I'm duly warned. Don't worry. I'm not interested in attention. I'm interested in Anna."

"For two weeks?" Bill asked.

Two kids popped out the door, and Stacey asked if the food was almost ready because she was starving. Sharon and Anna followed behind them with two chairs from the table. Steve grabbed both chairs so they could manage the door and set them next to the lawn chairs on the edge of the grass. Hot dogs in hand, the kids seemed content while the four adults ate their burgers and visited.

"We get hot dogs, Stewart, but the grown-ups are eating hamburgers, but they're not really made out of ham, so that doesn't make any sense," Stacey informed him. "My mom doesn't usually let me eat hot dogs, though."

Anna had just taken a bite of her burger and waved her arm at her daughter, trying to quell whatever she was about to say, but Stacey failed to notice her mother's attempt to silence her.

"My mom says hot dogs are made out of toots and snouts. You know what toots are, Stewart? . . . They're butts."

Anna choked on the bite in her mouth while the men found the information chuckle-worthy. Embarrassed by the desperate need to cough, Anna tapped her chest a few times and stood up to go back into the house.

"Anna, are you all right?" Sharon asked.

She shook her head and made an OK sign as she stepped into the kitchen. Once inside, she tried to cough the food out of her throat, but it wouldn't budge.

"Steve," Sharon said, handing him Anna's water, "will you see if she needs a drink?"

Steve stepped through the door. "Are you in need of this?" he asked.

She grabbed the kitchen counter as panic began to set in—she couldn't breathe.

"Anna!" Steve watched her for one more second before whipping her back against his chest and forcing his clenched fist into her diaphragm.

A chunk of soggy food landed on the floor a few feet in front of her. She sputtered for a few seconds, gasped for air, and then sucked in a few deep breaths.

"Better?" he asked as he turned her toward him, holding on to her arm. He handed her the glass of water from the counter with his free hand.

She took a few small swallows. Steve could tell she was extremely embarrassed.

"I knew I'd get my arms around you sooner or later," he said, trying to ease her tension.

She gave him a sideways glance and an uncomfortable grin. "I thought you were going to give yourself credit for taking my breath away," she said, the tone in her voice revealing she was now more friend than foe.

Steve didn't miss the rosy blush making its way across her cheek. "Okay, if you insist, I'll take credit for that as well," he said, shrugging his shoulders and hoping to pull her thoughts away from any embarrassment. "Are you ready to go back outside?"

"Yes . . . I . . . need to . . . I want to . . . " Anna struggled to put together what she wanted to say.

"*Thank you for saving my life, Steve.* Is that what you wanted to say?" he asked with a sly smile.

She shook her head. "You're such a humble guy, aren't you?"

He threw his hands in the air. "How am I to answer that question? If I say no, I'm rather insensitive, and if I say yes, then I've proven I'm not humble at all. Do you see the predicament you've put me in? Now then, what were you saying about me saving your life?" He bent his knees and leaned against the counter next to her, putting himself at her eye level and making it more difficult for her to avoid looking at him.

"Thank you, Steve. It's very nice to be able to breathe again. I owe you one."

"How about tomorrow night then?" he asked.

"What are you talking about? And would you stand up, please? You're making me nervous."

"You owe me one—like you said—and I have a limited amount of time to collect. So, I will take you out tomorrow night, say . . . seven o'clock? I'll pick you up—you and Stacey, that is—nothing fancy. How does that sound?" Steve smiled at her, a look of exaggerated expectation painted on his face.

"Smooth," Anna replied. "I think I'm being hustled." She squinted at him, clearly mulling over optional responses before she committed to anything.

"I'll take that as a yes, then? You took far too long to think about it, so you might as well give in and humor me." He moved toward the door as if the whole business was settled and held it for her.

"Okay, you win," she said. "Tomorrow at seven, but then we're even. I said I owe you *one.*" She pointed her finger in his face and moved toward the door.

"One at a time," he whispered as she stepped past him.

They returned to their chairs, sitting on either side of Sharon and Bill. Sharon put a hand on Anna's knee and asked her if she needed anything.

"Like a restraining order?" Bill teased.

Anna laughed politely and didn't offer any of her usual barbs. "No, I'm fine."

The four of them enjoyed another fifteen minutes of conversation until Anna thanked the Websters for dinner and regretfully said she needed to get Stacey home before the little princess turned into a pumpkin.

"Mom," Stacey lamented, "the stagecoach turns into a pumpkin—not the princess."

"My bad," Anna responded. "Now help put the toys back in the living room. We need to get going."

"I don't know why I have to do everything," Stacey challenged.

"Stacey Hayes," her mother warned.

"Sorry, Mom," she replied as she collected an armload of toys.

Bill and Sharon gave Anna and Stacey a hug goodbye.

Before leaving, Anna offered her outstretched hand to Steve. "Truce?" she said with a mischievous smile.

He shook her hand gently, not trying to hide how pleased he was with her gesture. "Truce. Looking forward to seeing you two tomorrow."

Stacey looked at her mother with a confused expression.

After Anna was a good distance up the sidewalk, Bill and Sharon stared at Steve.

"What am I guilty of this time? She seemed perfectly fine," Steve said, like a kid caught with stolen candy.

Bill raised his eyebrows. "*See you two tomorrow*—what's that all about?"

"What's with the goofy smile, Steve?" Sharon chimed in.

"You'd better go ahead and take me home, Bill. I have a date scheduled with two beautiful redheads tomorrow, so I need to be quite rested up," he said proudly. "Besides, you two are about as innocent as thieves."

"What's that supposed to mean?" Bill asked, trying his best to appear guiltless.

"*Why don't you come over for burgers tonight?* I wasn't born yesterday, Bonnie and Clyde. You two set this up. Not that I'm complaining about it. Really, I'm honored."

"I'm not admitting to anything," Sharon said. "It was Bill's idea, and he didn't tell me until after lunch."

"Honey, throw me under the bus, why don't you?" Bill said before giving her a hug. "You are an accomplice, which makes you just as guilty."

"Guilty maybe, but not *as* guilty," she corrected before planting a kiss on his cheek.

"That's enough, you two. Your crimes have clearly drawn you closer," Steve said, "but the third wheel needs to go home now."

Bill had Steve take his car, certain he wouldn't need it until after Steve's date the following evening. They had a plan to visit with Nanna May and Earl, and then they would spend the bulk of their Saturday packing up boxes and getting things ready for the movers. Steve offered to help, but they declined. They weren't pressed for time and were looking forward to a slow and easy day.

* * *

After Bill tucked Stewart into bed, he helped Sharon put a few more things away in the kitchen. "What do you think?" he asked. "I thought our meddling was going to backfire there for a minute."

"I didn't," Sharon said confidently.

"Why not? Is there some sort of secret sixth sense women have that men aren't privy to?"

"Yep," she replied as she flipped off the light switch and grabbed his hand. "No more talking. It's time for bed, Mr. Webster."

"Is that secret code for sleep . . . or no sleep?" he asked with a hint of hopefulness.

"Come to bed and find out."

CHAPTER 29

Sharon headed down the sidewalk toward the Clarks' for a quick visit. Earl invited her in, and they sat in the comfortable living room waiting for Nanna May.

"I have a confession to make, Sharon," Earl whispered with a guilty grin. "You know the stool that was set by your back gate?"

"The one Stacey had brought over so she could scale the fence?" Sharon asked.

"Yes, that one. Well, here's how it is . . . Stacey didn't put it there. I did."

"You did? But Nanna May told me Stacey put it there."

Earl chuckled. "That's 'cause I didn't tell her any different. One day the stool was gone, so Maybeline thought Stacey took it down the alley to your house, and she did, in a way. She was with me when we put it there, and really, it was her idea. I just carried it."

Sharon was humored by Earl's confession. "So, you're saying nothing is really your fault, right?"

"That's right." The furrows deepened at the corner of his eyes, and a childish grin spread across his face. "I feel justified in passin' the buck to Stacey on this one."

They had a good laugh, and then Sharon had another question. "I thought Stacey just decided she wanted to play with Stewart and climbed over the fence without you and Nanna May knowing where she was. But that's not the truth, is it?"

"Yes and no. You see, Stacey did make a few trips down the alley by herself. And she saw Stewart playing in the sandbox, but she couldn't get his attention or get over the fence. She told me one day that if she could get over the fence, the blond boy would be her new best friend. I asked her why she didn't knock on your front door and ask if she could play. That was a terrible idea, I guess, 'cause she said best friends don't have to use the front door." Earl mimicked Stacey, rolling his eyes, throwing his hands up and popping his hip to the side. His little-girl impression was pretty convincing, earning him a good laugh from Sharon.

Earl continued, "Her idea seemed reasonable enough to me, so on our next trip down the alley, we brought the stool with us, but no one was in the yard that day. We set the stool by the fence, and I planned to go with her the next day and see if it was okay for her to play. Now . . . if I remember right, Anna's car wouldn't start, so I gave her a ride to work. When I got home, Stacey was already playin' in your backyard. I wasn't surprised she didn't wait for me, so I walked down the alley and saw them two kids havin' a good time and figured I'd go back a bit later. She was already headin' through our back gate when I planned to go get her from your place. That's when we read your note. Maybeline broke out in song when she realized Stacey had found herself someone to play with. With all that was goin' on, the details of who carried the stool down the alley didn't seem important, so I let it be. Now, I'm all squared up then, right? I don't want to be in no trouble, but there's no need to tell Maybeline," he teased.

Sharon schooled her features and put on her serious mom face. "For every crime, there is a fine. It's only fair."

"That's what I's afraid of. I'm used to getting into trouble, though, so what's it gonna be this time?" He tried to appear serious, a tight-lipped smile turning up the corners of his mouth.

"Earl Clark, due to the nature of your crime and your own admitted propensity toward trouble, not to mention the fact that you passed the buck to a little girl, your penalty—due immediately—is one hug."

Earl laughed at the charade and hugged her. "Only one?"

"Okay, two. You can owe me," she said with a warm smile.

* * *

It was Saturday afternoon when Steve arrived at the Webster' house to return Bill's car.

"Hey, I didn't think I would see you so soon. Come on in," Bill said, with a confused look on his face. "You don't need my car tonight?" He hoped Anna didn't change her mind, although it wouldn't surprise him.

Steve walked into the living room and sat on the couch. "Everything's fine, Bill, but I need to talk to you."

"Hi, Steve," Sharon said, poking her head around the kitchen doorway. "I thought I heard you."

Stewart joined the men in the living room and tapped a picture on his tablet. *I would like a cookie,* his tablet informed them.

"You can have a snack, son, but you can't have a cookie until after lunch. Pick something else," Bill instructed.

His son scrolled through a few pictures until he found a suitable option. *I would like a cracker.*

"Come in here, honey," Sharon said from the kitchen doorway. "I'll get you a snack."

As Stewart passed him, Steve held his hand out. "Here, mate, give me five." The gesture had become a welcome routine.

Stewart slapped his hand with gusto and laughed. "Tee," he said with a smile and then joined his mother in the kitchen.

"Did he not just say my name?" Steve asked, surprised.

"Stewart is full of surprises lately, and I do believe you are *Tee*," Bill said proudly. "Now, is your date with Anna still on for tonight?"

"Yes, it is, but there's another matter in need of discussion. I wanted to talk to you before I speak to Dwayne. It's about moving to Washington state. Bill . . . I'm not going." Steve rubbed his hands together and looked at the floor before trying to read his friend's reaction. "This whole move was my idea, and now I feel as if I'm leaving you hanging, but I can't go, at least not yet—if at all. I know what you're thinking, and it's not because of Anna."

"You're sure about that?" Bill pressed.

"I know you don't believe me. As much as I'm interested in her, and I've done some dodgy things in the past to get a lady's attention, it's more than that.

I can't escape the feeling that this move was for you, Bill, not me. I've already informed the firm in Pullman that I'm not accepting the position."

"You're not messing around, are you? Will you stay on with Davis?" Bill asked.

"Yes, I already phoned Dwayne. He bit my hand off he was so excited to have me back. He wants me to pick up one of the new company cars straight away." Steve hesitated and then added, "I'm sorry to be such a duffer on all this."

"Listen, Steve, I'm not going to be upset with you for staying here. Maybe God needed you to plant the idea in my head, and that was the end of it."

"I think I fancy you as a preacher," Steve said, clearly relieved by his friend's understanding.

"I was your congregation for years, so don't you think it should be my turn now? Besides, it sounds like you're going to need some long-distance relationship advice. I'll send you my hourly fee schedule."

"Look who thinks he's the funny one now!" Steve said, acting more like his comfortable, easy-going self.

"Now? . . . I've always been funny," Bill replied as Sharon and Stewart walked into the room.

"Honey, I'm funny, aren't I?" Bill asked, more interested in including her in the conversation than getting an answer to his question.

"Super funny," she offered in monotone assurance.

Steve laughed and stood up to leave. "That was really convincing." He handed Bill his car keys and walked over to the door.

Bill offered to take him to pick up his company car, but he wanted to walk to the end of the block and catch a cab.

"Have a wonderful evening," Sharon said with a wink.

"Plan to, luv—thanks to you two meddlers," he replied as he walked out the door.

* * *

Monday morning Bill walked into Davis Engineering and met Dwayne in the hallway.

"You haven't changed your mind, have you?" his boss asked. "It's not too late, Bill. I haven't found the right person to replace you yet. Maybe we can take another look at your options?"

"Sorry, Dwayne, this is my last week," Bill replied.

"I figured as much, but it was worth a try." Dwayne patted him on the back, a gesture that insinuated the need to leave all bridges intact.

Bill popped into Steve's office. "Just checking to see if you have a big, stupid grin on your face from Saturday night."

Steve leaned back in his chair and put his hands behind his head. "It was all right."

Bill wasn't buying it. "Whatever. I can tell you're already done for," he said, shaking his head. "I wasn't sure I would ever see it, but it looks like big Steve is off the market. There's going to be wailing in the streets tonight."

"Those poor women," Steve agreed as he looked somberly out the window. "Thousands of hopes, dashed to pieces."

"Thousands, huh?" Bill smirked.

"Yep . . . thousands," Steve repeated with a huge grin, suggesting he had never been happier.

"Did Anna tell you she and Stacey rented the house across from the Clarks?" Bill asked. "The one I almost leased."

"She did. I'm helping her move in next weekend."

"Already have a honey-do list, huh? That was quick." Bill chuckled.

"While we're on the topic of houses," Steve said, changing the subject, "I know someone interested in making an offer on your house."

"Really? Let me guess . . . *you* would?"

Steve nodded. "Do I need to wait until you move out to call your realtor?"

"No, but the value of my house just went up. Let's get together for lunch and haggle over the price tag," Bill said as he stepped back into the hall. "You buy my house, and I'll buy lunch."

"Now who's funny?" Steve called after him.

"Me . . . like Sharon said, I'm *super* funny."

* * *

The last box was loaded and the moving truck drove away, leaving an empty house and a tired moving crew behind.

"This place is a lot bigger without all the junk in it," Stacey announced.

"Stacey Hayes," Anna scolded, "where are your manners?"

"Sorry, Mom, my manners are hungry," Stacey whined.

The smell of hamburgers on the grill wafting from the Clarks' backyard beckoned the work party.

"I think all of our manners are a bit hungry," Steve said as he poked Stacey in the ribs. "And there isn't any meat on these skinny bones, so I'll settle for a burger this time."

Stacey giggled and grabbed Steve's hand as they made their way down the sidewalk.

"Would you fancy holding my other hand and skipping down the pavement as well?" Steve asked Anna, with a flirtatious glint in his eye.

"Nice try, Mr. Darcy," Anna replied, trying to appear unaffected.

As Stewart happily tromped along in front of them, Bill and Sharon shared a knowing grin as they witnessed the exchange between Steve and Anna.

* * *

When they were done eating, Earl took a few pictures, and Nanna May gave the Websters a basket of fresh sweet rolls for their busy morning the next day. They would spend the night in a hotel and leave for Washington state before the sun came up. Bill and Sharon thanked Nanna May, and Bill confessed that he was not going to wait until morning to eat the rolls.

"You all come back here for Christmas and see us," Earl said as he gave each of them a hug.

235

Sharon helped Anna bring a few things into the house from the backyard, and when they were alone in the kitchen, Sharon looked at her friend with love and appreciation, not sure how she would tell her goodbye.

"Give me a hug already," Anna said, her eyes tearing up. "You know I'm going to miss you like crazy."

Sharon swallowed hard and swiped at a tear trailing down her cheek. "Anna, you've been more than a friend. You're more like a sister to me. I'm really going to miss you—and Stacey, too."

Anna dabbed at her nose with the back of her hand. "I hope it works out for you guys to come back for Christmas. And now that you have a phone that works, you keep me posted on life in Washington state, okay?"

Sharon promised to call and gave her a final goodbye embrace, wishing she could take her friend with her; then she reluctantly joined the others gathering around the car outside.

Steve was passing out hugs and reached over to hug Anna, who pushed him away, earning him a giggle from Stacey.

"Steve, Mommy isn't leaving. Only the Websters are leaving. Didn't you already know that?"

"Oh . . . that's right," he replied in mock confusion and then turned to the youngest Webster. "I'll miss you, Stewart. You send me some pictures, all right?" Steve held his open hand out, and Stewart slapped it with enthusiasm.

"Bye, Stewart," Stacey blurted awkwardly as he walked toward the car.

Stewart looked at her and grinned but didn't offer her any sign of communication. He slid into the back seat of the car and fumbled with something. Stacey looked disappointed, obviously more affected by the pending separation than he was. Stewart stepped out of the car and handed something to Stacey. It was his favorite toy: the fur critter his father had given him for Christmas.

Sharon knew Stewart's gift was a sacrifice on his part and was deeply touched with her son's desire to give it to his friend.

Looking at her mother, Stacey seemed conflicted, as if she should return the toy.

"Stewart would like you to have it," Sharon assured her. "He wants you to know that you're a very special friend. He's really going to miss you."

Stacey thanked Stewart for the furry toy and then threw her arms around him. "Goodbye, Stewart!"

Sucking in a quick gulp of air, Sharon hoped her son wouldn't be too upset with the surprise show of physical affection. Stewart looked off into the distance and patted his friend on the arm. Deeply touched, she wondered if her son would ever have another friend like Stacey.

The Websters waved goodbye to everyone as they pulled away from the curb, headed toward the hotel and their last night in DC. After twenty seconds of silence, Bill went over a few details with Sharon and then asked her if he could have one of the rolls.

"No. They're for breakfast."

"Stewart, should Daddy be able to have one of those rolls now?" he asked.

Stewart rocked his fist up and down.

After a minute of friendly banter, Bill decided to surrender to Sharon's wishes. He didn't want a roll. What he relished was the secure sense of belonging that flows between family members in ordinary conversation—no veiled questions or cautionary responses, just people feeling free enough to say what's on their mind. Sharon policing the rolls, that's what wives do when they're comfortable with life—they police rolls.

In the morning, the three of them devoured the sweet bread as they packed their things up to leave for the airport. Sharon noticed a small item wrapped in tissue and tucked in the basket. Unfolding the paper, she recognized the magnet she'd seen months earlier on Nanna May's refrigerator. She slipped it into her pocket and headed to the car with Bill and Stewart.

CHAPTER 30

Bill shoved their carry-on suitcases into the overhead compartment while Sharon situated a pair of noise-reducing headphones on Stewart. He resisted them until he realized the difference they made, lifting them off and on a few times before leaving them in place. Sharon handed him his tablet so he could shuffle through the new games his father had loaded earlier, something special to interest him during the trip.

"Here, honey, can you try not to swallow this? Only chew it, but don't swallow it, all right?" Sharon handed him a piece of gum and slid the headphones back down over her son's ears.

Stewart chewed the gum for about ten seconds and then swallowed it.

"Don't worry about it. He'll be fine," Bill assured her as the plane climbed into the sky over DC.

* * *

While they waited in Denver to taxi onto the runway, a young girl seated in the aisle seat across from Bill asked a man a few rows in front of her if she could trade seats with him. She wanted to sit by her sister, if he didn't mind. The man was happy to comply.

They were soon in the air and headed to their final destination: Spokane, Washington. Stewart seemed content to manipulate a new game on his tablet, and Sharon allowed herself to relax, thankful that her son had adjusted to unfamiliar surroundings far more easily than she thought he would.

"That's a pretty bright young man you got there," a man said, sitting across the aisle from Bill. "How do kids know how to work all those gadgets at their age?"

The friendly man had thick black hair with white streaks above his ears, bushy salt-and pepper eyebrows, and a deep crease in his chin. He visited with Bill for a few minutes, admiring how quickly Stewart had been able to figure out the game he was playing, and then he and Bill moved on to discussing their destinations and the various reasons for their travels. Sharon thought the man had a smile that looked like he'd probably been in trouble a few times as a schoolboy, and his voice reminded her of John Wayne, slow and deliberate with more than a hint of humor.

She listened in as Bill visited with him. The stranger had introduced himself earlier, but she hadn't been paying attention then and couldn't recall his name. She found it odd, as her husband continued to visit, how easy it was to hear the man talk over all the other noises on the plane. He wasn't shouting, but something about the tone of his voice made it unusually easy to hear him.

"I'm coming back from a special friend's wedding," the man said, pulling a folded paper out of his blazer pocket.

He handed Bill a program, a happy couple pictured on the cover. They were older, and there appeared to be more to the picture than a wedding. He told them the groom in the picture had been a resident in a shelter he directed in Spokane, but three years ago, the new groom was a homeless addict. Now he had a job, was drug free, and newly married. Sharon could see the care and pride the man had for the groom in the picture, but he didn't offer any more information about the couple.

The stewardess pushed a drink cart through the aisle, drawing Stewart's attention away from his game and interrupting the conversation across the aisle. After the cart rolled away, Bill asked the man a few more questions about the shelter he directed. Sharon listened in as he talked about the way God was using a group of faithful people to reach the broken-hearted with the good news that Jesus loves them. A woman seated behind the man rolled her eyes as if his beliefs were foolish. Sharon felt embarrassed for him until it dawned on her that the man wasn't worried about seeming foolish or he wouldn't have been so comfortable sharing. He reminded her of Nanna May and Earl. Jesus was a part of their everyday life, and they wouldn't have considered keeping it a secret from anybody.

A feeling of shame needled Sharon's conscience. When had she been taught that the name of Jesus, spoken in public, was a faux pas or something to be ashamed of—as if proper etiquette relegated it to Sundays and secret conversations between believers?

Stewart interrupted Sharon's thoughts, tapping her on the arm and then placing his hands near his armpits and rocking them down.

Sharon recognized the new sign. "Are you tired, honey?" she asked as she copied the sign herself.

Stewart nodded his head forward. Minutes later, he was asleep, covered with his favorite blanket. Shane had given them some helpful information on sign language, and within a week, the communication barrier that had been between them and their son was quickly crumbling.

Bill and the stranger continued on in casual conversation, and then something the man said caught her attention, making her wish she'd been listening more closely. Bill was looking at another brochure the man handed him. She leaned over Stewart to get a better look at the picture on the front. It was a shelter for women, and something on the cover caught Sharon's eye.

"Can I see that, Bill?" she asked, reaching for the paper in his hand.

He gave it to her and continued visiting. She took a closer look at a woman in the back of the picture and felt a tightness building in her throat.

"Bill, can you ask him who that woman is?" she said, pointing to an older woman, partially hidden in the grainy photo.

Bill had a questioning look as he took the folded paper from her and asked the man, "Do you know who that is?" pointing out the woman Sharon had referred to.

"I do," he replied. "That's Shirley. She's been at the women's shelter for about six months now."

"What do you know about her?" Sharon asked with a quivering voice.

"Are you okay, honey?" Bill asked. "Do you know who it is?" he asked her quietly.

"I think it's my mother," she whispered, pressing the back of her hand to her mouth.

The man asked if everything was all right, not able to hear what Sharon was saying.

"What are you able to tell us about Shirley?" Bill asked.

"Well," he began, "Shirley divorced her first husband when he had an affair. She remarried shortly after her first marriage and had two more children. She had a daughter from her first marriage but tried to keep her away when she was about fifteen because of the way her second husband was watching her. When she refused to invite her older daughter to their house for Christmas a few years later, he hit her and didn't stop for several years."

Sharon froze in her seat—she was that daughter. She knew it.

The man continued, "From there, she tells us her second husband had a bit of money and a few connections, and when her second divorce was final, he was able to get full custody of his two children, and she had to move out on her own. She had a few jobs that moved her from place to place, and then she met someone she thought cared about her. He introduced her to heroine. After realizing she was working to support both of their habits, she left that relationship and came to the women's shelter, not wanting to be who she had become any longer." The man shook his head. "Shirley is full of guilt, though, and won't accept that there is a God that loves her. She's too ashamed to find her older daughter, and she's not allowed to contact her other two children. She's a lonely woman that won't accept forgiveness. It's too bad when you see people broken like that." The man looked at Bill and glanced briefly at Sharon. He pulled a card out of his pocket and handed it to Bill. "You can reach me at this number. I encourage you to call, even if you only need some answers," he said quietly.

Bill shook the man's hand and slipped the card into his wallet. Sharon faced the window, releasing muffled sniffs and brushing her hand over wet cheeks. Bill handed her a handkerchief. She dabbed at her nose a few times before noticing the initials on the corner: SYW. He'd given it to her when he proposed and must have seen it in her things when they were packing. She looked over and caught Bill watching her with a concerned look on his face.

"I love you," he whispered over Stewart's head. "We can work this out together."

She shook her head in agreement. "Thank you . . . I love you, too."

* * *

Bill signed for the rental car at the Spokane airport, and they headed for the freeway exit that would take them south to Pullman, Washington.

"Do you want to wait to visit your mother?" Bill asked. "We can call this number and let her know we're coming," he offered, pulling the card out of his pocket.

She wasn't sure what she wanted to do.

"You need to see her, don't you?"

Tired from the trip and nervous for what lay ahead, Sharon looked at the card in her hand. "I want to call."

She dialed the number. A friendly voice answered and promised to let her mother know she was coming to see her. After receiving a few directions, Sharon ended the call and let out a deep breath. "We should be there in about fifteen minutes," she said as she entered the address into her phone.

"Do you want us to go in with you or wait until after you've had a chance to talk to her?"

"Just me . . . at first."

"Stewart and I can wait in the car." Bill offered, rubbing her leg to reassure her.

"Thank you." Sharon slid her hand over her husband's and looked back at Stewart. "How are you doing, honey?"

He swiped at his tablet until it sounded a request: *I would like a hamburger.*

"That's a good idea," Bill agreed. "Do you want one?"

"No, you guys go ahead. I'm not hungry."

After getting their order, Bill followed the GPS to the shelter on the card. "We'll be right here eating our burgers if you need us. This is a good thing, honey . . . You can do it."

Sharon stepped out of the car and up to the front door. The shelter wasn't anything like she had expected, with its stately white columns and manicured lawn. A friendly, older woman greeted her when she opened the front entrance door.

"Hello, are you Sharon?" the woman asked.

"Yes, I'm here to see Shirley . . . ." She let her voice trail off, not sure what her own mother's last name was.

"It's so nice you could visit today. Shirley is in the room right through those doors. She's expecting you."

Sharon rubbed the dampness collecting on the palms of her hands across her waist and pushed the handle on the door in front of her.

A woman that seemed too old to be her mother stood up from a recliner in the corner. "Sharon . . . Sharon, it's you, isn't it?" she asked softly, struggling to maintain her composure.

"Yes, mother, it's me," she said nervously, giving the frail woman, only a shadow of the mother she remembered, a gentle hug, then sitting in a chair across from her.

"Let me look at you for a minute," her mother said, her eyes red and puffy from freshly shed tears. "I can't believe it's you . . . so beautiful . . . so grown up." She continued to pat Sharon's hand. "Sweetheart?" Tears continued to trickle down her mother's deeply furrowed cheeks, etched by abuse and years of disappointment. She tried to say something, but a wave of emotion rendered her speechless.

Sharon pulled a few tissues from a box on the table next to her and handed one to her mother, using another to dab at her own tear-filled eyes. "It's okay. I'm here now."

"Are you going to come back again, after everything I've done?" she asked, another wave of emotion overwhelming her.

Sharon's throat tightened as she ached with sympathy for her mother, so burdened with regret. "Yes . . . don't worry, Mother. I'm coming back, and not only me. There are a couple of people outside that I want you to meet."

"Wait!" her mother said, grabbing both of Sharon's hands. "Before we go out there, I want to tell you I'm so sorry, sweetheart . . . so sorry. I should have been there for you. I'll understand if you don't want to come back."

Sharon interrupted, "Mother, I want to come back, and I will come back. I promise. You need to know that I love you . . . I really do."

243

"How can you?"

"The same God that let us know you were here gave me a heart that loves you because he loves you, too. It wasn't a coincidence that I found you." Sharon wrapped an arm around her mother's and walked with her to the parking lot, aware that the surprise visit needed to be kept short.

Bill and Stewart stepped out of the car as Sharon and her mother walked slowly into the parking lot.

Sharon smiled at her husband and son. "Bill, this is my mother, Shirley . . ." she stammered, still not sure what her last name was.

"Henderson, Shirley Henderson. It's so nice to meet you, Bill. And who is this?"

"This is Stewart. Stewart, this is your grandmother," Sharon said, wondering how her mother would react to her son.

Stewart smiled and scrolled through some pictures on his tablet. *Hello,* his tablet chimed, and he reached a hand out for her to shake.

Bill looked at Sharon with a surprised expression. She smiled, remembering who had taught him the proper greeting.

Shirley clasped his hand in hers. "It's nice to meet you, too, Stewart."

"I'll see you in a few days, okay?" Sharon said as she rubbed her hand over her mother's boney shoulders and gave her one more hug before opening the car door.

"I love you, sweetheart." Shirley put a hand over her mouth to stifle an apparent wave of emotion and then added, "I never stopped loving you."

"Thank you . . . I love you, too, Mom." Sharon replied before shutting the car door.

Her mother continued to wave from the columned porch of the shelter until they were out of view.

"How are you doing?" Bill asked after they had driven a few miles.

"I didn't really know what to expect. She looks so frail and . . . empty, as if she had given up on life years ago. I wish things could have been different for her."

"They can be different for her now."

"Yes, they can." Sharon pulled Bill's hand into hers. "Thank you for bringing me here . . . with you."

Bill swallowed hard as if food was lodged in his throat and choked out, "Yes . . . Yes."

I would like some ice cream, Stewart's tablet chimed in the backseat.

Sharon turned around. "I would like some ice cream, too."

"Me three," Bill added and took the next exit.

As they drove to Pullman, eating their ice cream, Sharon considered everything over the last few months that had brought her to this moment in her life. She reached into her pocket and pulled out the magnet Nanna May had given her: *All things work together for good, to them that love God, and who are called according to his purpose.*

"What do you have there?" Bill asked.

She held it up. "Nanna May put it in the basket with the rolls, as a reminder to trust God, even when things seem to be falling apart. If I were honest, I would have to say I didn't believe it." She looked at him thoughtfully. "Until about a month ago."

It was dark by the time they reached the vacation house Bill rented online. It was comfortable, clean, and fully furnished. Once Stewart was situated in his bed, Bill went over their plans for the next few days.

"Here's a few places I thought we might want to look at with the realtor tomorrow." He tapped the list on the screen. "See if there's anything else you like."

Sharon scrolled through the page and pointed out one she was interested in. "If it's all right with you, I'd like to consider the possibility that my mom could live with us someday."

"No way," Bill replied.

Sharon stared at him in surprise.

The corners of his mouth turned up. "Kidding, I'm just kidding. I'm sorry, hon. I couldn't resist," he said with a guilty smile.

"You're terrible."

"I am terrible . . . and sorry," he said, planting a quick kiss on her cheek. "Do you think we need that much house, though? There are a few other places with mother-in-law apartments." He scrolled down the page. "Like that one. See, it has two bedrooms and a mother-in-law."

"But we're going to need three bedrooms," Sharon said.

"Why? . . . Wait." He gave her his full attention. "*When* are we going to need three bedrooms?"

"In about eight-and-a half months," she replied with a glowing smile.

"Really?" He pulled her onto his lap. "You're not messing with me, are you, to get back at me for what I said about your mom moving in? Seriously . . . Sharon, are you kidding?"

"Not *kidding*, at least not for another thirty-eight weeks," she said with a silly smile. "Did you catch that?"

"Yes, pun intended. Are you going to be cheesy your whole pregnancy?"

"Likely. Is that going to work for you?"

"Yes . . . yes it is." He brushed his hand over her waist. "Oh, my goodness, I can't believe it. You know, when I was overseas, I asked God to give me a chance to make things right, to be the father and husband I was called to be. There isn't anything in the world I want more than to be here with you and Stewart and now this baby. God gave me back far more than I ever deserved or hoped for."

Sharon slipped her arm around Bill's neck and kissed his cheek. "When he answered your prayer, he answered mine, too."

Bill kissed her softly and held her close to him. "Can we just go to sleep right here?"

"Come on." She pulled him off the couch and pushed him toward the bedroom.

"I'll be there in a minute. I need a drink." Sharon leaned against the refrigerator, her dry throat relieved after a few swallows of ice-cold water. She rested her hand in her pocket and felt the magnet, took it out, and placed it on the refrigerator.

"Thank you, Lord . . . for working all things together for good. It wasn't easy, but life wasn't intended to be easy, was it? Thank you for loving us so much that it cost you *your* life. It's hard to understand sometimes, but you never stop loving us, do you?"

* * *

Earl Clark secured the new picture into a frame and brought it into the living room. "I don't know if we can fit too many more on this wall, Maybeline." He shifted a few pictures to make room for the new one.

"That's good right there, babe."

He hammered a small nail into the wall and hung the silver-framed family, tipping it slightly this way and that until it appeared level. The two of them took a few steps back to inspect the new addition. Bill, Sharon, and Stewart Webster smiled back from the satin paper.

"I wasn't sure we were up to the challenge on this one, May," Earl said as he placed his arm around the love of his life.

Patting her husband's back, Nanna May replied, "We weren't, but the Lord was."

"Do you think Anna's gonna give that Steve a chance?"

Maybeline rested her head on Earl's shoulder. "That's a tough one to call. She ain't in no hurry."

THE END

Acknowledgements

A friend of mine, Dr. Monica Hardie, came into my coffee shop nearly every day to write. We went to high school together, in Walla Walla Washington, but hadn't seen each other for three decades. Being one of few that remain alive after Hospice care, and no longer able to practice medicine, she continues to use her limited energy on writing and research. While getting reacquainted with her, she influenced me to consider writing. The one, non-fiction character in *Six Houses Down,* is Dr. Hardie. You'll find her briefly in chapter ten. She encouraged me to give writing a chance for a year. If not for her, I would not be a writer.

To my family, who received a play-by-play of every scene and indulged me in my quest for opinions, thank you, and yes, I owe you, Steve, Heather, Heidi, and Holly. And to my first grandchild, Avery, thank you for being you and giving me an abundance of material for the character, *Stacey.* To my son-in-law that formatted my manuscript, thank you.

Instrumental in the revision process, the Judges from OCW and ACFW highlighted both strengths and weaknesses, assisting me in a much needed skin thickening. I also need to thank my dear friend, Melissa May, who helped me see what I should let the readers see for themselves.

I'd also like to thank Terry Whalin and Morgan James Publishing for giving a new author a chance.

And to my parents, whose faith and love for those in need have made this story possible, thank you.

About the Author

Kari Rimbey began to write after her youngest of three daughters left for college. *Six Houses Down* is her first novel. Her short story, Who Is Maria, earned an award in the 86th annual Writer's Digest short-story competition.

Throughout most of her childhood in Walla Walla, Washington, her family took in foster children of all ages. At the age of nine, three young children came to her home in need of care, one of them five-year-old Scotty, the inspiration for her character, Stewart Webster.

Pursuing a career as a writer after a decade of youth ministry and teaching at her church,

Kari lives in the beautiful Palouse region of eastern Washington where her and her husband entertain a growing herd of grandchildren.

Morgan James makes all of our titles available
through the Library for All Charity Organization.

www.LibraryForAll.org

CPSIA information can be obtained
at www.ICGtesting.com
Printed in the USA
BVHW072347200519
548886BV00001B/2/P